Praise for the novels of Paula Treick DeBoard

"*The Drowning Girls* left me awestruck, revealing DeBoard's true brilliance as an author. Spellbinding."
—Mary Kubica, *New York Times* bestselling author of *The Good Girl*

"*The Drowning Girls* is cleverly plotted, full of twists and turns and so well-written.... Impossible to put down."
—Heather Gudenkauf, *New York Times* bestselling author of *The Weight of Silence*

"Heart-pounding."
—Sophie Littlefield, bestselling author of *The Guilty One*

"Fans of *The Good Girl* and *The Luckiest Girl Alive*...have found their next must-read."
—Catherine McKenzie, bestselling author of *Hidden* and *Smoke*

"Suspenseful and compelling."
—Karen Brown, author of *The Longings of Wayward Girls*

"[E]xpertly told... It will move you."
—Lesley Kagen, *New York Times* bestselling author of *Whistling in the Dark*

"Assured storytelling propels DeBoard's first novel."
—*Publishers Weekly*

"Tautly written and beautifully evocative."
—*Bookreporter.com*

Also by Paula Treick DeBoard

THE FRAGILE WORLD
THE DROWNING GIRLS

PAULA TREICK DEBOARD

THE MOURNING HOURS

If you purchased this book without a cover you should be aware that this book is stolen property. It was reported as "unsold and destroyed" to the publisher, and neither the author nor the publisher has received any payment for this "stripped book."

Recycling programs for this product may not exist in your area.

ISBN-13: 978-0-7783-1961-0

The Mourning Hours

For questions and comments about the quality of this book, please contact us at CustomerService@Harlequin.com.

www.MIRABooks.com

Printed in U.S.A.

For my Tea Time friends, because I always said I would.

THE MOURNING HOURS

prologue

October 2011

Just outside Milwaukee, I saw the lights behind me—Wisconsin Highway Patrol—and pulled over to the shoulder.

Even before the cop tapped on the window, I started fumbling in the shoulder bag I had been lugging around since that morning, since San Francisco. I had packed in a hurry—my cell phone, a tube of lip gloss, a stack of undergrad papers to be graded, a dog-eared copy of *US Weekly*.

While I searched for the power window button, I caught a glimpse of myself in the glass: wrinkled clothes, grease forming at my hairline, mascara from twelve hours ago smudged under my eyes like twin bruises.

"I know, I was speeding," I said, even before the window came to a stop. The night was cold—was it really almost winter in the Midwest? I had been living in a mild haze of seasonless fog, and this chill nipped straight through my T-shirt. It was as if I had spent years walking on a treadmill and was just now finding my real footing.

"License and registration," said the cop, an automaton. I peered out the window at him, but his face was hidden in a pocket of darkness, only his badge winking back at me, his stiff jacket collar standing at attention. From his waist, a radio crackled.

"I just rented this car at the airport," I said, producing the plastic pouch from Hertz, full of shiny brochures and a contract that unfolded like a fan to reveal my sleep-deprived scrawl at the bottom. It could have been anyone's signature, really.

He scrutinized the contract with his flashlight, more carefully than I'd studied it at the airport with a line of twenty people shifting behind me. I suddenly worried that with this, like most things in my life, I hadn't taken the time to read the small print, to look for loopholes.

"Your license?" he asked.

"Yes, my license…" I dug in my shoulder bag for my wallet, where an empty space gaped at me from behind a plastic window. Credit cards, my Berkeley ID, a Starbucks gift card with a grand balance of fifty-seven cents. I could feel the cop's eyes on me. To speed up the search, I turned my shoulder bag upside down. A dozen pens, the wad of Kleenex I'd cried into on the plane, a Life Saver clinging to a bit of aluminum foil—but no license. I started babbling away like a psychotic on a weekend pass. "I'm so sorry, officer. I'm usually a very cautious driver. But my flight got in late, and I was anxious to get going and there's almost no one on the road…."

In the midst of my rambling, my right hand brushed against the ID carrier still looped around my neck. "Oh!

Here it is!" Thank God. I'd been about to throw myself on the mercy of the Wisconsin justice system, which had never impressed me. Instead I handed it over, the driver's license that expired on my next birthday: my tentative smile, the vital statistics I had improved upon slightly, adding an inch, subtracting ten pounds.

"California, huh?" he said. "I bet it's a bit colder here."

I laughed with relief, playing along. Everyone in California lives in L.A., after all. We're all sun-bleached blondes who load our kids into shiny SUVs and cart them off to surf camp.

"They might drive faster there, too," he said. "I clocked you going twelve over."

"I'm sorry," I repeated, twisting the hem of my T-shirt.

He ignored me and tapped something into the keypad of the radio receiver. The license plate—to see if it would come back stolen? My name to check for warrants or a skipped court date, a charge or possession or prostitution or burglary?

My name. I stiffened, a reflex for someone who has heard her name on the news, enunciated carefully by well-coifed reporters. I worried that the cop might feel my nerves, the way a dog can sniff out the presence of a cat. In California my name didn't matter; it didn't ring any bells the way it might here. The officer was old enough to remember the case, the name Hammarstrom on the front page of every Wisconsin paper.

He handed back the Hertz packet with my license balanced on top. As he leaned into the window, his face was visible—pale, mustached, his forehead topped by a receding brown hairline. "So, where are you headed?"

My eyes drifted back to the road. Highway 43 would

take me past Port Washington, Oostburg, Sheboygan. Before Manitowoc, I would branch off onto 151, taking the various twists and turns through the country roads that would bring me to Watankee, to Rural Route 4, to the gravel driveway and the light over the back porch.

Except it would all be different now, since he wouldn't be there to greet me.

Suddenly I felt the pull of the place, like the insistent tug of a magnet buried deep down, beneath the asphalt. It was something I had never been able to properly explain to my Cultural Geography undergrads, maybe because I'd never been able to explain it to myself. *A sense of place.* I smiled at the cop, at this stranger leaning in through the crisp evening air. Somewhere deep inside, where I'd been clutching my childhood in a tight invisible fist, I felt myself slowly releasing, releasing. *Let it go, Kirsten. Let it go.*

"Home," I said, swallowing hard. At that moment it felt like the only truth, the deepest possible truth of them all. "I'm going home."

one

1994–1995

Everything you needed to know, Dad said, you could learn on a farm. He was talking about things my mind, shaped by Bible stories and the adventures of Dick and Jane, could barely comprehend—the value of hard work, self-sufficiency, the life cycle of all things. Well, the life cycle—I did understand that. Things were always being born on farms, and always dying. And as for how they came to be in the first place, that was no great mystery. "They're mating," Dad would explain when I worried over a bull that seemed to be attacking a helpless heifer. "It's natural," he said, when the pigs went at it, when the white tom from Mel Wegner's farm visited and we ended up with litters of white kittens.

Nature wasn't just ladybugs and fireflies—it was dirt and decay and, sometimes, death. To grow up on a farm was to know the smell of manure, to understand that the gawky calves that suckled my fingers would eventually be someone's dinner. It was to witness the occasional birth of a half-formed calf, missing eyes or ears, like some alien-headed baby. We couldn't drive into town without seeing the strange, bloodied remains of animals—cats, opossums and the occasional skunk who had risked it all for one final crossing. By the time we got Kennel, our retriever-collie mix, we'd had three golden Labs, each more loyal than the last, until they ran away during thunderstorms or wandered into the path of an oncoming semi headed down Rural Route 4. When Dad had spotted him at the county shelter, Kennel had a torn ear, a limp in his back left leg and ribs you could spot from a hundred yards away—the marks of an abusive owner.

Even humans couldn't avoid their fates. Sipping lemonade from a paper cup after the Sunday morning service, I weaved between adult conversations, catching little snatches as I went. A tractor had tipped over, trapping the farmer underneath. Cows kicked, and workers were hurt. Pregnant women, miles from any hospital, went into early labor. Machines were always backfiring, shirtsleeves getting caught in their mechanisms. This was to say nothing of lightning strikes, icy roads and snowdrifts, or flash floods and heat waves. This was to say nothing of all the things that could go wrong inside a person.

So we were used to death in our stoic, farm-bred way. It was part of the natural order of things: something was born, lived its life and died—and then something else replaced it. I knew without anyone telling me that it was this way with people, too.

Take my family, for example—the Hammarstroms. My great-great-grandpa had settled our land and passed on the dairy to his son, who passed it to Grandpa, who passed it on to Dad, who would pass it on to Johnny.

Dad and Mom had gotten married and had Johnny right after Dad graduated from high school, leaving Mom to get her degree later on, after Emilie and I were born. I'd always thought it was extremely cool that our parents were so much younger than everyone else's parents, until Emilie spelled out for me that it was something of a scandal. Anyway, when Johnny had been born, Grandpa and Grandma had moved to the in-law house next door, where Dad and Mom would someday move, when it was time for Johnny and his wife to inherit the big house. This was simply the expected order of things, as natural as the corn being sown, thinned, watered, fertilized and harvested. Everything that was born would die one day. I knew this, because death was all around me.

There was Grandma, for one. I was too young to have any concrete memories of her death, although I'd pieced together the facts from whispered conversations. She'd been standing in her kitchen, peeling apple after apple, when it happened. A *pulmonary embolism,* whatever that was. A freak thing. I couldn't walk into Grandpa's kitchen without thinking: *Was it here? Was this the spot?* But life had gone on without her. Grandpa stood at that sink every morning, drinking a cup of coffee and staring out the window.

The first funeral I remember attending was for our neighbor, Karl Warczak, who'd collapsed in his manure pit, overwhelmed by the fumes. An ambulance had rushed past on Rural Route 4, and Dad and Mom had followed—Mom because she had just completed her training as a nurse, Dad because he and Karl Warczak had worked together over the years, helping with each other's animals, planting, harvesting, tinkering with stubborn machinery. By the time they'd pulled in behind the ambulance, Dad had said later, it had already been too late—sometimes, he'd explained, the oxygen just got sucked out of those pits.

Mom had laid out my clothes the night before the funeral—a hand-me-down navy wool jumper that seemed to itch its way right through my turtleneck, thick white tights and a pair of too-big Mary Janes with a tissue wadded into the toes. She'd always been optimistic that I would grow into things soon. During the service I'd sat sandwiched between Mom and Emilie, willing myself not to look directly at the coffin. The whole ashes-to-ashes, dust-to-dust thing made me feel a little sick to my stomach once I really thought about it, and so did Mom's whisper that the funeral home had done "such a good job" with Mr. Warczak. It was incredible that he was really dead, that he had been here one minute and was gone the next, that he would never again pat me on the head with his dirt-encrusted fingers. There had been such a solemn strangeness to the whole affair, with the organ music and the fussy bouquets of flowers, the men in their dark suits and the women in navy dresses, their nude pantyhose swishing importantly against their long slips.

"It is not for us to question God's perfect timing," Pastor Ziegler had intoned from the pulpit, but I remember thinking that the timing wasn't so great—not if you were Mr. Warczak, who thought he could fix the problem with the manure pump and then head inside for lunch, and not for his son, Jerry, who had been about to graduate from Lincoln High School and head off to a veterinary training program. The rumor had been that Mrs. Warczak's cancer was back, too, and this time it was inoperable. "That boy's going to need our help,"

Dad had told us when we were back in the car, riding with the windows open. "It's a damn shame."

"Why did it happen?" I'd asked from my perch on top of a stack of old phone books in the backseat. I could just see out the window from that height—the miles of plowed and planted and fenced land that I would know blindfolded. "Why did he die?"

"It was an accident. Just a tragic accident," Mom had said, blotting her eyes with a wad of tissue. She'd been up all morning, helping in the church kitchen with the ham and cheese sandwiches that were somehow a salve for grief. When we'd parked in our driveway, she'd gathered up a handful of soggy tissues and shut the door behind her.

"Oh, pumpkin," Dad had said as he sighed when I'd lingered in the backseat, arms folded across my jumper, waiting for a better answer. He'd promised to head over to the Warczaks' house later, to help Jerry out. "It's just how things go. It's the way things are." He'd reached over, giving my shoulder a quick squeeze in his no-nonsense, farmer-knows-best way.

Somehow, despite all the years that passed, I never forgot this conversation, the way Dad's eyes had glanced directly into mine, the way his mustache had ridden gently on top of his lips as he'd delivered the message. He couldn't have known the tragedies that were even then growing in our soil, waiting to come to harvest.

All he could do was tell me to prepare myself, to buck up, to be ready—because the way the world worked, you never could see what was coming.

two

I would always remember the summer of 1994 as an unbroken string of humid days, the air thick and sticky late into the evening. It was the summer of the Fifth Annual Watankee Softball Tournament, and a summer I'd never forget. Mom had seen the announcement in the St. John's Evangelical Lutheran Church bulletin on a Sunday morning and, looking for an activity to keep us from uninterrupted hours in front of the television, had signed us up by that night.

"It'll be fun," Mom said, urging us into action. "I can see it now—The Hammarstrom Hitters."

Emilie rolled her eyes. "More like The Hammarstrom Quitters."

We practiced on our front lawn, using tree trunks as bases and chasing Johnny's powerful home runs until they disappeared into our cornfield. Johnny had been dying for action all spring, ever since he'd dislocated his elbow during wrestling semifinals and had been forced to sit in the bleachers at State, his left arm swaddled from shoulder to wrist. By June, Johnny's arm had healed and he was ready to resume his status as a local hero.

We piled out of Mom's Caprice Classic an hour before our first game at Fireman's Field, Johnny leading the charge. Dad followed him, whistling, tossing a ball and catching it in his glove. Emilie slumped behind Dad, her hands in her jeans pockets. "This is going to be so *boring,*" she'd protested on the way over. "Almost as boring as staying home."

Mom waited for me to free myself from my roost in the middle of the backseat and leaned over, shutting the door behind me. She pointed to the encyclopedia-sized book I carried, *Myths and Half-True Tales*. "You're bringing that with you?"

I considered. I was too small for softball, too small for most things—I needed a boost from the top rung to reach the monkey bars and a step stool to see the top of my head in the bathroom mirror. It went without saying that I couldn't swing a bat by myself, and that a fly ball would probably knock me down.

"What if I get bored?" I replied.

Mom and I walked toward the infield, where Bud Hirsch, captain of Hirsch's Haybalers, waited with his clipboard. He took one look at me and, with his massive gut thrust forward, said, "You here to watch, shorty?" He chuckled as I sidled away, offended, and turned away to bark orders at the rest of the team. Johnny was going to start out in left field, Dad at first base.

Mom leaned down to me. "Never mind him. You can share my position with me if you want."

"No, thanks," I said. "I'll just watch."

During the warm-up, I sat cross-legged on the bench in the dugout, leaning back against the chain-link fence. Bud Hirsch's son, Raymond, was pitching slow arcing lobs to Sandy Maertz, a member of our church. Dad, Johnny and the rest of the men in the infield passed the ball back and forth, rolling grounders and tossing fly balls. Mom stood awkwardly in right field, waiting to be included.

The other team, Loetze's Lions, was starting to arrive, and the bleachers on both sides were beginning to fill up. Someone unlocked the concessions stand, flipped the wooden door down, and raised the Watankee Elementary Academic Boosters Club banner. The money raised tonight would finance our school field trips to the Wisconsin Maritime Museum in Manitowoc and our less academic but equally inspiring annual visits to Lambeau Field in Green Bay.

I tracked Emilie as she made her way up to the top row of the bleachers, her honey-blond hair swinging behind her. It amazed me how she moved, how much confidence she had. A year ago she'd been a clumsy eighth grader. Now she was ready to take Lincoln High School by storm. "I'm going to join pep band," she'd announced to me proudly when we were lying side by side in our twin beds one night. A shard of moonlight had fallen through the curtains and cut her slim body in half—her hipbones and long legs on one side, the small buds of her breasts, like plum halves, on the other.

"Why do you want to be in pep band?" I'd asked, thinking of the few football games I'd attended in my life. The pep band was a group of shivering kids who took the field at halftime after the cheerleading routine, right about when half the stands decided they needed a hot dog or a trip to the bathroom. "Those kids never get to watch the game."

"I don't care about the stupid game," Emilie had said, sighing dramatically. "I want people to watch *me*."

Bud Hirsch called my attention back to the game with

two toots on his whistle. "All right! Switch it up!" Our team started a slow jog through the infield to our dugout, and Loetze's Lions took a turn at their warm-ups.

Panting as he came off the diamond, Dad gave me a high five—as if by staying out of the way, I'd performed some huge feat.

I slid from the bench. "Can I have a dollar?"

"Sure." Dad dug in his pocket and came up with a handful of change.

"Stay close," Mom said.

I could feel her eyes on me as I walked behind the batter's box, my feet kicking up little swirls of dust that instantly coated my tennis shoes. I resisted the urge to hike up my shorts, Emilie's from years before. Sometimes I hated the way Mom looked at me, like I was a medical specimen.

A dollar bought me a can of Coke and three blue Pixy Stix, the kind of pure-sugar pleasure I was never allowed at home. Clutching the soda in one hand and my book in the other, I scanned the bleachers for a place to sit. A few people from church smiled encouragingly in my direction, but I spotted Emilie in the center of a tight, whispering circle of recent Watankee Elementary graduates and changed course. A few of my own soon-to-be-fourth-grade classmates were sitting in the stands with their parents, but we glanced away from each other with summertime awkwardness, as if we knew we weren't meant to connect again until the Tuesday after Labor Day.

I lugged my volume of *Myths and Half-True Tales* to a shady spot beneath the bleachers and opened to the dog-eared page on Atlantis. The game began and cheers erupted.

We were only a mile or so from our farm, but to

hear Dad yell, "Hammer one home, Hammarstrom!" during Johnny's turn at bat was to imagine that we'd been transported somewhere far away, like an island in the South Pacific. Dad was only here at all because he'd worked out a deal with Jerry Warczak: Jerry, who had no interest in softball, would cover Dad's last milking on these nights if Dad and Johnny would lend him a hand on Saturdays with the chickens. This was typical of the sort of deals they worked out. "It's just being neighborly," Dad had explained to me, but it had seemed that he was being more than neighborly when he'd clapped Jerry on the shoulder and said, "He's like another son to me."

When the noise of the game finally faded into the background, I spent the next few innings reading about Atlantis and wondering how a city could go missing—*poof!*—just like that. What would happen if Watankee, Wisconsin, and all the people I knew were to fall off the face of the earth one day—a sudden crack, then a quick slide into Lake Michigan? How long until the rest of the world missed us?

I lay back and closed my eyes, listening to the crack of the bat, the sudden burst of applause. I imagined the ball hurtling through a blue sky deepening into purple with the sunset. The tall grass under the bleachers prickled and dented the undersides of my legs, and a mosquito seemed intent on sucking my blood. I was swatting my ankle when a shadow covered me.

"Hey, you're Kirsten Hammarstrom, aren't you?"

I struggled to sit up. For a moment, it looked like an angel was standing over me, even though my Sunday school teacher Mrs. Keithley said there was no such thing anymore, unless maybe you were a Catholic. The voice belonged to a girl who wore cutoff denim shorts and a checked shirt with the tails knotted at her waist, so that just a teensy strip of skin at her stomach showed. I realized that what looked like a fiery halo on top of her head was actually just her red hair, backlit by the stadium lights.

"Yeah," I confirmed. "I'm Kirsten Hammarstrom." Suddenly I felt guilty, as if I'd been caught sneaking a sliver of pie before dinner.

"Your brother's Johnny Hammarstrom, right?" she said, bending down to my height. Up this close, she was the loveliest person I'd ever met. Creamy white skin, a tiny bridge of freckles spanning her nose. A smile so wide and welcoming, she might have been pictured on a travel brochure.

"Yeah," I said again, suddenly ashamed of my dirty hands, my teeth sticky with the residue of Coke. "Why?"

She smiled and held out a hand, poised as any church greeter. "I'm Stacy Lemke."

We shook hands. Nothing drastic happened, no fireworks or a sudden crack of thunder, but somehow the moment felt significant.

Stacy's hands were cool, her nails painted the softest pink, like cotton candy. If she noticed that my nails were ringed with dirt, she didn't say anything. "Kirsten. That's such a pretty name," she said.

I smiled. "Do you know my brother?"

She laughed. "Everyone knows Johnny Hammarstrom."

This hadn't really occurred to me until I heard it said that way, so boldly, like a biblical fact. During wrestling season, Johnny's name was a regular appearance in the sports section of the *Watankee Weekly;* whenever I was in town with Dad, someone always approached him to ask about Johnny's prospects for the fall.

"I go to school with him, but we don't really know each other," Stacy said, smiling a little sadly. "I mean, I don't think he would ever notice someone like *me*."

I looked at her more closely. Her tiny freckles glistened under small bubbles of sweat, but I didn't see any kind of defect—no eyeteeth or harelip or deformed thumbs. If my brother hadn't noticed Stacy Lemke, he was either blind or stupid or both. "Why not?" I asked, blushing. "I think you're really pretty."

"Oh, you're so sweet!" She gave me a quick touch on the knee and stood up, brushing invisible dirt from her legs.

"I would have noticed you," I said, swallowing hard.

"Aren't you just the cutest thing in the world!" She laughed, tossing her head so that her red hair briefly covered her face and then swung free again. "Well—it was nice meeting you."

She started to walk away. I watched her until she got to the edge of the bleachers, where she stopped and did a little rubbing thing with her shoes in the grass, to toe off the dust. I was still watching her when she turned back to me, and I looked down, embarrassed.

"You know, maybe you could tell Johnny that I said hi."

"Sure." I smiled. She could have asked me anything, and I wouldn't have said no.

When she smiled back at me, I could see a little tooth in the back of her mouth that was turned sideways and slightly pointed—the only thing about Stacy Lemke that wasn't absolutely perfect. It made me like her even more.

three

The crowd dispersed, and the Hammarstroms reassembled in the infield, half of us sweaty and all of us satisfied.

"Watch out, shorty!" Johnny yelled, appearing from the dugout. I pretended to dodge his grasp, but he caught me by the arms and hoisted me to his shoulders. I shrieked while he ran the bases, my hands grabbing on to his neck for dear life.

"Be careful!" Mom called from somewhere, her voice lost in the darkness.

I screamed as Johnny gained speed, heading for home plate. I squeezed my feet against his chest, too terrified to look until he eased up and carefully deposited me on the ground. That was Johnny—rough and gentle at the same time.

It wasn't until later, when we were gathered around the kitchen table dunking chunks of apple pie into bowls of soupy vanilla ice cream, that I remembered about Stacy. For a moment I hesitated to say anything, wanting to hold Stacy's existence close, like a treasure gathered in my fist.

Johnny had finished giving Grandpa the play-by-play, and Grandpa was just about finished pretending to be interested in his analysis of Sandy Maertz's triple, when I managed to get a word in.

"A girl named Stacy Lemke says to tell you hi," I said.

"Who's that?" Johnny asked gruffly, looking down into his bowl. His cheeks suddenly flamed pink.

I shrugged, trying to be casual. "Stacy Lemke. She has red hair and freckles." *She has creamy skin, the softest handshake in the world. She said I was adorable.*

"That must be Bill Lemke's daughter. He played for the other team tonight. Is she in your class, Johnny?" Mom asked.

"I don't know," he said, shrugging.

"Sure you do," Emilie piped up. "Stacy Lemke? She used to go out with what's-his-name, the Ships quarterback."

I smooshed my finger into a drop of ice cream. "She says she goes to school with you."

"Well, I don't know. Maybe I've seen her around," Johnny said. He brought his bowl to his lips, trying to drain the last of his ice cream into his mouth. Mom cleared her throat pointedly, and Johnny set the bowl back on the table.

"Bill Lemke, the tax attorney?" Dad asked.

"O-o-o-h, someone's got a crush on you," Emilie teased.

Johnny clanked his spoon against his bowl. "Shut up, that's not true."

Dad said, "He's the guy who helped Jerry hold on to some of that land after Karl died. Decent guy."

Emilie sang, "Johnny's got a girlfriend.... Johnny's got—"

"I said shut up, already." Johnny stood up and Mom sent Emilie a warning look sharp as any elbow. I had to hand it to Emilie; she wasn't a coward. She was a master at pushing Johnny right to his very edge.

"Look, she's just some girl." Johnny turned away from us. His bowl and spoon landed in the sink with a clang, and the back door slammed a few seconds later.

Mom called, "Johnny! You get back here!" but Johnny was already gone.

"What's got into him?" Dad demanded, his voice caught between annoyance and amusement.

Mom shrugged, getting up to rinse out Johnny's bowl.

Dad stood then and stretched, the same stretch he did every night when the day was just about over. "I guess it's time for me to make the rounds one last time," he announced. "I could use a bit of company, though."

This was my cue. I stood, following Dad to the door for our nighttime ritual. Kennel trotted behind us to the barn, where I dumped out some cat food for our half-dozen strays and Dad walked up and down the calf pens, whistling and cooing to the youngest, reassuring them. "Hey, now, baby," I heard him say, and the calves responded by tottering forward in their pens, all awkward legs and clunky hooves.

I waited for Dad in the doorway of the barn with Kennel rubbing against my legs. From this perspective, slightly elevated from the rest of our property, it seemed as if all we needed was a moat and we would have our own little kingdom. Our land, all one hundred-and-sixty acres of it, stretched away farther than I could see into the deepening darkness. On the north side of the property the corn grew fiercely, shooting inches upward in a single day. Beyond the rows of corn was our neighbor Mel Wegner, beloved because he let me feed apples to his two retired quarter horses, King Henry and Queen Anne. In the opposite direction, our cow pasture joined up with what had been the Warczaks' property, until Jerry had had to sell most of it to cover legal and medical expenses. These days, the bank rented him part of the property for a chicken farm. Sometimes, when the wind carried just right, I could hear the confusion of a thousand chickens pushing against each other. Other times, days in a row might pass without us seeing any of our human neighbors.

Our house, beaming now with yellow rectangles of light from almost every window, was set back from the road by a rolling green lawn that Grandpa Hammarstrom tended faithfully. Peeking behind it, closer to the road, was Grandpa's house, newly remodeled to be in every way more efficient than ours. On the east end, our property ended in a thick patch of trees that started just about at one end of the county and ended at the other, a green ribbon of forest that more or less tended to itself. In the middle of it all was our barn, which Johnny had been painstakingly repainting, plus our towering blue silo, the sleek white milk tank.

"Ready, kiddo?" Dad asked, appearing behind me. He cupped his hand around the back of my head, and my silky, tangled blond hair fell through his fingers.

"Race you," I said, suddenly filled with the night's unspent energy, and started back. Dad was a superior racing companion, pushing me to go faster and farther, but never getting more than a step ahead of me. We arrived breathless at the back door. Mom was alone at the sink now, and she turned to grin at us.

"Another tie," Dad announced.

When I thought about this day later, I wished I could have scooped up the whole scene in one of Mom's canning jars, so I could keep all of us there forever. I knew it wouldn't last for that long, though—the fireflies I captured on summer nights had to be set free or else they were nothing more than curled-up husks by morning. But I had always loved the way they buzzed frantically in the jar, their winged, beetlelike bodies going into a tizzy with even the slightest shake. If I could have done it somehow, I would have captured my own family in the same way, all of us safe and together, if only for a moment.

four

Suddenly, I was seeing Stacy Lemke everywhere. A few days after that first softball game, I saw her at Dewy's, where I was sucking down a chocolate shake while I waited for Mom to place an order next door at Gaub's Meats. The instant Stacy stepped through the door with two other girls, my heart performed this funny extra beat.

"Hey, Kirsten!" she called loudly, and everyone in the whole café turned for a second to look at me.

I beamed back at her. She put her arm around me in a quick hug, as if we had always known each other. She was wearing a yellow T-shirt, a denim skirt and sandals, and her reddish hair, hanging loose around her shoulders, smelled like gardenias.

She gestured behind her. "These are my sisters, Joanie and Heather."

I smiled shyly into the whipped cream residue of my shake. Heather was in the sixth grade at Watankee Elementary, and I'd seen her on the playground, walloping a tetherball over her victims' heads. She was basically a giant. Joanie, strawberry-blonde and shorter, was what

Stacy would look like if she went through the wash a few times. We smiled our hellos.

"When's the next softball game?" Stacy asked as her sisters stepped up to the counter to order.

"Next Tuesday, I think."

She smiled that Stacy smile, wide and white. "Well, maybe I'll see you then."

My eyes tracked her as she placed her order, produced a folded bill from her skirt pocket to pay and made small talk with the girl behind the counter. I remembered what Emilie had said the other night, that Stacy used to date the quarterback of the mighty Lincoln High Shipbuilders. Even though what I knew about football was limited to helmets and "hut-hut" and touchdowns, I knew that the quarterback was a big deal. Everyone in all of Wisconsin knew who Brett Favre was, after all.

I saw Stacy only a few days later at the library, while Dad was down the street at the feed store. I was curled up in a bean bag, leafing through an encyclopedia and wondering for the millionth time why reference books couldn't be checked out like anything else. It hardly seemed fair.

Suddenly, Stacy was squatting beside me, a book in her hand. "Oh, hey! I keep bumping into you!"

I beamed. It would be fair to say that by this time I was already half in love with Stacy Lemke. She looked happier to see me than the members of my own family did, even the ones I saw rarely. Only this morning Emilie had thrown a hairbrush across the room at me for losing her butterfly hair clip. Stacy would never throw a hairbrush at her sisters—you could tell a thing like that just by looking at her. I wondered if there was some way I could trade Emilie for Stacy, as if they were playing cards.

"So," she said as she smiled, "how's your family doing?"

I thought about mentioning that Emilie was in trouble for cutting five inches off the hem of one of her skirts, but figured that probably wasn't what Stacy wanted to hear. I took a deep breath and said, "I forgot to tell you last time. Johnny said I should say hi if I saw you." It was surprising how easily the lie had come to me, and how smoothly the next one followed on its heels. "He said he would see you at the game on Tuesday."

"He did? Really?" She rocked backward on her heels and then straightened up, until she was standing at her full height. Her cheeks suddenly looked more pink, her tiny freckles like scattered grains of sand. I remembered what she had said: *I don't think he would notice a girl like me.*

"Really," I said. It wasn't a lie if it was said for the sake of politeness, right? Didn't we always compliment Mom's casseroles, even as we shifted the food around on our plates without eating it? Besides, to repeat the truth would be rude: *She's just some girl.*

Stacy grinned at me. "Well, tell him hi back."

"I will," I promised.

After she returned her book and left, smiling at me over her shoulder, I went to the checkout counter where Miss Elise, the librarian, was stamping books with a firm thud. "Can I check out that book?" I asked, pointing to the one Stacy had just returned.

"What, this one?" Miss Elise said, holding up *Pride and Prejudice.* "Are you sure? Might be a little hard for you."

"I think I'm ready for it," I said.

She smiled, handing the book over, but she was right. I wasn't ready for it; I gave up after the first page. But I liked knowing that Stacy had held this very book in her hands, that her fingers with the perfectly painted nails had turned these very pages.

And, of course, I saw Stacy in the stands at every softball game for the rest of the Haybalers' short season. At our second game, Stacy walked right up to where Mom and I were sitting, and I said, "Mom, this is Stacy Lemke. Remember, I was telling you about her?"

"Of course," Mom said smoothly, standing. They shook hands politely.

"I go to school with Johnny," Stacy explained.

The Haybalers took the field just then, and there was a general roar from the hundred or so of us in the stands.

"Well, I should probably find my seat," Stacy said.

"Good to meet you," Mom said a little dismissively. She turned her attention to the game, and Stacy winked at me. I winked right back, glad I had perfected the technique during a particularly long sermon last winter. It felt as if we were secret agents with the same mission: to get Johnny to fall in love with her.

With Stacy for me to watch, softball was much more interesting. She sat next to a friend or two, girls who seemed boring compared to her. I couldn't help but notice how Stacy watched Johnny while she pretended not to, distributing her gaze equally among all the players, and then homing in again and again on Johnny at shortstop. When he was up to bat, she joined the crowd in chanting, "John-ny! John-ny!" She cheered when he broke up a double play at second and whooped with pleasure when he crossed home plate.

During the game, Johnny was all focus, an athlete's athlete. He had always been a competitor, no matter what the sport. It was clear, watching him, that he had a natural talent—he could hit farther, run faster, field better, throw harder than anyone else. He also took failures more personally than anyone else, cursing when Dad dropped a throw to first, kicking divots in the dirt to shake off a bad swing. If he noticed Stacy Lemke watching him, it didn't show.

It was Stacy who approached him first after that second game. I know because I was watching, holding my breath, clutching my fists to my side like the freak Emilie always said I was. If asked, I couldn't have explained why their meeting was so important to me, but maybe it had something to do with ownership. In a way, I owned a part of Johnny Hammarstrom, who was star athlete for the Lincoln High Shipbuilders, but my own brother, too. And since I'd met Stacy first, since she'd sought me out under the bleachers that day, I felt I owned a part of her, too.

Stacy had walked right down the bleachers, not on the steps but on the seats, confident. She moved with purpose around the chain-link fence and out onto the field, her legs creamy white in her short shorts, a checked shirt pushed up past her elbows. She was headed right for him, and Johnny must have realized that at some point, too, because he froze, his cheeks flushed with sweat, his jeans filthy along the left side from a slide into third base.

I don't know what she said to him and what he said back to her, but my mind filled with a million possibilities, talk of baseball and school and plans for the rest of the summer and deep dark secrets. Well, maybe not that—it was hard for me to imagine that Johnny, who most of the time seemed as complicated as a June bug, could keep any kind of secret. But something was being said, and something was happening between them. At one point Stacy gestured to the stands—to *me?*—and Johnny followed her gaze, scanning the crowd. Before she walked away, Stacy reached out her hand and touched him on the arm, just lightly, such a small and insignificant touch, but I reeled, gasping. This was *flirting.* This was something.

"What's wrong with you?" Emilie asked, joining me in the stands.

I shook my head. Nothing. Everything. The way I was sweating, it might have been me out there, falling in love.

Mom turned from the conversation she'd been having with an internist from the hospital and studied me. "I think you've been having too much sugar, Kirsten."

"No, I haven't—" I protested, and by the time I looked back, Stacy was gone and Johnny was standing with the guys in the dugout.

It was like this at every game for the rest of the tournament. Bud Hirsch led the team in a cheer for the competitors, and the men worked their way through the line slapping sweaty hands: "Good game"…"good game"…"good game." Then Stacy and Johnny began a slow, purposeful wandering toward each other while I held my breath. Even Mom had started to notice, and the two of us would watch them together, Mom shaking her head, and me grinning like an idiot.

With everyone else packing coolers and blankets and finding rides home, Johnny and Stacy stood in a little bubble of quiet, whatever words they said meant for each other alone.

"Don't stare, shrimp," Emilie nudged me once when I was lost in their romance. "Isn't it past your bedtime, anyway?"

I followed her to the car, kicking against the grass with the toes of my tennis shoes. When I looked back, Johnny and Stacy were still talking, and his truck didn't pull into our driveway until we'd been home for twenty minutes.

five

It was a hot, lazy Wisconsin summer. In the barn, flies descended by the thousands onto the backs of our cows, but it was too warm for them to protest with even the simplest flick of a tail. It was too warm in our house, too—upstairs, Emilie and I opened our bedroom window one day in June and didn't bother to close it for weeks. We woke up sticky in the mornings, the humidity coating our bodies like fur. It seemed to me that the whole world was taking a break, holding its breath, waiting for Johnny and Stacy to fall in love.

Aunt Julia rescued us on weekday afternoons, inviting us to cool off in her aboveground pool. Emilie and I traipsed the half mile down Rural Route 4 to her house, our beach towels draped over our shoulders. I lagged behind, pulling at fuzzy cattails and listening to mosquitoes swarm over the stagnant water in the ditch. Toss a stone through their midst and they would part like the Red Sea letting Moses and his people cross, then swarm back in a rush. Emilie marched ahead, preening for the service vehicles that lumbered past on the road.

Aunt Julia, older than Dad by almost twelve years,

was my favorite aunt. Her husband, Uncle Paul, was a general manager for John Deere in Manitowoc, and their son, Brent, only a few years older than Johnny, was training to be a firefighter in Milwaukee. Emilie and I were the girls she'd never had. Uncle Paul had built them a fancy deck around a four-foot Doughboy, and she loved to serve us Popsicles and sugary glasses of lemonade and lay her wrinkly, too-tan body on the deck while we swam. Sometimes she smoked cigarettes, too, although about this we were sworn to secrecy. "I'm supposed to be quitting," she had explained, although she never seemed to try all that hard.

"What's new, girls?" she asked from beneath a broad sun hat.

"Unfortunately, nothing is ever new around here," Emilie said, splashing dramatically onto her back. "That's the problem."

"Well," I said, staying close to the deck, "I think Johnny has a girlfriend." Suddenly Johnny had been asking to use the phone every night after dinner. On weekends, he showered after the last milking and disappeared in his truck.

Aunt Julia's eyebrows rose over the tops of her sunglasses. "I think I've heard that myself."

"Really? From Mom?" I asked.

"From everyone in Watankee, more like it," Emilie scoffed. "He took her on the youth group rafting trip last weekend, and they're going to a movie tonight. In Watankee terms, they are officially a couple." She lifted her hands out of the water to put air quotes around the word.

Aunt Julia laughed. "So what do you think? Do you like her?"

Emilie made a sound like "ehh." She wobbled her hand in the air in a so-so motion.

"I like her! She's really nice," I said. In Stacy's defense, I splashed in Emilie's direction, but the water landed a foot short of its mark.

Emilie laughed. "You don't even know her."

"I do, too! You don't know who I know." I *did* know Stacy. She had visited our house twice now, and each time she'd asked me about what I was reading, what I liked to do during the summer. She and Johnny and I had walked out to the barn, and I'd convinced her to let a calf suckle two of her outstretched fingers. She'd squealed at first and then got used to it and started stroking the calf behind its ears with her free hand. This felt like the most essential thing to know about a person.

There was a familiar hissing sound as Aunt Julia struck a match to light her cigarette. "What don't you like about her, Emilie?"

Emilie considered for a moment. "She's just so clingy, you know? She hangs all over him."

Aunt Julia blew some smoke out of the side of her mouth and gave a little chuckle. "Seems like she's the kind of girl who likes to have a boyfriend. Plenty of girls like that."

"I think it's pathetic," Emilie pronounced. "She spent the whole past month just trying to catch his eye—"

"She did not!" I sputtered defensively. Of course she hadn't. She'd only been at that softball game because her Dad was playing; she'd only talked to Johnny in the first place because I'd passed on her message. "You're just jealous because you don't have a boyfriend."

Emilie shrieked with laughter. She tipped her head backward into the water and came up again, her hair lying sleek against her head. "Oh, puh-lease. Plus, ask anyone at school. She was dating this guy last year and she just about drove him insane, she was so needy."

I flopped onto my back, kicking my legs angrily in her direction. She skimmed her arms across the surface of the pool in response, serving up an impressive wall of water that splashed onto the deck.

"All right, girls." Aunt Julia sighed, a gray strand of smoke curling out of her mouth.

"I'm only *saying,*" Emilie smirked.

"Well *I* like her," I announced.

"I do, too, sweetie," Aunt Julia said. "And I bet Johnny's big enough to handle himself."

Emilie rolled her eyes but let it go. "I'm going to start a whirlpool," she announced, kicking off from the edge of the pool.

Aunt Julia laid her head back, closing her eyes, and I flopped back onto an inner tube, letting the momentum from Emilie's vigorous one-person whirlpool spin me in lazy circles. Every now and then I splashed water onto the inner tube to cool off my legs. The sunscreen that had been slathered on me only an hour before had melted away with the heat, and I could feel my skin pinking from head to toe.

That night, with barely any warning, a thunderstorm rolled through on dark, menacing clouds that hung low on the horizon over our still-fragile cornstalks. It was still blazing hot, eighty degrees but dripping with humidity so thick that the air seemed to splinter and shape itself around us as we moved. Dad and I were coming back from the barn when the first bolt of lightning split the sky in two. We were drenched by the time we made it to the back door. Upstairs, Emilie and I sat on her bed, watching while rain swept the fields and battered the house. Suddenly, there was a crack; the oak tree on the front lawn had been hit by lightning. I screamed when a large branch hit the ground, shaking the house and all of us inside it. In the morning, Dad and Johnny dragged the limb across the grass to the side of our shed, where it lay like a carcass, its sad branches splayed to the side.

six

One night that August, Stacy Lemke showed up unannounced at our back door.

Johnny was in the living room practicing moves with some of his wrestling friends, Peter Bahn and Erik Hansen. Johnny was always conditioning—hefting feed bags and doing chin-ups at a barn in the hayloft, but he saw these nights as serious training sessions. Dad was there, of course, and Jerry Warczak had stopped by to talk with Dad about some new fencing he would need help installing. Grandpa took a seat in one of the out-of-the-way recliners and cheered at all the wrong times. Somehow, despite watching dozens of Johnny's matches, he'd never figured out the scoring system.

Johnny's coach was there, too; he liked to stop by from time to time to check in with Dad and throw around words like "scholarship" and "state title." Coach Zajac was Johnny's height but twice as wide, his shoulders straining the seams of the warm-up jacket he wore year-round, no matter the weather. His ears were puffy, bulbous even, like an early version of human ears, before God ironed out all the kinks. Cauliflower ears,

Dad had explained to me once. "It's just fluid that gets trapped in there." But every time I saw him, I was reminded of the jar at Wallen's Pharmacy, where people dropped their spare change to help end birth defects.

When Stacy arrived, I happened to be in the kitchen, helping myself to a glass of lemonade. I didn't recognize the white sedan that dropped her off, but there was Stacy, striding across our lawn as if she'd done this a million times before.

"Oh!" Mom said, opening the door but standing in front of the doorway, as if she wasn't going to let Stacy inside. "You know, this might not be the best time, honey. Johnny's in the middle of some wrestling with the guys."

"I know," Stacy said, smiling sweetly. "I came over to watch."

Mom didn't respond; she just stepped out of the way. Stacy gave me a little wave, passing right through the kitchen into the living room, as if she belonged there. I saw Mom raise an eyebrow; she didn't approve. It wasn't personal, but as far as she was concerned, Johnny was too young to have a serious girlfriend.

I followed Stacy into the living room, noticing the way her jeans hugged her thighs, the way her hair floated over her shoulders. She didn't fit in here, I realized. Everything we owned was shabby, from Mom's hand-me-down furniture and the worn carpet that had been here since Dad was a boy and the peeling wallpaper we always meant to take down. Everything about Stacy was new and fresh, as if it had just been invented that day.

The men in the doorway stepped back to let Stacy into the room, and Grandpa looked up from the recliner.

Dad looked from Stacy to Johnny and back, as if he was trying to figure out the joke. Only Johnny and Peter Bahn, wrestling in the middle of the floor, didn't notice her right away. I said loudly, "Stacy's here," and Johnny froze, his glance drifting over his shoulder. Peter took advantage of the moment and flipped Johnny over, pinning him. Grandpa clapped. Johnny swore.

"Got you," Peter said, laughing.

Johnny rolled out from under Peter's grasp, his chest heaving. "Caught me off guard," he panted. "That's no fair."

Peter shrugged. "Fair's fair," he said, pushing himself up to a standing position.

Johnny stood, too, scowling. He hated to lose.

"I didn't mean to break anything up," Stacy said, smiling uncertainly.

"What are you doing here?" Johnny demanded.

Stacy's smile faded. "I just wanted to say hi."

Johnny shook his head. "You could have just called."

Dad cleared his throat. "Johnny, why don't you introduce Stacy around."

Johnny hesitated a long beat, breathing through his nose. Only after catching Dad's eye did he relax. "This is Erik, Peter, Grandpa Hammarstrom, Coach Zajac," he said, gesturing. Erik and Peter smiled, Grandpa gave a slight, confused nod of acknowledgment, and Coach raised one hand in a meaty salute. "And this is Jerry, who lives next door."

Jerry reached out his hand a little bashfully, and Stacy shook it.

She turned to Johnny playfully. "And you are?"

"We were in the middle of something," Johnny said, still not letting it go.

Dad cleared his throat again, trying to diffuse the awkwardness. "How about a breather?" he asked, motioning toward the kitchen. The men followed his cue and trudged off obediently, even Grandpa, who seemed to greatly resent having to move. I stayed in the doorway, nervous for Stacy.

"Really, I didn't mean to break up anything," Stacy said. She reached for Johnny's hand, threading her fingers through his. Johnny was as unyielding as a plastic dummy. "Okay. Look, you're right. I should have called first."

"Yeah," Johnny grunted, relenting. He locked his fingers with hers, bringing her hand to his chest. "We were about done anyway."

I knew that wasn't true. It was barely eight o'clock, and sometimes they wrestled past ten, until Mom started hinting about an early shift in the morning, and Dad drifted off to check the barn one last time. This was the power Stacy had over him, then; she could interrupt his wrestling night—that most sacred of Johnny's rituals—and be forgiven.

"Are you sure?" Stacy gave him a playful smile. "You might need more practice. Looks like you were getting whipped right there."

"Oh, yeah?" Johnny grabbed her by the waist. "That's it, Lemke, you're going down." He scooped her up in his arms like she weighed nothing at all. I held my breath, trying to figure out if he was joking or angry. It was hard to tell from the way he handled her—swinging her around a little too fast, depositing her a little too roughly on the carpet. Stacy shrieked but didn't struggle as he pinned her down, his knees on either side of her legs, his hands on her shoulders.

"Say that again?" Johnny asked.

Teasing, I thought, relieved. *He's only teasing.*

"I said it looks like you need a little more practice," Stacy said, smirking.

"You're going to help me with that?" Johnny leaned over her, pressing his weight against her.

"You bet."

Johnny brought his face down to hers and kissed her so hard that it made me dizzy. Stacy grabbed him around the neck and somehow they were rolling, her over him and him over her, not coming to a stop until they bumped up against the sofa. Stacy was on top, grinning.

"Looks like I win," she said.

Johnny laughed. "This is only round one, Lemke," he said, and rolled her onto her back.

I slipped into the kitchen, joining the men for a piece of pie.

By the time Johnny and Stacy came in, red-cheeked, all the men had left, except Grandpa, who was picking at a few last crumbs on his plate.

"Everyone's gone?" Johnny asked, looking around.

No one answered. Mom was at the sink with her back to him, running water, and Emilie stood next to her, scowling, a dish towel in hand.

"I should probably go, too," Stacy said. "Good night, everyone!"

"Good night," Mom murmured.

"Good night, Stacy!" I called, and she gave me a little wink.

"Umm… Stacy's going to need a ride home," Johnny announced, jiggling his keys. "I'll be back in a half hour." I watched the two of them head down the sidewalk together, with both of her arms wrapped around his waist. Johnny opened the passenger door of his truck and escorted her inside with a flourish.

"It doesn't take half an hour to get to the other side of Watankee and back," Emilie observed drily.

Mom gave Dad a look—*the* look.

"I don't think we were ever like that," he said, giving her a playful nudge with his foot. His sock, I noticed, was worn thin at the heel.

In the moment before the interior light in the truck was extinguished, I saw that Stacy had scooted across the bench seat, so she was riding with the left side of her body pressed up against Johnny.

"No," Mom said, refusing to take the bait. "I don't think we ever were."

I never learned where Stacy had seen Johnny for the first time. Maybe it was between classes and he was shelving books in his locker, or maybe he was standing in line at the cafeteria, but I liked to believe that she first saw him when he was wrestling, crouched in the stance perfected on all those long summer nights, a number on his back, battling his way through the bracket and coming out, just about always, on top.

seven

After that evening, Johnny's wrestling nights became rarer and then tapered off for good. There was something a little awkward about being around Johnny and Stacy, something that made everyone else feel like a third wheel. They couldn't stop touching each other, and they practically sat on top of each other on the couch, even though, as Mom liked to point out, there was plenty of room to spread out. On warm-weather weekends, Johnny's friends used to congregate in our driveway, their Fords and Chevys idling, finalizing plans for cliff jumping in Manitou Park or riding their bikes down Clay Pit Road to the old quarry. But once Johnny and Stacy were officially dating, the guys Johnny had known his whole life—guys he'd played with since elementary school—basically disappeared.

Stacy's sixteenth birthday coincided with Labor Day weekend, our last truly free moments of life before school began. Stacy delivered the party invitation herself, her hair swinging in a thick French braid.

"It'll be small, just family and a few friends," she said at dinner. She'd become a regular fixture in our lives in a short span of time. "My parents just want to meet everybody, you know, officially." She grinned at Johnny, and he smiled back at her.

"Well, that sounds very nice," Mom said with a tight half smile she generally reserved for the women she didn't like at church, or the times when Grandpa invited himself over and didn't seem inclined to leave. "Doesn't that sound nice?" she continued, looking around the table. "Please tell your parents we wouldn't miss it."

Later, Emilie made a valiant effort to plead for freedom. "When you said *we* wouldn't miss it, you meant you and Dad, right?"

Mom stiffened her jaw. "We're all going," she said, throwing her gaze onto me.

I tried to shrug casually, but it was no secret to anyone that Stacy Lemke had become my idol. When I was alone I tried to imitate the way she walked, with just a little slouch to her shoulders. I loved how she parted her straight hair right down the middle and had tried it with my own, wetting my hairbrush under the faucet. Emilie had studied the end result critically. "What happened to your hair? You look like a drowned rat," she'd pronounced.

As it turned out, the Lemkes lived less than two miles from us, on the south side of Watankee, not far from the juncture at Passaqua Road. I noticed right away that their white house looked neater than ours, as if it were standing up a little straighter in its frame. Half a dozen kids were bouncing on a huge trampoline on the lawn—the sort of thing Dad would never approve of because it killed the grass. Behind their house, tucked between a row of evergreens and a three-car garage, the yard was set up for Stacy's party. Crepe-paper streamers twisted from surface to surface, and bouquets of helium-filled balloons floated from the backs of folding chairs.

"I thought this was just a small thing," Mom said as we pulled into the driveway, which was lined with parked cars. Johnny's truck was already there, behind a shiny burgundy Buick.

Stacy, wearing a white dress with eyelet trim and red sandals, rushed over to greet us, followed by her parents. Mr. and Mrs. Lemke, tall and tanned, might have been siblings. If they were cookies, they would have come out from practically the same cutter. I couldn't stop staring at Mrs. Lemke; she looked pretty enough to be on television. Her hair was sprayed upward and rode on her head like a reddish-blond helmet. She wore a pink shift dress with platform sandals, and her fingers glittered with rings. Mr. Lemke wore a bright Hawaiian shirt with white pants and navy deck shoes. They were as polished as a pair of Kennedys.

"Looks like they've come straight from the country club," Mom muttered under her breath. But she smiled broadly; a second later she held out a hand to shake with Stacy's parents.

"Oh, homemade potato salad, Bill!" Mrs. Lemke exclaimed, taking the dish from Mom, followed by a conspiratorial whisper in Mom's direction, as if she were revealing a state secret, "It's his favorite, and I just don't have time to make it from scratch anymore."

"Oh, I'm so glad," Mom said. Without the salad bowl to hold, she clasped her hands in front of her stomach awkwardly.

I set our gift—a soft white cardigan with tiny pearl buttons that Mom had picked out and Emilie had judged "too fussy"—on a card table already heaped with presents, and then stood uncomfortably in the middle of a circle of strangers. Emilie spotted a group of teenagers that included Joanie Lemke and wandered over, perfectly at ease. It wasn't difficult to spot Heather Lemke; even in a sundress, she was just as fearsome as she was on the playground. She was giving a piggyback ride to a little boy about half her size, who wobbled on her back like an oversize doll. I made my way over to the drink table, where my parents stood uneasily, sipping out of plastic cups. I reached for one of the massive plastic ladles but was redirected by Mrs. Lemke.

"Oh, no, Kirsten. Have some punch from *this* bowl," she said and laughed, steering me by the shoulders to a bowl floating with lumps of orange sherbet.

Sipping the too-sweet punch, I joined my parents, who were in the middle of a polite set of introductions.

"John's a farmer and Alicia works at the hospital in Manitowoc," Mrs. Lemke announced to the group. "Can you believe that? She's a lot tougher than me, working around blood and guts all day long."

Dad and Mom grinned and nodded, looking as out of place as I felt. We had dressed carefully, with Mom ironing out our wrinkles, but in this crowd of linen dresses and polo shirts, we might have been the Beverly Hillbillies. I spotted Johnny and Stacy coming out of the house holding hands and marveled at how comfortable Johnny looked here, as if he belonged.

"And over there, that's their daughter Emilie, and this is Kirsten." Mrs. Lemke leaned down to me with a wide pink smile. "And Kirsten will be starting…?"

"Fourth grade," I said loudly. Mom gave me a little nudge from behind, which I knew meant—*Be polite.*

Mrs. Lemke wrinkled her pretty face inquisitively, as if there was a joke she didn't understand.

"She's just a little small for her age," Mom said quickly.

I looked around for Stacy and saw her standing with some of the other high school kids. Then Johnny came up behind her and dropped something down the back of her dress, and she screamed, swatting him away. She wriggled an ice cube free and tossed it playfully after him.

"Who wants the grand tour?" Mr. Lemke asked, and Dad and I, not sure what to do, followed him. Mr. Lemke led us into their rambling house, pointing out the upgrades such as the finished basement with a pool table and the master suite addition, which he joked had cost "an arm and two or three legs." Everything looked bright and new, down to the dozen red pillows on the white living room couch. A white living room couch? Between Mr. Lemke's white pants and Stacy's white dress, I was beginning to believe that dirt didn't exist here.

When we got to Stacy's room, I lingered behind, giving the open door a slight nudge. Inside, the walls were a pale yellow, and the furniture was white, from her nightstand to her headboard to a double chest of drawers. I pinched myself: *I was inside Stacy's bedroom.* There was a massive "Shipbuilders" banner on one wall and a bouquet of red roses on the nightstand, which I guessed were from Johnny. Her room was so white, so clean and sterile, it might have belonged in a hospital. Emilie and I had filled about every inch of our room with our junk—where were Stacy's bunched-up socks, her bottles of perfume, the paper fans folded from church bulletins?

I peeked into the hallway, but Dad and Mr. Lemke

had continued on without me. I stepped farther into the room, cautiously. *Stacy slept here, in this very bed,* I thought as I ran my finger along her pillow, over her crisp pillowcase. I scanned her bookcase. A King James Bible, *The Adventures of Huckleberry Finn,* a set of pristine leather-bound classics. Through her filmy white curtain, I could see kids bobbing up and down on the trampoline, their heads coming in and out of view. I sat gently on the edge of her bed, and slid open the top drawer of her nightstand.

I wasn't looking for anything exactly—just evidence of the girl I knew in this too-perfect room, or maybe evidence of how much she loved Johnny, and me, too. But right on top was a picture of Stacy and someone who wasn't Johnny. His arm was tight around her shoulders, and she was grinning so widely that I could see her one pointed tooth. Someone had drawn a heart in red marker around their heads—and then, more recently I suspected, the boy's face had been blacked out with a ballpoint pen. I ran a finger across the snapshot, imagining Stacy wielding the pen, digging the deep hash marks across his face until it was gone, obliterated. She had pressed so hard that she'd almost poked a hole through the back of the picture. He didn't matter anymore, but Stacy was still there, beaming.

I dropped the picture as if it was on fire and slid the drawer closed, my heart pounding. Standing, I straightened the edge of the bedspread to erase my presence. Maybe Emilie was right—Stacy had loved someone else before, as intensely as she loved Johnny now.

"We spent the most money in the kitchen, of course," Mr. Lemke was saying when I caught up to them. "You know how these old farmhouses are, with the outdated plumbing and electrical."

Back outside, Mrs. Lemke removed a store-bought cake from its pink bakery box and poked sixteen candles through its stiff loops of white frosting. We sang a wild rendition of "Happy Birthday," with Mr. Lemke holding all the notes too long and stretching out his hands dramatically, as if he was performing for the back row of a crowded theater. Mrs. Lemke clapped excitedly when Stacy blew out all the candles in a single shot.

"No candles left? You know what that means, don't you?" Mr. Lemke bellowed. "No boyfriends!"

Everyone laughed, and Johnny pretended to look offended. Stacy leaned over to give his cheek a loud smack. "*One* boyfriend," she clarified. My cheeks burned, thinking of her in the picture with the other boyfriend, scratched out of existence. Mom forced a polite smile and excused herself to the bathroom.

Mrs. Lemke stepped up to cut the cake, and Heather and Joanie came forward to pass out plates and forks to the guests.

I picked at my slice, slipping a red rose of frosting into my mouth and holding it on my tongue until it dissolved. The adults, finding it difficult to balance their drinks and their slices of cake, found their way back to the folding chairs. I sat cross-legged on the grass, my own plate in my lap.

The frosting had melted in my mouth, sickly sweet. I felt a little bit like throwing up, whether from the sun or the sugar, or thinking of Stacy with a boyfriend she had loved as much as Johnny.

One of the ladies, passing by, said under her breath, "They've sure got their hands full with that one." I turned around, trying to pinpoint who she was talking about, but got only a sharp glare of late-afternoon sun.

Suddenly Mom was standing over me, her shadow like a soft blanket. "Did you save any cake for me?"

I held out my plate. "You can have the rest."

I lost count of how many boxes Stacy opened, carefully working her finger under the wrapping paper and gently separating layers of tissue. Instead I was watching her carefully, looking for any hint that Stacy was somehow less than perfect, not the angel I'd thought. She cooed over each sweater, shirt, skirt, necklace, bracelet and earring, holding it up for our appraisal. When she got to our gift, she said, "Oh, I love it! It's perfect. Tell the truth—who picked this out? It wasn't Johnny, was it?" Everyone laughed, Johnny loudest of all. I was irritated with him then; he looked like a buffoon, like just another big, dumb guy. "And now, the best for last," Mr. Lemke said, setting a huge box in front of Stacy. "Go ahead, baby."

Stacy ripped off the paper and opened the box—only to find another wrapped box inside, and another inside that. She tossed the wadded-up pieces of paper at her dad in mock frustration. Finally she came to a tiny velvet jewelry box in the middle, and opened it to pull out a single key. She screamed. "Oh, my goodness. You didn't! You didn't!"

"Follow me, everyone," Mr. Lemke said, and the whole party trooped behind him to the shed, clutching cameras and glasses of punch.

Stacy squealed at the sight of what was plainly a car shrouded in white sheets.

"Nothing but the best for my girl," Mr. Lemke said, whipping off the sheets to reveal a shiny red Camaro.

Everyone gasped and applauded, as if he had just pulled off a daring magic trick.

"I can't believe it!" Stacy cried, tugging open the driver's door.

"Not bad." Johnny grinned, running a hand along the hood.

"We needed a way to get her to and from school," Mrs. Lemke explained, her cheeks pink. "She's getting so independent now, always needing to go somewhere."

I caught a glance between Dad and Mom that was half smirk, half eye-roll. Maybe their look was in reference to our own 1985 Chevrolet Caprice station wagon, which was fast approaching the ten-year mark, or Johnny's '69 Chevy, dubbed the Green Machine, which he'd inherited from Dad when he turned sixteen. We'd all figured Dad would buy himself a new truck at that point, but instead he'd come back from Manitowoc with an even older model, one that was so stripped down on the inside, Mom refused to ride in it. "It runs fine," Dad had said, shrugging.

After the grand unveiling, Stacy's party fizzled out. One by one, we wandered back to gather the plates and napkins that had scattered in the breeze. Dad and Mom moved silently, helping to stack folding chairs against the side of the garage. There was another round of handshakes before we left, with Mrs. Lemke insisting we simply had to get together again soon, and Mom answering, "Of course!"

The next time we would see each other, Stacy wouldn't be there. The next time we would see each other, the Lemkes and the Hammarstroms wouldn't even pretend to be friendly. But that afternoon, we all smiled and said polite goodbyes, and Johnny announced, "Think I'll stick around and give Stacy a driving lesson."

"Don't be too late," Mom said automatically, which was funny, because Johnny had been coming home later and later, and no one seemed to know what too late was anymore.

When we were at the end of the driveway, Emilie and I craned our necks to look back at them. "Look at them—they're like a magazine advertisement," Emilie marveled.

Even from that distance, we could see Mrs. Lemke standing on a folding chair, unpinning a row of streamers. Mr. Lemke was scraping down the grill with a long-handled brush. As we straightened out of the turn heading onto Passaqua Road, we got a clear view of the Camaro behind the shed. Stacy was sitting on the hood, her arms wrapped around Johnny's neck, her legs hooked around his thighs. He was standing, his body pressed tightly against her in a way that was—well—

Mom cleared her throat suddenly, and all four of our heads swiveled on our necks, facing the road in front of us once again.

"I'll bet he teaches her how to drive," Emilie whispered, but I knew better than to laugh.

eight

Fourth grade wasn't much different from third grade, with its spelling tests and vocabulary words and the maps of Wisconsin we traced diligently from our social studies textbook. In gym class, my teacher seemed to plan our activities around things a small person simply could not do—shoot baskets, break through the chain in Red Rover. It was shocking how tall my classmates had grown over the summer. Mom resisted my constant pleas to write a note that would excuse me, permanently, from gym. In retaliation I lugged several of her old medical books to the hayloft and spent my afternoons trying to pull off a case of rheumatoid arthritis or intestinal polyps.

Emilie, with her hordes of friends, fit in perfectly at the high school. She was one of only two freshmen chosen to play clarinet in pep band, and she already knew that she wanted the lead in the spring musical, *Annie Get Your Gun.*

And Johnny—well, Johnny had wrestling and Johnny had Stacy. "You should see them at school," Emilie told me one afternoon, pointing a finger down her throat in a fake gag. "It's disgusting. I'm so embarrassed to know them."

After only a month of school, Johnny's English teacher called to report that Johnny hadn't yet turned in his *Macbeth* essay—hadn't, for that matter, seemed to have read a word of *Macbeth.* Mom repeated the conversation to Dad in the kitchen while I eavesdropped from outside the kitchen window, where I was brushing some burrs out of Kennel's coat.

"This is his *senior year,*" Mom said to Dad. "He only has a few classes left, and all he has to do is pass them. Instead he's spending all his time with that girl—"

I paused, midstroke. *That girl.*

"I'll talk to him about the essay," Dad offered. "He's going to have to keep his grades up if he's going to be eligible."

They lowered their voices, but I could tell they were arguing. Then the door slammed, and Dad came down the porch steps. "Hey, kiddo," he said, spotting me. Kennel jumped up, abandoning his brushing to follow Dad, whose long legs seemed to cover the distance between our house and the barn in only a few steps.

Whatever talk Dad had with Johnny did prompt a slight change in Johnny's behavior. He spent more weeknights in his room, presumably catching up on homework—although in reality he seemed to be doing nothing more challenging than throwing a bouncy ball against his bedroom wall and catching it with a loud clap. Throw, clap, throw, clap, until I thought I'd go insane.

One night after dinner, Emilie ran into our bedroom and thrust her hand over my mouth. "Ssshh!" she hissed.

"I wasn't saying anything," I protested into her hand. At the moment I was nose-deep in *The True Story of*

Bonnie and Clyde. I'd skipped ahead to the pictures, fascinated by Bonnie's tiny, gun-toting, cigar-smoking figure. When they were ambushed and killed in Louisiana, Bonnie had been twenty-three years old. She was four feet, eleven inches tall and officially my hero. I wondered if she had been routinely chosen last for P.E., and if her classmates regretted that later.

"Listen," Emilie said, still holding me around the neck.

"You're hurting me," I seethed back.

And then from downstairs, I heard raised voices—Mom's and Johnny's.

Emilie loosened her grip on me long enough for me to whisper, "What's going on? Where's Dad?"

She whispered back, "He went over to Jerry's for something. I guess Mom found a note from Stacy."

Uh-oh. I knew this could be bad. Stacy was the queen of writing long notes—it was what she did instead of homework on the nights she came over, a math book open on her lap, bent over pages of dense writing in purple ink, with tiny hearts to dot her *i*'s. Plenty of times, at the end of the night, she'd fold the note into an ingenious little package and pass it over to Johnny.

"We could hear better from the stairs," I suggested. For once, Emilie paid attention to me. She released my neck, which had started to cramp at that point, and we crept halfway down the stairs, stepping carefully to avoid creaks, and wedged ourselves onto the same step.

Johnny's voice was raised, easily traveling across the kitchen, through the closed door and up the stairs. "I don't understand. You were going through my stuff?"

"I was not going through your stuff," Mom clarified, her tone deadly. "I was simply doing the laundry like

I always do, and part of doing the laundry is to empty all the pockets."

"Okay," Johnny huffed. "But you didn't have to read it. That's an invasion of privacy!"

Emilie let out a small wheeze, a stifled laugh.

Mom laughed, too, a hard laugh, the kind I knew better than to cross. "Invasion of privacy! Do I have to remind you that I'm the parent and you're the child?"

"I'm seventeen! I'm an adult."

"Not yet. Not an adult—yet."

"I'm old enough to get a letter from my girlfriend without you—"

"This isn't just any ordinary letter, Johnny!"

I heard a rustling of paper.

"You're going to read it?" Johnny's voice was incredulous.

"First it starts with how much she loves you. She probably says that a dozen times. Then, 'The whole school could have caught on fire and I wouldn't have noticed, because I was just looking at you. I would have kept staring at you until my hair was singed and the skin started to drip from my bones…'"

"Whoa!" Emilie breathed into my ear.

Ick, I thought.

"Give it back to me!"

"And here she says that she might as well be dead if she can't be with you…."

Johnny bellowed, "You have no right!"

"I have every right! Later on, and I quote, 'It's like you're the best drug in the world and I need you in me all the time, pulsing through my veins.'"

I didn't realize how clenched my body was until I bit my tongue sharply and tasted warm blood in my mouth.

"All right! You've made your point!"

"No, Johnny. I haven't. The point is, this isn't just puppy love. It's getting way out of hand. Stacy is just getting way too obsessed—"

"She's not obsessed! What are you saying?"

"She says in this letter that she can't live without you. She says if she can't see you every day, she'll kill herself. It's not normal, Johnny!"

I shivered, remembering the picture in Stacy's night-stand again, with the boy's face obliterated, the pen almost wearing through the paper. Had she felt like that with him, too, that she would kill herself if she couldn't see him?

Johnny's voice was quieter when he spoke, as if maybe with Mom reading the note he'd heard Stacy's words for the first time. "She's not being serious, though. She's only trying to say..."

"Johnny." Mom's voice was lower now, more controlled. "I'm worried that you're spending so much time together. You're not seeing your friends, you're not keeping up with your grades. The things she says in this letter—they're not things a sixteen-year-old girl should say. You're both very young to be so serious."

"Oh, no," Emilie said. I felt her grip on my arm, tightening like the blood pressure cuff in the doctor's office.

"We're too young to be so serious? *I'm* too young?" Johnny's voice escalated with each syllable. "You know, that's really rich, coming from you!"

"Here we go," Emilie whispered.

I pinched her arm. "What? I don't get it."

Emilie pinched me back, hard. "I'll explain later."

Mom's voice had escalated again. "Johnny, you have

no right to say that. It was a different time, a different situation!"

Johnny's laugh was mean. "I can't believe you're using that on me. Somehow you're going to make even that be my fault."

"Johnny, that's enough!"

It occurred to me that somehow Johnny had never learned to be submissive, to roll over and give up like Kennel when we caught him gnawing on one of Dad's work boots. Emilie and I might push the boundaries from time to time, but we gave in just before getting ourselves in trouble. Johnny didn't stop, and that's what made him tenacious in the ring. But it also made him act impulsively, and earned him more than his share of punishments over the years.

"So it was okay for you, it was okay for you and Dad, but it's not okay for me? Stacy's 'obsessed,' but you were just, what? A normal teenage girl in love? You must not have been so pure and innocent, because—"

A slap—a sound so vivid that I could almost see Mom's palm connecting with Johnny's cheek. He must have stumbled backward; there was a thud as his body connected with the table. Emilie gasped. I winced, as if it was me who had been slapped.

"Never mind," I whispered to her. "I get it now."

Mom's voice was shaky. "You apologize for that. You apologize right now."

Johnny didn't say anything. There was a scraping sound, as if a chair was being dragged across the linoleum, followed by a heavy thud. Emilie's fingernails dug little half-moons into my arms.

"Johnny!"

But the screen door was already slapping behind

him, and before Emilie and I made it to the kitchen, Johnny was down the porch stairs and getting into his truck.

"We're not done!" Mom yelled, but the Green Machine had already shuddered to life, stirring up a spray of gravel before roaring away on Rural Route 4. I didn't have to be a genius to know that he was going to see Stacy.

Mom's words lingered in the kitchen like an ugly bruise. Looking around, I saw what had caused the crash. Johnny had thrown one of our heavy kitchen chairs against the wall; it lay toppled on its back, one of the spindles hanging loose.

Mom tucked her T-shirt into her jeans and, without saying a word, righted the chair. With a little pop, the spindle slipped back into its place, and she slid the chair under the table.

Back upstairs, I lay on my bed, facing the wall, staring at nothing. Maybe Mom was right—Johnny and Stacy were getting too serious. I blushed, remembering how Johnny had pinned Stacy to the ground, the breathless way her chest had heaved beneath his. Did she really think of Johnny as a drug, that she needed to keep coming back for more? Would she really kill herself if she couldn't see him every day? I pulled my quilt over my head, feeling suddenly as if I knew too much.

nine

That fall, tension in our house lurked around every corner. Stacy still came over sometimes, but she didn't always come inside. Instead, Johnny went out to meet her, and Emilie and I would spy on them as he leaned her back against the Camaro for one of their long, passionate kisses.

Mom would watch from the kitchen window, flicking the porch light on and off, like some kind of Morse code: *I'm watching you. I see what you're doing.*

Each night was its own battle, but the afternoons were generally quiet and peaceful, with Mom still at work and Johnny and Emilie at one sort of practice or another. When the bus dropped me off from school, I'd run down the driveway to check in with Dad in the barn, give Kennel a hundred kisses, fix myself a peanut butter sandwich and curl up in my own secret fort—the back of the hallway linen closet.

This was one of the few benefits of being short, I'd discovered—I could squeeze my body into unexpected places. When Johnny and Emilie used to play hide-and-seek with me, I was always the winner. I could slide into the narrowest of cracks behind an open door, climb into dresser drawers and stand upright in a vacuum cleaner box with inches to spare. Then a few years ago, I'd discovered the hollow at the back of an upstairs closet. It was just a narrow space behind the closet shelves, about four feet high and two and a half feet deep—too small to bother sealing, too awkward for storage, and perfect for me. It was a great place for reading; all I had to do was move our guest towels out of the way and I was in.

With a couple of Grandma's old quilts and the flickering light of a Coleman lantern, my hiding place was as neat and comfortable as any hobbit hole—and no one could bother me. I could spend uninterrupted hours with books of true crime, or my new favorite obsession, the *Guinness Book of World Records.* I marveled at the world's tallest person, who had reached eight feet, eleven inches and only lived to be twenty-two. Eight feet—I couldn't imagine. He wouldn't have survived long in our house, where his head would have brushed the ceiling and smacked against every doorway.

One afternoon, when Dad was up in Green Bay and I was up in my hideout studying a photo of Kara Gordon, the world's shortest person at twenty-three inches tall, I heard the back door bang open. I heard the unmistakable sound of Johnny hammering his boots against the door sill, a habit Mom had drilled into each of us, and then faintly, Stacy's laugh. This surprised me—since Stacy was only welcome in our house if Mom or Dad were there. And even then, she wasn't truly welcome.

Straining, I could hear the winter undressing sounds associated with snow—hats and scarves and gloves peeling off with a whack, coats unzipping, feet working their way out of boots. Then two sets of footsteps on the stairs. I held my breath.

"Shh…shh!" Stacy's hissed whisper.

"We don't have to 'shh.' No one's here," Johnny said, whispering anyway. "Mom's at work, and Dad's out of town for the day."

"What about your sisters?"

"Emilie's at band practice and Kirsten's probably in the hayloft or something."

"Are you sure?"

Johnny laughed. "Are you kidding me? If Kirsten were here, she'd be hanging all over you by now."

That was mean, I thought, my cheeks hot. But not as mean as Stacy's laugh of agreement. I would have expected her to protest, to say that I wasn't a pest, that she loved talking to me.

Instead, she hollered, "Hello! Hellllllloooo! Emilie and Kirsten! Come out, come out, wherever you are!"

They laughed as if this was the most hysterical thing ever.

Quietly, I folded my legs and brought my knees to my chin. I heard Johnny's bedroom door squeak open, then thunk as it caught on something, a pair of shoes, maybe, or a football.

"God, your room is such a *sty,*" Stacy said. "No wonder you've never let me in here before." She laughed again, and I remembered Stacy's bedroom from her party: the white bedspread, the neat line of books on her shelf.

"Jeez, Lemke. Let it go."

There was the sound of metal coiling, and I realized they were on Johnny's bed. My little hideout was situated between the linen closet and Johnny's bedroom; I might as well have been perched in his closet.

Listening to Stacy's giggles, my hearing suddenly felt very sharp. I plugged my ears and counted to twenty, then unstopped them and listened to their quiet sucking sounds. This was kissing—real kissing, late-night TV kissing, not the short pecks my parents planted on each other's cheeks on their way out the door or the dry forehead smacks Mom gave us when we professed to have fevers, kisses that were more thermometer than affection. Once, Emilie had shown me how to practice kissing, and we had sucked on the insides of our arms until they were covered with purplish hickeys. It had taken a full week for mine to disappear, and Mom had frowned, noticing my arm as I got ready for bed. "You must be playing too hard in the barn," she said. "You're all bruised up."

Now I imagined Johnny and Stacy burying each other's bodies in hickeys, a more private version of what Mom termed their "make-out sessions" when Johnny walked Stacy to her car. I wondered if her pink lip gloss, which she reapplied constantly from a little tube that bulged in her back pocket like a strange tumor, had transferred onto Johnny's mouth, his neck, leaving sweet raspberries on his skin.

I've got to say something now, I thought, *make some noise, get myself out of here.* I had a basic idea of what was happening—anything from necking to going all the way, which I'd learned about from Katie and Kari Schultz, twins in my grade whose college-aged babysitter had filled them in on everything from periods to where babies came from.

Then I heard something else—a zipper?

"What are you doing?" Johnny groaned, loud and low.

Stacy laughed again. "I thought you might like that,"

she whispered, a throaty sound that didn't sound like Stacy at all, but more like an actress in a love scene the moment before Mom changed the channel.

What would happen if someone came in now, like Grandpa with one of his shirts to be mended, or Mom, released from her shift early?

"You are such a tease," Johnny moaned, and Stacy laughed again.

"Good?" she asked.

"Mmm..."

I started to count in my head again, just wanting this to be over. *One, two, three...* Something soft like a sweater smacked against the wall, and then there were more sounds, like someone tugging off a pair of jeans. Were these, I wondered, the pale blue jeans with heart-shaped appliqués on the back pockets?

All of a sudden, the sounds stopped, and Johnny said, clear as anything: "I don't know about this."

Fifteen...sixteen...seventeen...

"I told you, I'm ready," Stacy whispered.

"But I just—I don't want you to think you have to—"

"I don't think I have to. I know I want to."

"You're sure about this? I mean, really sure?" Johnny's voice was husky, too. All of a sudden I realized it was a man's voice, not a boy's.

Twenty-seven, twenty-eight, twenty-nine.

"I told you, yeah. I'm sure. What can I do to get you to believe me?" She laughed then, and Johnny groaned.

"But what about...?"

"Don't worry about it. We'll be careful." She gave him a light smack, her voice teasing.

"Everyone always thinks they're being careful."

"I never thought *I'd* be the one who had to convince

you," she said, sounding almost annoyed for a second. Then she switched back to her throaty, teasing voice. "I mean, most guys wouldn't mind..."

Johnny's voice then was husky. "All right, you've convinced me."

There were more kissing sounds, the bedsprings creaking. Even if I wasn't hiding in the linen closet, I would have heard this. I started again. *Forty-eight, forty-nine, fifty...* My cheeks burned. The bed frame rattled against the wall.

Katie and Kari had illustrated the process for me in a notebook, behind pages of multiplication tables. It didn't make much sense until I equated her drawing with bulls and heifers. "So the man puts this—" a crude mushroom-shaped object "—into this—" a petal-shaped fissure I only vaguely equated with my own body "—and the woman gets pregnant," Katie had told me.

"And then her breasts get really big because they've filled up with milk," Kari added. I suspected they were missing a few steps in between, but still, I was unnerved to realize that this scene from the animal world in our barn translated so closely to human life. It shocked me to think that this happened all around me, to my parents, to my married cousins, even to people from church.

Johnny and Stacy were panting now, and it was as if they were breathing directly into my ear. I got stuck for a second: *Seventy-one, seventy-one, seventy-one...*

"Ouch!" Johnny's voice. "Did you just bite me?"

Stacy laughed. "Go ahead, bite me back."

Eighty-six... There was a rhythm to the bed creaking, the groans. I could hear—or was I imagining it?—two pairs of lungs, breath heavy, in sync. I hit one hundred and started working my way down. *Ninety-six, ninety-five...*

"Oh, Stace, Stace, Stace," Johnny said, his voice high-pitched and rapid.

What if I stood up, announcing my presence right then? I wondered if I could sneak out of the closet, down the stairs, out the screen door and then in again with a slam, the world's smallest superhero, here to save the day. I'd come charging up the steps and bang on Johnny's door, yelling, "Stop—or you'll have a baby!"

Seventy-five, seventy-four...

It was suddenly quiet, their bodies still. I felt as if I was going to suffocate in my hideout, I was so warm. If I moved, they would hear me. I had no choice but to stay still, breathing in the stale closet air until there was no more oxygen and I passed out. They would find my body there days later, and Johnny and Stacy would feel horribly guilty for what they'd done. I counted all the way down to zero and sat, listening to their silence. I imagined them together on Johnny's bed, skin against skin, and felt a warm flush on my neck.

"Shit," Johnny said suddenly, his voice startlingly close. "Look at the clock—it's after five. We've gotta get moving."

Stacy giggled. "Nah, I think I'll stay here."

Johnny was getting up—the bedsprings protesting, his voice moving farther away. "I don't think so."

"Why? Because your mom wouldn't approve?" Stacy laughed her lilting laugh. "Come on, Johnny. I'll be really quiet. I could camp here for a few days, and no one would even notice."

"Very funny."

I could hear Johnny moving around the room, dressing.

Stacy continued, her voice wistful, "If you want, I'll explain it all to them. I'll say, 'Mr. and Mrs. Hammarstrom, I know you don't really like me, but I'm moving in with your son.' I'll tell them that we love each other and that I'm already physically your wife."

"That's ridiculous," Johnny said, annoyance creeping into his voice. "Put your clothes on. Let's go."

Stacy's voice was smug. "Nope—I told you. I'm not leaving. I'm going to have a little talk with your parents when they come home, mister."

She seemed pretty pleased with herself for coming up with this bizarre plan. I tried, and failed, to imagine a world where my parents would let Stacy Lemke live in my brother's bedroom.

"Stacy, come on." There was an edge to his voice now, something I'd heard often enough as his sister. I remembered how angry he'd been when Stacy interrupted the wrestling night, that breathless moment when I couldn't tell if he was serious or joking, when it could have gone either way. Stacy had won that match, but I knew she wasn't going to win this one.

Again she laughed. "Sorry! No can do. I guess you're just stuck with me, Johnny Hammarstrom."

"I'm serious." Johnny's voice was level, but there was an edge to his calm. If Stacy got up right then, everything would be fine. If she didn't…well… "Any second now my sisters are going to be here, and we need to be gone."

"I'm perfectly serious, too," Stacy purred. "I'm just going to lie here on your bed, all stretched out, deliciously naked…."

"Stacy—now!"

They were both alike, I realized. Johnny never knew

when to stop being the aggressor, and Stacy didn't know when to stop egging him on.

Stacy ignored him. "I'd be like your own little princess in the tower, catering to your every whim. And I'd be good to you. I'd be so, sooo, soooo good to you. Come over here, we have time for more—"

There was a slapping sound, as if Johnny was batting Stacy's hands away. "What are you, crazy? Get dressed! You're going to get me in trouble!"

I'd been holding my breath for so long that I felt dizzy.

"Well, we wouldn't want that." Stacy sounded hurt, but as far as I could tell, she hadn't moved yet.

Johnny sighed, trying to be patient. "Are you going to get up?"

"I don't know," Stacy said simply.

"What the fuck, Stacy!" Johnny exploded suddenly. There was a thunk, like he'd kicked something—an open dresser drawer or his bed frame. He swung his bedroom door open, banging it against the wall, and took the stairs two at a time. At the bottom of the stairs, he called back over his shoulder, "I'm going to be in the truck, and if you're coming, you'd better get moving."

Slowly, too slowly, Stacy stood up. She seemed to be muttering under her breath while she gathered her clothes. I pressed my ear to the wall, trying to pick out her words. But, no, she wasn't muttering. She was *humming*—as if she had all the time in the world.

Johnny's voice carried up the stairs, dangerously. "Stacy…"

"All right, I'm coming," she called finally, starting down. "What's the hurry, Hammarstrom? Got another girl to visit before dinner?"

When I heard the back door slam behind them, I unfolded myself from my hiding spot, taking in fresh gulps of air like a deep-sea diver coming to the surface. I rushed to my bedroom window, careful not to disturb the curtain as I peeked out. Johnny had already started his truck. Hands on the steering wheel, he stared straight ahead. Stacy only had one leg inside when he gunned the engine. As they made the half turn in the driveway, I saw her reach unsteadily out with one hand and, straining, pull the door shut.

ten

There was no way I could tell anyone about that afternoon. Mom and Dad would yell loud enough to be heard in three counties. Emilie would use the information as a bargaining tool in the future.

Besides, I wasn't exactly sure how to describe what had happened. The sex wasn't even the bad part, not really. There was sex in just about every movie on TV, even though Mom cleared her throat pointedly and Dad changed the channel before anything got too detailed. Sure, Pastor Ziegler said every single Sunday that "sexual impurity" was explicitly forbidden by God, but the act itself didn't seem that strange. My parents had done it, and their parents before them, and even, presumably, Pastor Ziegler and his wife. It didn't seem all that crazy that Johnny and Stacy would give it a try, too. No, what I kept replaying over and over in my mind was their argument afterward: Stacy refusing to leave, Johnny kicking his dresser, then gunning the engine of the Green Machine.

And of course, I couldn't say anything to Johnny. I'm not sure what I would have said, even if I had dared, but the thing that kept coming to my mind was that I was sorry. Maybe I shouldn't have talked to Stacy that day under the bleachers. I shouldn't have given her message to Johnny. I shouldn't have encouraged her. Up until that afternoon, I'd been obsessed with Stacy myself. Now she scared me—she was too intense, too demanding. The further things went between Stacy and Johnny, the worse things got at home with Mom, the more I felt the heat of guilt creeping up my skin and sinking low in my stomach.

But if Johnny had been bothered by Stacy that day, he quickly forgot it. That very weekend, they went to a concert with friends in Green Bay. The next week she came over for dinner, and they held hands underneath the table. Their kisses, with her back pressed against the Camaro, were just as passionate as they had been before.

By mid-October, Johnny's mind was more or less occupied with wrestling, anyway. His schedule was packed with predawn runs, after-school practices and weekend scrimmages. Mom and Dad agreed that this would be a good distraction for him, and things seemed to be settling down. There had been no more notes in the wash—either Stacy had stopped writing them or Johnny had become better at hiding them, and after a while, Mom started to soften toward Stacy, encouraging Johnny to invite her over on weeknights to study. "Better to keep them under our noses," she'd say to Dad.

Stacy stopped by now and then in the evenings that fall, when Johnny was newly showered from practice, wet hairs still curling on his neck. She and Johnny "studied" in the kitchen, their feet entwined beneath the table, while Mom banged dishes noisily in the sink. They "studied" on the living room couch, textbooks balanced on their knees, Stacy's head fitting perfectly into the crook of Johnny's neck, while Dad snoozed in his recliner. Watching them, it seemed to me that they were drawn together like barbed wire to cow magnets.

I kept a close eye on Stacy at all times, half in love with her, half scared of what she might do. Sometimes it felt as if I'd imagined the whole scene in Johnny's bedroom, the bedsprings squeaking, her protests that she wasn't going to leave.... Sitting on the couch next to Johnny, she seemed as sweet and harmless as a slice of apple pie.

I couldn't help watching her stomach, too—to see if it began to pooch out the way it happened with the married women at church. First it was a rounded blip, then a tight waistline, and before you knew it we were gathered in the church basement among streams of blue or pink crepe paper, discussing stretch marks and twenty-hour labors.

If it happened to those women at church, it could happen to Stacy Lemke, too. I spied on her whenever I got a chance, peeking at her stomach around the edges of my history textbook. I tried to imagine slender Stacy with her belly button protruding, her hands gripping the sides of her stomach, lowering herself carefully to sit. And what would Johnny be like as a father? Proud? Embarrassed?

It was funny because this—or something like this—was what I'd wanted last summer, when my heart had done a lopsided somersault every time I'd bumped into Stacy Lemke in town. I'd wanted Stacy for Johnny so that I could have a bit of Stacy for myself. But somehow, I thought, it had all gone wrong.

"Let me braid your hair, Kirsten," Stacy coaxed on one of those fall evenings.

I considered, then shook my head slowly.

"Aw, come on," Stacy said, reaching for me playfully.

"I don't know."

She reached for me anyway, her hands gathering a mess of hair at the back of my neck. Last summer I would have loved this. I would have melted into a puddle at her touch. Now I remembered the way she and Johnny had laughed at me, and I pulled back. "I don't want to."

Stacy sank back into the couch, frowning, her arms folded across her chest.

Johnny sighed. "Don't you have some homework to do, pip-squeak? Something upstairs?"

I slipped off the couch and plodded to my room, where Emilie was engrossed in this month's *Seventeen.* The cover read, "Thirteen Ways to Wear this Skirt." How could there be thirteen ways to wear a skirt? I could only think of one.

"Do you think Johnny and Stacy will get married in our church or her church?" I asked.

Emilie gave me a look of disgust and went back to her magazine. "They're not getting married, dummy," she said. "They're just dating, that's all."

"But if they really love each other—"

Emilie dog-eared a page of the magazine and set it aside. "Let's put it this way. If they get married, it's because she's pregnant. If she gets pregnant, her parents will kill Johnny, then her. So there won't even be a wedding to worry about. *Capisce?*" That was her new word, picked up from TV.

I sighed. *"Capisce."*

Even after careful watching, I really couldn't tell if there was a difference in Stacy. Johnny, on the other hand, had become suddenly gaunt. He had gone on the wrestler's diet like he did every fall, shedding the weight he'd gained during the spring and summer. It wasn't unusual for Johnny to hit 190 pounds in the off-season, although he wrestled in the 160s. In the past, he'd eaten egg-white shakes for breakfast, ran laps around the barn, jumped rope, sprinted up the bleachers, lifted weights in the gym. Sweated, then sweated some more.

But this year, he'd lost much of the weight without even trying. I didn't notice it when he was bundled up in sweatshirts and warm-up pants, but when he sat across from us at the kitchen table in just a T-shirt, his arms looked positively scrawny, his chest sunken. Any sign of a bulge on his stomach—Aunt Julia's lingonberry kuchen, Mom's beef brisket—had completely disappeared.

"Are you trying to drop another weight class or something?" Dad asked one night when Johnny refused a second helping of Mom's turkey tetrazzini.

Johnny shrugged. "I ate something before practice."

Dad sat back in his chair, studying Johnny carefully. "Does Coach want you to drop more weight?"

Johnny looked back at him. "I'm not dropping weight."

"Sure looks like you are."

Johnny shrugged again. He brought a spoonful to his mouth slowly, as if in rebuttal. "Well, I'm not trying to."

"But you are," Mom said pointedly. "Are you feeling sick?" She reached across the table for his forehead, but withdrew her hand when he pulled back.

"I'm fine," Johnny insisted. "You're making too big a deal out of this."

Later that evening, Dad called Coach Zajac, and Coach recommended less running and more weight lifting, more carbohydrates and fewer vegetables. "Coach says we'll get him back on track," Dad said, hanging up the phone. "Although he might not be a bad wrestler in the 150s, if it came to that."

Mom pursed her lips together, shaking her head. "You two wouldn't care if Johnny was a skeleton, so long as it gave him an advantage."

When I dreamed that night, it was of Johnny on the mats, a skin-and-bones cadaver performing some strange, macabre dance. In the stands, Stacy was watching him, her hands folded beneath her belly.

eleven

Winter, which had only been flirting with us up to that point, made a serious appearance in the weeks between Thanksgiving and Christmas. Overnight, everything green disappeared beneath thick white snowdrifts. Mom dragged the boxes of our heaviest winter sweaters down from the attic, and we began listening to the local news each morning, praying for a snow day. It was so cold that Kennel was allowed inside the barn, where he terrorized our farm cats, essentially treeing them in the hayloft. One Saturday, Dad and Jerry cut down a fir from the woods behind our property and lugged it inside our house, then left it to Emilie and me to decorate with looping strings of tinsel and uneven rows of blinking lights. Mom brought down boxes from the attic, and we dug out our favorite ornaments—the clothespin reindeer Grandma Hammarstrom had made for us when we were little, the palm-print casts from our years in kindergarten, Johnny's palm then as big as mine now. I ate almost as much popcorn as I strung.

We hosted Christmas dinner, complete with too-dry turkey and Mom's creamy green bean casserole. Uncle

Paul and Aunt Julia were there, as well as our cousin, Brent, and his fiancée, and a few of Mom's cousins from northern Wisconsin. Jerry joined us, helping to cut the turkey with slow, precise strokes. "This man knows his way around a bird," Dad had announced, clapping Jerry on the shoulder. With an apron tied around her neck and pot holders for hands, Mom was in her element. Grandpa gave horse rides on his knee to the toddlers, and Stacy stopped by, too, after the Lemkes' family meal. Through it all, Johnny picked at his food like a fussy toddler.

It snowed every day of our Christmas break, and once the excitement of our presents had worn off, Emilie and I were mostly cooped up. She practiced the clarinet for hours on end, until even Dad requested that John Philip Sousa be confined to the basement, *please.* A friend rescued Emilie for a day of shopping in Milwaukee, and Mom took me ice-skating at the indoor rink in Waukesha with Katie and Kari Schultz and a few other girls from school, but otherwise, the weeks passed in a blue chill of boredom. Even as we watched TV or read books or played marathon games of double solitaire, it seemed our whole family was holding its breath for Johnny.

We didn't miss a meet that season. Piled into the Caprice, we followed the Ships' bus to tournaments in Kiel and Fond du Lac and Menomonee Falls, then spent entire Saturdays in the bleachers waiting for Johnny to wrestle, standing every so often to stretch our backs or relieve our behinds. Even Grandpa came along, although he complained that the car ride was too long and we sat in the bleachers too long and it took too long to make it all the way through the brackets.

Stacy was at every tournament, too. During the long

lulls between Johnny's matches, she sat in a corner of the gymnasium with the other kids from Lincoln High. The girls took turns braiding each other's hair or passing around homework to be copied; they snapped gum and sucked lollipops and leaned close, heads together, for a whispered conversation that ended in a bout of hysterical laughter. Stacy carried a thick binder that was completely covered with doodles. *Stacy and Johnny. I love Johnny H. Stacy Lynne Hammarstrom.* It made me feel funny, to see her trying on our name for size.

She always crossed the bleachers to say hello to us, to chat about how Johnny was doing or how Johnny was feeling or who Johnny was up against. She had become a wrestling expert overnight. "See that one there, in the green sweatshirt? That's Crowley, he's in the 160s, too. That's Johnny's toughest opponent of the day," she would say, bent into our airspace. From her necklace dangled the gold heart locket that Johnny had bought her for Christmas, with the money he'd saved from doing his chores and other odd jobs around our farm.

When Johnny was on the mat, Stacy was a ball of nerves. She whispered, over and over, "Get him, Johnny, pin him, Johnny" like a breathless rosary. Once, when the tension became too much, she grabbed my hand and squeezed it until tears pooled in the corners of my eyes. Even when I tried to wriggle free, she hung on, not noticing.

Johnny qualified for regionals at the end of February, and Stacy made the drive to Wausau with us. Wrapped in a navy peacoat over her Ships sweatshirt, she perched in the middle of the backseat between Emilie and me and insisted that she was perfectly comfortable, even though her long legs were wedged against the front seat. Mom turned on the radio and hummed along to the Top 40. Mostly we watched the frozen Wisconsin countryside pass in a dull blur through our windows.

"You know what?" Stacy confessed into my ear at one point. "I have this theory. If I'm watching Johnny's match, then he'll win. If I don't watch, he'll lose. Like it's all up to me. Is that crazy, or what?"

I looked up to see Dad glancing at Stacy in the rearview mirror. I could tell from the rigid way that Mom was holding her neck that she was listening, too.

We were joining Johnny on the second day of regionals; to move on to state, he would have to wrestle his way through a thirty-two-man bracket. Coach Zajac spotted us in the gym immediately and waved us over.

"How's he doing?" Dad asked, extending his hand for a shake.

"Three wins. First guy, he pinned in only twenty seconds. He ran into a tough guy in the second round, kid who kept shoving him around, and the ref wasn't calling it. So Johnny roughed him up a bit."

"Oh, yeah?" Dad asked.

"Got him in an arm bar, twisted it too far, and all of a sudden the kid's screaming." Coach shook his head, a smile playing on his lips. "Your kid doesn't take crap from anyone, that's for sure. Come on, let's say hi to some folks."

Coach walked Dad around the gymnasium, introducing him to scouts and WIAA officials and reporters who had come all the way from Milwaukee. Stacy and Emilie found friends to sit with, and Mom, with a spirit of abandon, ordered us greasy slices of cheese pizza and bottles of Coca-Cola from the snack stand in the foyer. When we took our seats in the bleachers later, my stomach was protesting.

Johnny, prepping for his matches, kept to himself. He seemed to lurk in one corner of the gym or another, his face mostly hidden by the hood of his sweatshirt. We watched him pin his opponent from Sturgeon Bay easily, securing his place in the final. Someone behind us said, "Watch out for that one. He nearly broke a kid's arm last night." I turned around, trying to identify the speaker, but no face stood out of the crowd.

Then Johnny wandered over to us, the straps of his singlet hanging down, a few ribs and curly golden chest hairs visible. Sweat shone on his forehead.

"How are you holding up, kiddo?" Dad asked.

He shrugged. "Okay."

"Are you hungry?" Mom asked.

Johnny pulled his warm-up jacket over his head. "I guess."

Mom produced her wallet and handed over a five-dollar bill, carefully, as if she was parting with a small fortune.

"Thanks," he said, and wandered off in the direction of the Ships cheering section. Stacy was waving her arms back and forth beneath a sign that read "GO JOHNNY H!" in three-foot letters, and Johnny raised one hand in greeting and moved toward her.

"When's his next match?" Mom asked, checking her watch.

"Probably an hour, hour and a half."

Yawning, I stretched out on the bleacher, my head on Mom's lap. While we waited in the stands, people from Watankee and Manitowoc kept wandering over to talk to Dad and Mom for prolonged congratulations and rather boring discussions about wrestling. Another Ships teammate, 119-pound Dirk Bauer, was headed for the finals, too, and all in all it was a good showing for the Ships. I sneaked a few pieces of hard candy from Mom's purse and let them dissolve, one by one, on my tongue.

Then the first call for the middleweight classes was announced over the loudspeaker. I sat up, paying attention. That meant Johnny would be taking the mats within half an hour. I suddenly started to feel a bit of Stacy's nerves—my brother could be a regional wrestling champion in only thirty minutes.

We waited anxiously as skinny, pale Dirk Bauer vied for victory. I looked around for Johnny, but it was hard to see with the cluster of people near the mats.

As if reading my mind, Mom asked, "Where's Johnny? I don't see him out there." She craned her neck around a family walking in front of us.

"He's gotta be down there somewhere," Dad said, unconcerned. I stood in the bleachers, straining to see over the heads of the people in front of me, but couldn't find Johnny, either. Of course he was down there—the whole team was there to support Dirk Bauer. Curious, I looked over at the small student cheering section in the far corner of the bleachers. Stacy's sign was propped against the wall, but I didn't see her. I waved at Emilie, who nodded her head ever so slightly in recognition.

The 125-pounders took the mats, shook hands and the referee started the match.

Over the loudspeaker, the announcer's voice said, "Second call for 160 pounds, Hammarstrom from Lincoln."

Dad stood, looking around. "Johnny's not down there?"

"He's here somewhere," Mom reasoned, standing, too. "Where could he be?"

I spotted Coach Zajac at the same time Dad did. He was standing at the foot of the bleachers, surveying the stands. Dad raised his hands palms-up, asking the question. Coach shook his head.

"Jesus!" Dad swore. "Where the hell is he?"

From the center of the gym, we heard the ref's hand slap the mat, setting off a wild celebration. Someone had been pinned.

"He doesn't get his ass on that mat and he's out," Dad said, loud enough that the family sitting in front of us turned to look. He started down the bleachers in a quick jog, taking the steps two at a time.

"Where could he be?" Mom moaned. "Do you see Stacy anywhere?"

I'd been looking but still hadn't spotted her.

We followed Dad's progress around the perimeter of the gym floor, wending his way brusquely between slow-moving groups of parents.

"Shit," Mom said.

Dad reached the set of double doors leading into the foyer at the exact moment that Johnny burst through them with Stacy in tow. I didn't need to be in hearing range to know exactly what Dad said; Johnny started across the floor in a quick sprint, wriggling out of his warm-up jacket as he went. For a second, Dad glared at Stacy. It looked as if she was trying to apologize, but Dad wasn't having any of it. He turned his back on her and marched back to the bleachers. Stacy followed slowly, walking past us and up the bleachers to her section. One of her red barrettes was missing, I noticed, and the hair on the top of her head was mussed.

Mom was shaking her head when Dad rejoined us in the stands. "Do you see what I'm talking about now?" she hissed.

Dad was still seething, but more quietly now. "I swear, I'm going to kill that kid," he said under his breath.

And Mom said, half joking, "Which one?"

Stacy found a seat in the bleachers, but now she was sitting a little apart from everyone else, hugging her arms to her chest. What had happened in the hour or so when they'd been alone? I remembered with a shudder that afternoon in Johnny's bedroom, with Johnny insisting they had to leave, and Stacy refusing.

It was eight-thirty when Johnny took the mat for the championship match against Plinker, a squat kid from Onalaska. Watching them face off in the circle, I was amazed they were in the same weight class. Plinker was almost a head shorter than Johnny, his body tense with muscle and movement. Johnny was tall and powerful, but looked as if he could use a good meal or three.

Our part of the gymnasium chanted as one: *John-ny, John-ny!* On the other side of the gym, fans took up a cheer for his opponent.

Photographers crouched at the edge of the mat, focusing their lenses.

"You get him! You get him, Johnny!" Dad yelled.

"Come on, Johnny, come on!" Mom called.

Johnny entered the circle, crouched, shook hands with Plinker.

The ref blew the whistle, stepped back, and the two began stalking each other, their bodies circling, teasing, tangling, positioning.

From the mats, I could hear Coach Zajac's voice, although his exact orders were lost in the din. Calls of encouragement came from the stands. "Let's go, already!" someone yelled close to my ear. The wrestlers from the lower weight classes formed a loose ring around the perimeter, chanting.

Johnny lunged, and Plinker caught his arm. Using Johnny's momentum against him, Plinker caught him off balance and threw him to his back. Johnny hit the mat with a thud, his legs flipping over his body.

"No!" I screamed.

Johnny had three seconds to get out of the pin. I'd seen him do this before on our living room carpet. Feet on the mat, he arched his back, bridging to keep from being pinned. Johnny rolled to the right, grabbing Plinker's arm. I was watching it as if in slow motion, Johnny on his knees, finding his footing with Plinker behind him, trying to bring Johnny back to ground. Within seconds, Johnny was up, and they separated.

Dad had been clutching Mom's arm, and his grasp slowly eased in relief.

The circling began again. Johnny was moving faster now, angered by the close call. He lunged forward, reaching for Plinker. There was a blur of limbs, a mad scramble of maneuvering, two sets of thigh muscles quivering. Johnny got hold of Plinker's arm and moved behind him, twisting. The *arm bar,* a position of strength—I remembered that. Johnny had the leverage and drove forward until Plinker went down. Then he was on his stomach, struggling for position, and Johnny was on top, forcing Plinker's shoulder down for the roll.

"That's it, Johnny!" Dad screamed, his voice hoarse. "Drive, drive, drive!"

Plinker tried to work his way up, but Johnny wasn't giving an inch. It was the beginning of the end, a battle Johnny was not going to lose. He was simply stronger. Johnny wanted this. Every muscle in his body was straining…and just like that, Plinker collapsed on his back, his shoulders down.

The ref smacked his hand on the mat, and everyone around us screamed. The Ships went crazy, jumping up and down. Hands reached out, slapping Coach on the back. In the stands, Dad was suddenly mobbed by Ships fans.

Johnny hopped to his feet, the victor. Plinker rolled himself into a standing position, and they took the circle again, one with his shoulders back, the other with his shoulders forward. The ref seized Johnny's hand, showing it first to one corner, then to the other. Mom, jostled by the crowd in the stands, snapped a quick photo that would come out too blurry months later, when she finally developed the roll.

I turned again to spot Stacy in the top row of the bleachers. While the rest of her schoolmates screamed and jumped, Stacy stood perfectly still, a smile spread across her glossy lips.

We didn't get back to the car until after ten o'clock, and there was still a drive ahead of us. As excited as we'd been in the gym with all the cheering and congratulating and snapping pictures, that feeling seemed to disappear the second we were back in the station wagon. Dad and Mom talked to each other, replaying the action. They deliberately ignored Stacy.

At one point, realizing this, Stacy leaned forward. "I just want to say I'm sorry. I didn't know—"

"Could have been the end for Johnny right there,"

Dad responded immediately, as if he'd been waiting for the opening to rebuke her. "All those years of practice, and that would have been it."

"I'm sorry," Stacy said again, her voice small in the interior of the car.

Mom said, "It's still cold in here, John," and Dad cranked up the heat until the windows were fogged up on the inside. Emilie took off her coat and bunched it up to use as a pillow. She fell into a noisy, mouth-breathing sleep, but the rest of us sat quietly, staring at the same dark countryside, mile after mile.

Once I caught Dad glancing in the rearview mirror—not checking up on me or Emilie, or the dark road behind us, but staring directly at Stacy.

And although she didn't say a word, Stacy was looking right back.

twelve

We came home from Wausau to a sign on the Stop 'N' Go marquee: *Go Dirk B! Go Johnny H! Make us proud!*

On Sunday afternoon, Aunt Julia and Uncle Paul stopped by to congratulate Johnny. Aunt Julia brought a chocolate cake that said CONGRATS in white icing, and we ate it like gluttons, picking directly at the cake with our forks.

Grandpa came over, too. He might not have understood the rules of wrestling or why sports were important, period, but even he could understand that Johnny had done something well. "All right, Johnny, all right," he kept repeating, clapping Johnny roughly on the back.

Jerry came over to shake hands with Johnny, too. "What's it gonna be, you think—University of Iowa?"

"It's looking that way," Johnny said, grinning. His picture made the front page of the afternoon paper, and Dad drove into town to pick up a stack of copies. Stacy didn't stop by, which seemed a little weird to me—she was usually the first person to point out Johnny's name on the local sports page.

On Monday, the boys at school who usually ignored

me now included me in their conversations. "Hey, Kirsten—is your brother going to win state? What's he wrestling at?" I was only too happy to oblige with the details. If Johnny Hammarstrom was on his way to being the best thing to come out of Watankee, I saw no problem in going right along with it.

That Tuesday, the last day in February, Kevin Coulie and I won the class spell-off and were asked to stay after school to practice for the annual county spelling bee. We would be representing all the fourth graders at Watankee Elementary. In the next round we would face older kids—fifth and sixth graders—from much bigger schools in Manitowoc, and from smaller schools all over the county. This was rather intimidating news for someone who went down on *scissors* the year before.

Miss Swanson had copied about twenty pages of practice words for each of us, then placed them in crisp manila folders labeled smartly with our names. She thrust them into our hands at the end of the review session. "Study hard, okay? We're down to the last week."

Kevin's dad had agreed to give me a ride home, and his truck was idling in the parking lot when we stepped outside. Kevin climbed in first and settled into the middle, his knees banging into the stick shift. Mr. Coulie grunted a hello and was pulling out of the parking lot almost before I had the passenger door closed. I spent a fruitless minute digging for my seat belt, but its clasp was wedged deep beneath the seat cushions. I had to hold on to the door with both hands, or else bump knees with Kevin at each turn.

We rode through the dusk in an uneasy silence. I stared out the half-fogged windows at the frozen piles of snow that lined the streets of Watankee and sat heaped around the edges of parking lots.

We weren't far from my driveway, maybe a half mile or so, when I saw two vehicles pulled to one side of the road near a ditch—Johnny's hulking Green Machine, looking less and less green as more and more of its paint flaked off, and Stacy's Camaro, red and shiny as Christmas. It was strange to see their cars parked there, so close to our house.

I sat up, straining to see. Was something wrong? Had something happened?

I've gone back to the moment a thousand times, a million maybe, over the years, trying to see it from every angle, to read facial expressions or lips, to interject myself into the scene, not only as a witness but as the person who could put things right.

Nothing screamed *wrong,* exactly. They were standing between the tail of his car and the front bumper of hers, close enough to lean in for a kiss. The air between their faces was fogged with breath.

Kevin's dad slowed for the turn, and I put up my hand, ready to wave.

It happened in about a second, in about the time it would take to let out a laugh or blink or glance at the radio dial.

Just as we passed, Stacy put her gloved hands on Johnny's chest. I'd seen her touch him like this before—her hands reaching for his shoulders, inching around his neck. It looked like that now, too—the start of an embrace, one of her sweet "Come here, baby" moments—but instead she gave him a hard push. I gasped. Johnny took a rough step backward, off balance, righting himself with his hand on the tailgate. I had seen that look on Stacy's face before—her mouth tight, chin raised. It reminded me of the way she had squeezed my hand during Johnny's wrestling match, so hard that I'd felt as if all those little bones might snap.

Suddenly I was aware that I'd blundered yet again into a private moment, something I wasn't supposed to see or know. I ducked down in the seat, not sure what I'd seen, not wanting to be seen myself. I could feel Kevin watching me all the way down our driveway. Mr. Coulie, if he had noticed, said nothing.

My face felt hot, as if I'd been called on to read out loud but had lost the passage and even the page number.

When Mr. Coulie shifted his truck into Park, I was out the door instantly, slamming it behind me. Kennel came running around the side of the house, and I grabbed him by his collar. "Thanks. Bye!" I called over my shoulder, not meeting Kevin's eyes. I released Kennel at the back door and stepped inside, surprised to find that I was almost out of breath.

I replayed the scene in my mind, the way they stood, bodies tense, angry even, I saw now. Johnny at his breaking point, Stacy at her most intense. I tried to make her push into something playful, some kind of inside joke or rough sign of affection, but I couldn't. Maybe she had told him, finally, that she was pregnant. And he had said he couldn't be tied down right now.

"What's wrong with you?" Emilie said, coming down the stairs. I was still in my coat and scarf, snow melting off my boots, my backpack hanging from one shoulder.

"Nothing," I said. But I wasn't sure.

When Johnny came in about ten minutes later, I was still lurking in the kitchen, pretending to dig for something in my backpack. I needed to see him, to read anger or hurt or betrayal across his face. Maybe he would even make some kind of announcement, like he was done with Stacy or she was done with him or they were done with each other. I was poised to ask him something—anything—but when he opened the door, my mouth went dry.

Johnny's face was completely blank, as if he was numb. He didn't look up at me or Emilie, just kicked off his boots, dumped his jacket on the floor, and went upstairs. His bedroom door clicked shut, and I trailed after him, putting an ear to the door. I wanted to say something, to let him know that whatever it was, it would all be okay.

But then I remembered Stacy's hands on his shoulders, her chin thrust forward—and I knew it wasn't okay.

thirteen

On Wednesday night, Mom came home from Holy Cross with a stack of T-shirts that read *Johnny H. is our man! State Wrestling Champ 1995.* "From the other nurses," she gushed, passing them around the table. There was one for me, too, large enough to sleep in. "Isn't that thoughtful? We all have to wear them to Madison."

"Cool," Emilie said. She had stopped making comments about how wrestling was stupid. Maybe she felt, like I did, that it was pretty great to have a star for a brother.

Johnny shook his head, refusing to touch the shirt Mom was handing him. "What are you trying to do, jinx me?" he demanded. "It's a bit early for this."

"Oh, come on," Mom said, beaming. "We're just so excited. Everyone's so proud of you."

I watched Johnny over spoonfuls of baked potato that I'd smothered with sour cream. He had a plain potato in front of him, and rather than eating, he was concentrating hard on separating the skin from the rest of the potato. Since yesterday, since *the push,* I had been watching him closely, trying to figure it out. He hadn't called Stacy yesterday night after dinner for the nightly phone call that had been a staple of their relationship. Instead he'd spent the evening in his bedroom, grunting a tally of push-ups, collapsing every now and then for a breather and then starting back up.

But if something was wrong, I was apparently the only one who noticed.

I cleared my throat. "Is Stacy coming with us to Madison next week?"

Mom looked quickly at Dad, who was looking down. Maybe he was remembering the way he'd charged down the bleachers, looking for Johnny, or how Stacy's face had been flushed, a loose barrette dangling in her hair.

Mom said, "We'll see about that," at the same time Johnny asked, "Why wouldn't she?"

They stared at each other, and Dad repeated, "We'll see."

Johnny grunted and went back to picking at his potato.

"Just wondering," I mumbled.

Mom leaned over and tousled my hair affectionately. "What's wrong?" she asked, and I shook my head, not knowing how to tell her.

That weekend, with the break between regionals and state, Johnny had his first free Saturday in months. "I'm taking Stacy out later," he announced that morning while Mom and I were in the kitchen, putting away groceries.

"Where are you headed?"

"Movie and then dinner in Sheboygan."

"And you'll be home…?"

"I don't know. Eight. Eight-thirty."

"It might snow tonight," Mom said. "You make sure you drive careful, okay?"

"All right," Johnny said, rolling his eyes. He gave me a grin that I tried to return, not convincingly enough. "What's wrong?"

Mom was looking at me, too.

I didn't say, *Be careful, Johnny.* I didn't ask if he'd pushed her right back, once Kevin's dad had rounded the corner and we were out of sight. Instead, I only shrugged.

When Johnny left that afternoon, he looked the same as always. I watched out the window as he walked to his truck, tossing his keys into the air and catching them with a little flourish. It had started to snow, but only barely, not enough to cover some of the ragged melted patches on the lawn. He circled the truck with an ice scraper, his breath coming out in puffs as thick as summer clouds.

It was a normal evening. If I'd had the sense that our lives were about to change, that God was about to topple our little world like we were indeed bugs in a Mason jar, I would have paid closer attention to every little thing. Instead, it was the most normal evening in the world. We watched *Wheel of Fortune* with the TV muted while Dad talked on the phone with Coach Zajac. *Iowa*—he said, as if the whole state had been reduced to a single school. I listened while I lay upside down on the couch, with my head where my feet should be and my feet waving in the air, letting the blood pool in my head until it must have weighed a thousand pounds. When Mom finished working in the kitchen, she quizzed me on my spelling list: *Dexterous, immaculate, oscilloscope, millennium.* Words I'd barely heard before and couldn't define. Upstairs, Emilie ran through "Stars and Stripes Forever" until Dad hollered, "Enough, already," and she joined us in front of the TV to paint her toenails.

"Time to get ready for bed," Mom said at eight, and

I slumped upstairs for my evening routine—measuring my height against the mark on the door frame, brushing my teeth, selling an imaginary audience in the mirror a tube of Crest, and finally settling under the covers with a flashlight. I was halfway into *The Clue of the Dancing Puppet* when Emilie came in. Through the open door I could hear Dad and Mom's voices, arguing. Emilie shut the door and plopped on my bed.

I sat up. "What's wrong?"

"It's almost ten and Johnny's not back yet. He said they'd be home by eight-thirty. Mom called the Lemkes and they're not there." She pulled up her knees to her chest and hugged her legs.

"They're probably on their way back right now," I said, but my heart thumped in my chest. Something was wrong.

Emilie bit her lip. "It's snowing really hard, though."

I climbed out of bed and went to the window. She was right—the snow that had been a few friendly flakes in the afternoon was now coming down sideways, like millions of little polka dots against the night sky. "Let's keep the door open," I said, quietly twisting the knob.

Emilie stayed on my bed, knees tucked under her chin.

There were a few minutes of silence, and then, straining, we heard Mom say, "I think you should go look for them."

Dad said, "Let's give it another ten minutes."

"Aren't you worried?"

"Johnny can handle himself in a little bit of snow."

Ten-fifteen came and went. Then ten-thirty. Upstairs, I clutched on to the sleeve of Emilie's sweater, and she didn't push my hand away.

The Lemkes called, and we heard Mom's side of the conversation, "No, we haven't heard… Right. Well, we'll call you if we hear anything." And then to Dad: "Bill Lemke's been to Sheboygan and back and didn't see them, John. You have to go out there."

I could hear Dad grumbling under his breath, but he put on his coat and reached for his keys. His old truck grumbled to life, and I watched his headlights sweep across our house, across Grandpa's dark house, and then out of sight.

"He'll find them," I whispered, more confident than I felt. They'd been gone for hours. They could be anywhere. I pictured them driving through the night, the Green Machine navigating the country roads through Watankee, Manitowoc, Green Bay, up north, farther and farther away, with Stacy in the middle of the bench seat, urging Johnny forward. *Let's not go back,* she might be saying right at that moment.

"Yeah," Emilie said, but she stayed on my bed, chewing on her lower lip.

We waited.

Dad hadn't been gone five minutes when we heard footsteps on the front porch, and the door banged open. It was Johnny.

"The truck slid off the road," he was saying, by the time Emilie and I had raced downstairs to see him. His face was red with cold and his hat and coat were covered with snow. He tried to kick off his boots and ended up working his feet back and forth until he was free of them. "It's freezing outside."

Mom started to peel off his wet coat and saw us. "Put the kettle on," she barked to Emilie, who scuttled into action.

"Where's Stacy?" I asked.

"She's home," Johnny said. "We weren't far from her house when it happened, so she walked the rest of the way."

"She wasn't home ten minutes ago," Mom said.

"Really? She should be home by now," Johnny said. I would try to remember later how he said this, whether he was worried or certain, guilty or innocent, but everything happened so fast. *She should be home by now,* he'd said, and I'd let out my breath. Mom tugged on his sleeves and Johnny's coat came off. At the same time we saw the cut on the back of his hand, three inches long and gaping wide.

"Oh, my God," Mom said. "Let me see that."

"From the truck—I was trying to push it out of the ditch, but I just couldn't get it to move," he said. "Dad's gonna be mad—"

"He's out looking for you now," Mom said, examining Johnny's hand. "This might need stitches. Kirsten, get me the first-aid kit."

I jumped into action, running to the hall closet and back. When I came back, Johnny was saying, "I'm so sorry about the truck."

"Forget about the truck. I'm just glad you're safe." Mom ripped open a packet and began swabbing Johnny's hand. He winced, shutting his eyes against the pain.

On the stove, the kettle began to steam and whistle, a thin cry that escalated to a shriek by the time Emilie reached it. "What about the Lemkes?" Emilie asked. "Shouldn't we call them?"

"Yes," Mom said and reached for the phone. But before she dialed, we heard Dad's truck pulling in. He left it, lights blazing and engine running, and was up the steps in only seconds. Mom replaced the receiver.

"I found Johnny's truck— Oh, thank God," Dad said, spotting Johnny. His chest was heaving, and he knelt over to catch his breath. I felt out of breath, too, even though I'd done nothing more than watch Johnny's cut be cleaned. *Now we're all here,* I thought. *We're safe.*

"What happened?" Dad demanded.

And then Johnny said what I would hear over and over, repeated to my parents, Stacy's parents, the police, the newspaper, the district attorney: they were almost home when the truck fishtailed. "I must have hit a patch of ice or something," he said, "and we ended up in the ditch." Johnny said he tried to push them out while Stacy steered, and when that didn't work they waited to see if anyone came. "It was snowing harder and we were so cold. I thought we should keep waiting, but Stacy said she would walk to her house and get her dad. I guess—I mean—she was pretty mad at me. And then she didn't come back after a bit, so I just started walking home."

"Oh, my God. She might still be out there," Mom said, reaching for the phone. She punched in the numbers for the Lemkes. "Bill? It's Alicia. Is Stacy back yet?"

There was a silence that stretched just a second too long, and in that moment, all the relief I'd felt seeped out of me. As the five of us held our breath, waiting, it was as if we already knew. I choked that breath down my throat, as if I sensed that it might have to last me for the rest of my life.

Mom shook her head at us. With her index finger she depressed the switch hook and dialed again, this time to the police.

fourteen

While Mom talked to the dispatcher, Dad and Johnny went out in Dad's truck. From the kitchen we could see his high beams sweeping across the night, illuminating a gathering of fat snowflakes.

I bit my lip, staring into the night. "It's really coming down now."

Mom replaced the receiver and looked up at us.

"What did they say?" Emilie demanded.

"We're supposed to sit tight. They're sending an officer." Mom pressed her palms flat on the table, then curled her hands into fists, then latched them behind her head, her neck bent forward. There was nothing she could do that would make this better.

The phone rang a minute later, and Mom snatched it up. "John and Johnny are out there, too, and the police are on their way," she promised. "We'll call you the minute we hear anything."

She hung up, stared at us again. "An officer is already with the Lemkes, taking a statement."

"What does that mean, a statement?" Emilie asked.

Mom didn't say anything. She leaned forward so

that her forehead fell into the palms of her hands. "Oh, Johnny," she moaned. "What did you do?"

Thoughts were swirling in my head. The fight, the push, Johnny standing in the kitchen that afternoon, telling us about his plans for the evening.

Suddenly a truck came speeding down our driveway. Feet tramped across the yard while we sat, stunned, and then Aunt Julia slammed through the back door, wild-eyed. "Paul just heard on the scanner—" she began, and Mom filled her in on the details.

"Oh, my God." Aunt Julia sank back against the door frame. "It's been what, now? An hour?"

I tried to imagine an hour in that cold, the wind swirling, whipping through my coat.

The phone rang and Mom grabbed for it.

Aunt Julia rushed back outside, and I followed her onto the porch, the wind slapping against me like an open palm. The storm that had been only a mild blip on the morning weather report had gained intensity. Snow eddied around us, instantly wetting my pajamas.

Uncle Paul was coming up the walk, but Aunt Julia met him at the foot of the stairs and sent him back. "Go out there, go help them," she said, the wind carrying her words across the yard. Uncle Paul hesitated, then ran down the walk, threw open the driver's door and started his truck.

"Come on, now, you can't be out in this," Aunt Julia scolded, shooing me inside. "You don't even have shoes on."

I stared out the window as his truck made the turn. A dusting of flakes, wind-blown, had already covered their footprints.

Our phone had never rung so many times before in a single night. Mom snatched it on the first ring, greedily, while we waited, filling in the blanks in her conversation.

A shape passed in front of our window, and we all jumped to our feet. Grandpa pulled open the door, his eyes scanning the room. "What the hell is going on?"

"Stacy's missing," I said at the same time Mom told him, "There was an accident—"

Grandpa's neck swiveled from Mom to me and back. "What do you mean, an accident?"

Mom's look shushed me. "Johnny slid off the road. And then Stacy tried to walk home—"

"In this?" Grandpa demanded. "By herself? Why the hell—"

"Papa," Aunt Julia said, taking him by the arm. "John and Paul and Johnny are out there. It's going to be okay."

"Half the county is out there now, looking," Mom reported. I imagined the chain reaction of lights in windows as the people of Watankee woke up, the men pulling on their boots and heading out to garages to warm up their trucks. I shivered, thinking of the trucks driving along the country roads, their headlights cutting through the night, on the lookout for Stacy's green coat, the strands of red hair that had escaped her hat. Stacy's coat. Stacy's hair. They were looking for *Stacy.*

"What kind of damn fool lets a girl—" Grandpa barked.

"Papa, please," Aunt Julia said. "That's not helping."

Suddenly my body felt hot and cold at once. "I feel sick. It's my stomach."

"Oh, baby." Mom reached for my forehead. "You're warm. Were you feeling sick earlier?"

"I don't know. I don't think so." I remembered: Stacy had put her hands on Johnny's chest, as if she was going to pull him in for a kiss. But she hadn't kissed him, she'd pushed him, and he had fallen backward.

"You look kind of pale. Why don't you go on up to bed?"

"I want to stay here," I said. It was such a strange feeling to be up this late, with the members of my family scattered around the county. Dad and Johnny and Uncle Paul out in the snow, and Stacy unaccounted for. "I'm staying here," I repeated.

Mom stared at me across the table, and then once again headlights flashed across our house as a car pulled into the driveway.

"They're back," I said, hopeful. "Maybe they found her already."

Aunt Julia peeked out the window. "Police car," she reported. "It's just idling there. Looks like he's talking on the radio."

My stomach lurched again. I watched as Mom smoothed down her hair, straightened her sweater and put her shoulders back to answer the door. "Thank God you're here," she said, cold air leaking inside the door. "I'm Alicia Hammarstrom, the one who called. My husband and son are out there, looking."

"Officer Parks. We've got other cars responding, and they should be out there by now, too. And another officer is at the Lemkes."

Suddenly, unable to hold it in, I ran around Grandpa to the bathroom off the kitchen and retched the remains of the chicken potpie we'd had for dinner. The officer's boots banged across the linoleum, and I leaned back against the bathtub, shaking. Only a few miles away, the Lemkes were sitting in their remodeled house with the expensive master suite and the pool table in the basement, as sick as I was with fear for Stacy. I should have said something, I thought. I should have come clean, before it was too late. I echoed Mom's question: *Oh, Johnny. What did you do?*

"Is there any news?" I heard Aunt Julia ask, and from the way the officer didn't answer, I knew he had shaken his head. Or maybe it was one of those questions that a teacher sometimes asked, a *rhetorical* question, where everyone knows the answer but nobody was actually supposed to say anything.

I unwound some toilet paper, wiped a drip of vomit from the linoleum, and flushed the toilet.

"I need you to start from the beginning, Mrs. Hammarstrom," Officer Parks said.

"The beginning?" Mom asked. "Well, I don't know. I guess it was earlier tonight..."

I stood on my step stool and reached my mouth under the faucet, letting it run and run. My throat felt as if it had been scraped down with a giant spatula.

Emilie knocked on the door. "Kirsten? You okay?"

I dried my mouth on a hand towel and came out. Mom was sitting at the kitchen table, and Aunt Julia was standing behind her, her hands on the arms of the chair. Grandpa stood behind both of them, his arms folded across his chest.

Officer Parks, maybe a few years younger than Mom, sat in Dad's seat at the table, making notes in a tiny pad. He was tall, broad-shouldered, loaded down with official-looking gear once his thick snow jacket came off: a radio hooked to one side of his belt, handcuffs and a holster to the other. "And that was at approximately five-thirty?"

Mom nodded.

"Oh, Kirsten," Aunt Julia said, and I looked down,

noticing the murky streak of vomit down the top of my pajamas.

The officer looked up, gave me a slow appraising glance, and went back to his notes. "Have you noticed anything different lately? Any sort of strange behavior from either your son or Stacy?"

"Strange behavior? No, I don't think so," Mom said, her voice rising slightly. "I really don't see how—"

"Maybe something you noticed, something you overheard, any kind of plans they were making, anything out of the norm. . . ." Officer Parks prompted, his pen waiting.

I thought about Johnny at regionals, almost missing his call. I thought about their fight on Tuesday night—that was the right word, wasn't it? Not discussion or disagreement, but *fight.* I guess you could say something was out of the norm. But what was the norm for Stacy and Johnny—the love notes Mom found in the laundry? Stacy's desperate pleading after they'd had sex? I'd held it in all week, watching Johnny, listening for clues that hadn't been dropped. Now I needed to say something.

I opened my mouth, ready to speak, but my stomach leaped again. In reflex, I clapped a hand over my mouth.

"Julia—" Mom said, helplessly.

"Come with me, Kirsten." Aunt Julia turned me around by the shoulders and nudged me back into the bathroom. But this time when I hovered over the toilet, heaving, nothing came.

Aunt Julia held my hair back with one hand and wiped a long string of saliva from my chin with a wad of toilet paper. Her clothes smelled like smoke, but her breath against my cheek had the chemical sting of mouthwash. "It's okay. Everything's going to be okay."

I slid to the floor, tears rolling down my cheeks. "I need to tell the officer something."

Aunt Julia looked at me sharply. "What do you mean?"

"I think they had a fight. Earlier this week, I saw her push him—"

Aunt Julia crouched beside me, and I told her everything, although it came out in a messed-up rush, not at all orderly like it had been in my mind. Their fight, Stacy's hand on his shoulders, Johnny not calling her that night, the notes she'd written to Johnny, saying she would kill herself if he… "I think I heard them…in his bedroom…" I whispered.

"What were they doing in his bedroom?" Aunt Julia asked.

I looked at her desperately, trying to avoid the word. "You know."

Aunt Julia's eyes widened, but she only nodded. "Keep going."

"And sometimes she acts—I don't know. Crazy. And it makes him mad." My voice broke. "But what if something happened tonight, what if Johnny—"

"Oh, you poor girl," Aunt Julia said, pulling me tight against her skinny chest. "You've been holding this in for so long, haven't you?"

"I need to tell the officer—"

"Okay, honey." Aunt Julia pulled away, holding me by the shoulders. "Listen to me now. We don't know what happened out there yet. The men are out there doing their job, and they're going to find Stacy. I'm sure what you saw was nothing. Okay?"

I considered. "But if Johnny…"

"There's no sense in making people worry for nothing," Aunt Julia said, easing upward out of her crouch.

She pulled me to my feet and reached for a clean hand towel. “You’ll see,” she said into my ear. “Everything’s going to be okay.”

I nodded and let her pat my face dry, but I knew I hadn’t explained things well. I still knew more than Aunt Julia did, more than Mom, more than everyone.

And yet, I didn’t know anything at all.

fifteen

When we came out of the bathroom, Grandpa had pulled up a chair to the table, too.

Officer Parks continued to write, while Mom stared at his notes upside down.

"Stacy is out there somewhere," she said firmly. Her fingers worried the edge of our old blue tablecloth, the one we used when it was just the five of us. It was stained with dozens of spills that hadn't quite come out in the wash, faded into discoloration.

Without looking up, Officer Parks said, "I understand, Mrs. Hammarstrom. We have some of our first responders out there looking."

"Let's wrap you up real good," Aunt Julia said, and I hugged my arms to my chest while she wound me burrito-style into a quilt from the hall closet. She sat in a chair next to Emilie near the door to the living room, pulling me backward onto her lap. Emilie didn't take her eyes off Officer Parks—the handcuffs, his gun.

"It's very frustrating—" Mom began, but suddenly the windows lit up as a whole caravan of cars came down our driveway. I hopped off Aunt Julia's lap, shedding Grandma's quilt, and met Dad and Johnny at the back door. More car doors slammed, other voices following behind them.

"Oh, my God," Mom said, standing.

Dad pulled off his hat, shaking his head free of snow. His look said everything we needed to know.

Johnny stumbled in behind him, his fists jammed deep into his coat pockets. I tried to read his expression in a face blistered with cold. His eyes darted around the room, taking everyone in.

"What are you doing back?" Mom asked. "Shouldn't you still be out there?"

"We need to warm up a bit, and then we'll head back out," Dad said, unzipping his coat. Maybe it was the cold, the wind lashing against his face, but Dad looked older then, a decade older than he'd been that morning at breakfast. A decade older than he'd been a few hours ago, when we were sitting in front of the television. Mom held the door open again, ushering inside a half dozen men, including Uncle Paul and two more police officers. They instantly filled our kitchen, stamping snow off their boots and whisking snowdrifts from the creases of their clothes. Aunt Julia stood up to help. The rack by the door was already loaded with our own coats and scarves and hats, so she began stacking the men's coats on top of our counters.

Emilie disappeared into the living room and came back, thumping a set of folding chairs in each hand. Aunt Julia helped with the coffee. I took in the grave faces of the men, the official badges on their uniforms, and realized that this was the single biggest tragedy of our lives. Back when I was in kindergarten, an ice storm had felled trees across driveways and roads, but that had happened to all of Watankee. This was a tragedy all our own. Suddenly everything was important, every word, every movement. I felt dizzy, trying to take it all in at once.

"Let's take off your coat, Johnny," Mom ordered.

Johnny didn't react.

"Come on," she directed, holding out her hand. Johnny shook his head slightly and leaned back against the wall, closing his eyes. Against the yellow wallpaper with the brown teacups, he looked yellowish himself.

The men settled heavily into folding chairs and began working the cold from their bodies—flexing fingers, rolling ankles, rubbing their palms against their cheeks.

"We've got coffee coming in a few minutes, gentlemen," Aunt Julia announced.

Two officers who had just come in joined Officer Parks on one side of the kitchen table. They bent together, voices low, their shoulders touching as if they were in a huddle.

"What have they found?" Grandpa asked, too loud. Uncle Paul said something to him, and he boomed, "I'm just trying to find out what's going on here."

"We don't know anything, Papa. No one knows anything," Mom said, her voice sharp.

I heard barking and realized I'd been hearing it for a while. Someone had tied Kennel to the stake by his dog house, and when I glanced out the window, I could see him spinning on the end of his chain in nervous circles.

At the door, Mom shook snow from hats and gloves, letting it puddle on the floor in a way that would have been unthinkable at any other point in our lives. Dad stood next to her, his eyes darting from person to person as if he couldn't believe they were here, in his own house.

"It's not good, Alicia," Dad said, his voice low. "Bill Lemke is out there raising hell."

"Well, I would be, too, if that were my daughter," Mom said, just a bit too loud. Johnny turned, staring at her.

"We've got to stick together now," Dad hissed.

"Ready for some coffee?" Aunt Julia asked loudly, stepping forward with steaming mugs.

"We'll head back out in a minute. Just gotta get some of this cold off." I realized it was Sandy Maertz speaking, a member of our church and a player on that long-ago softball team.

"Hey, Kirsten," said a man who had kept his hunting cap on, the flaps dangling against his cheeks. For a moment, taking in his bulk, his ruddy cheeks, I couldn't place him. Then I spotted the name sewn on his shirt pocket: G. Coulie. Kevin's dad.

I wrapped my arms across my chest, suddenly conscious of the vomit stain on my pajamas.

It all seemed so civilized, so strange. *Surreal*—Emilie's word. It was the middle of the night, and people we barely knew were standing in our kitchen. It was embarrassing to have our lives opened up like this, to see Kevin Coulie's dad drinking out of the #1 DAD mug I'd given my own dad for Father's Day last year. When I was younger, I thought I could become invisible by closing my eyes. I tried it again now, hoping I could blend in with the wall.

Mom approached Johnny and, taking his coat by the lapels, eased him out of it. Underneath, he was wearing his Shipbuilders sweatshirt, a twin of the one Stacy had worn for weeks. Johnny looked annoyed but didn't protest. Aunt Julia handed him a cup of coffee, and he took it, wrapping his fingers around the mug and staring down into it as if it held all the answers, as if he was reading his future in a cup of tea leaves.

One of the officers had been sketching a crude map on a piece of notebook paper, and he pushed the finished product into the middle of the kitchen table. The men crowded around the table, studying it.

"If we can cover this area from Passaqua Road out..."

"Whose field is that there? We've got to get onto that property, too."

Johnny leaned over the table, too, his face blank.

"All right, then," Dad said. "Let's get back out there."

"I'll fill a couple of thermoses," Aunt Julia called.

The men snapped back into action, rising from their seats and collecting their coats. Johnny grabbed for his, too, but Officer Parks rose and stopped him, a hand on his arm. "Actually, son, for now I'd like you to stay behind with me."

Everyone turned to watch Johnny, whose face went from pale to red in a second. It looked as if he was about to say something, but then he slowly nodded.

The men lumbered out the door, calling thanks over their shoulders for the coffee. Dad and Uncle Paul hesitated at the door.

"Go on," Mom urged. "They'll need you out there."

Officer Parks said, "Mr. Hammarstrom, it might be best if you stayed behind, too."

Dad and Mom exchanged a long glance, and then Uncle Paul followed the other men out into the snow and Dad came back to the table. After a moment, engines started and the caravan reversed, winding its way past our windows and out to the road. Inside, it was as if a giant vacuum had sucked all the air out of the room. We stood silently, not sure what was next.

Aunt Julia said, “I’ll clean up this mess,” and Emilie rushed to help her with the cups and spoons. The two of them clustered silently at the sink, their backs to the room.

Officer Parks looked around, considering the rest of us. Seeming to make a decision, he settled back into his chair and flipped to a new page in his notebook. Silently, as if on cue, Dad, Mom and Johnny took seats across from him at the table. Grandpa hovered behind them.

Officer Parks cleared his throat. “So, what we’ll be wanting right now is a statement from you, Johnny. Just your version of what happened tonight.”

I noticed the *we.* He was probably referring to himself or the police department, but he might as well have been referring to the rest of us. We were all listening—we all wanted to hear Johnny’s version of what had happened.

Johnny licked his lower lip, which was cracked from the cold. “I already told this to one of the other officers when we were out there.”

“Yes, but we need to get an official account,” Officer Parks continued patiently. “So, why don’t you have a seat next to me, and we’ll start from the beginning?”

He asked it as if it was a question, but it was the sort of question that couldn’t be answered with a *no.* Johnny clasped his hands in front of him on the table, then took his hands off the table and nervously pressed his palms against his thighs.

“What happened to your hand?” Officer Parks asked,

his eyes narrowing, and Johnny held it up, turning it over, as if he were surprised to see his own hand wrapped in a fat bandage. A faint reddish stain showed the blood had seeped through the gauze.

"From his truck, when he tried to push it out of the ditch," Mom offered. "It was cut up pretty bad when he came in here, so I—"

"Mrs. Hammarstrom," Officer Parks interrupted. "I need to hear this from Johnny. And Johnny, we might need to take a look at that later on."

"Why did you do a damn fool thing like—" Grandpa began, shaking his head at Johnny.

"I was only trying—" Johnny began.

"Get your father out of here," Mom said to Dad.

Dad made a quick gesture over his head, and the rest of us dispersed—Aunt Julia to the living room, with Grandpa following, sullenly; Emilie and I halfway up the stairs, where by silent agreement we perched in our listening spot. It was a relief to sit down, even if it was on a wooden step. My stomach had finally settled, but my whole body felt wobbly and nervous and tired. I leaned my right side against the wall and closed my eyes.

"I can't believe this," Emilie whispered. She was wedged onto the same step as me, her long legs stretched out in front of us.

"It's like a nightmare," I said.

"I wish this was only a nightmare." Emilie took the quilt from around my shoulders and pulled it tight around both of us. It felt like the closest we'd ever been in our entire lives.

Officer Parks said something we couldn't hear, his voice rising at the end in a question mark.

Mom protested, "You know, I really don't think—"

"Alicia," Dad said, his voice a growl.

"It was just a stupid mistake," Johnny said. "I couldn't get the truck to move, and Stacy kept saying I should just leave the truck there and forget about it, and finally she just got up and left. She was mad at me. She just…just walked away."

Suddenly I saw it in my mind's eye, the way I would come to see it again and again. Stacy pulling the hood of her green coat tight, stomping away, her boots sinking into the new snow. Walking away, walking blind.

"She could be…" I whispered. "She could be dead." My voice caught, a funny little sound between a hiccup and a cry.

"Hush!" Emilie hissed, but it was too late. Dad had heard us on the stairs, and in a few smooth strides he went from the kitchen table to the doorway, firmly closing the door and pitching us into darkness.

sixteen

Even in our bedroom, we weren't entirely removed from the action. Downstairs, we heard the occasional raised voice, chairs squeaking against the linoleum. Emilie and I sat on the end of her bed, looking out the window. With our faces pressed almost to the glass, we could see the helter-skelter fall of snow, the faint outlines of the oak tree outside our window and the dark outline of Grandpa's house only a few feet away. I leaned my nose against the window, watching closely, as if maybe, just maybe, out of the darkness would emerge a tall sixteen-year-old girl with red hair, a green coat, leather boots. With each second I felt more and more panic growing inside me. She was dead…she was alive…she was dead…as if I were picking petals off a flower to determine her fate.

No, Stacy was alive. She had to be.

When I pulled back from the window, my nose half-frozen, all I saw were our reflections, pale and ghostly, in the window. Emilie was chewing on the end of her blond braid, staring at nothing. I had sleepy circles under my eyes; it had to be nearly two in the morning at this point, the longest night of my life so far. Emilie's head snapped up suddenly.

"What?"

She pointed. "Headlights."

Two more cars were coming down our driveway, slowly, as if this wasn't an emergency and they had all the time in the world. Even without lights flashing, I knew these were more police officers.

Emilie and I dashed downstairs and stumbled into the kitchen. Grandpa, hearing our footsteps, boomed from the living room, "What now?"

Dad and Johnny were still at the table, Johnny with his arm propping up his head as if his neck just couldn't do the job anymore. Dad raised his voice when he saw us. "I told you—"

"There are more officers," I whispered, pointing to the back door.

Emilie looked around. "Where's the cop that was here?"

"Emilie!" Mom barked from the sink, where she was rinsing out a coffee mug. She jerked her head toward the bathroom. "Shh."

"What 'shh'? He knows he's a cop, doesn't he?"

The toilet flushed at the same time we heard the footsteps on the back porch stairs. Officer Parks stepped out of the bathroom, drying his hands on his pants. I thought guiltily of the dirty hand towel Aunt Julia had tossed on the floor, after wiping the vomit from my mouth.

Two policemen came in, stamping their feet politely at the threshold. They introduced themselves as Officer Merrill and Officer Weil. Officer Merrill was baby-faced, looking not much older than Johnny, but I recognized the gray-haired, mustachioed Officer Weil instantly. He had come to Watankee Elementary last spring to remind us not to talk to any strangers and to stay away from people who took drugs. I remembered how my classmates and I had snickered at this. In Watankee? What strangers? What drugs?

Johnny rose to his feet. “Have you found her?”

There was a slight shaking of both heads at once.

“Shouldn’t you be out there looking?” There were tears in Johnny’s voice, although not on his face. He was at his breaking point. “Maybe I could go—”

“You’re going to stay put, son,” Officer Parks said.

From the doorway to the living room, Grandpa snorted. “Seems like a funny way to run a search, with everyone just standing around.”

“Papa—” Dad warned.

“Sir, with all due respect,” Officer Parks said, and Grandpa put his palms up in mock surrender.

“We woke up a judge in Manitowoc,” Officer Weil said then, pulling a folded piece of paper from his inside jacket pocket.

“I don’t understand,” Mom said, looking accusingly at Officer Parks. “What’s this?”

“It’s a search warrant,” Officer Parks said, and all of a sudden, it seemed as if I was no longer in the middle of a nightmare, but in the middle of a television drama, like *In the Heat of the Night* or *NYPD Blue. We have a warrant to search the premises....* Except there was no bad guy here, no criminal, no evidence. Was there? I shook my head, trying to clear it. This couldn’t be happening.

Mom unfolded the piece of paper, glanced at it and passed it to Dad. “I don’t understand,” she repeated, her voice rising. "Do you think she's here? Do you think we're hiding Stacy in our house or something?"

Officer Merrill explained, "We're following the proper procedure for an investigation, ma'am."

"And you're investigating *us?*"

Officer Weil was unruffled. "We need to pursue all possible angles, Mrs. Hammarstrom." There was no trace of the friendly voice he'd used in my classroom, when he'd informed my classmates that police officers were our friends, and we could trust them with anything.

"Clearly you think that we're hiding something," Mom continued, but Dad took her by the forearm, which seemed to silence her. He laid the search warrant on the table and nodded slowly.

I looked from Dad to Mom and Johnny and back; it was unthinkable that this was happening, that officers were standing in our house, about to look through our belongings.

Johnny said, "This is a waste of time. We should all be out there!"

"We have a full team of people out there looking, and more members of the community have joined in the search," Officer Parks said. "In the meantime, we need to let these officers do their jobs."

Mom shook her arm free from Dad's grasp. "I just can't believe this. We've been completely cooperative. And yet you think that..."

"Let's have everyone head into the living room," Officer Weil said firmly.

Aunt Julia came forward, taking Grandpa by the arm. "Maybe I'll walk you home. Nothing you can do here right now anyway."

Grandpa huffed a bit but let himself be led to the door. "You call me with any news," he said over his shoulder.

"Your room upstairs?" Officer Merrill asked abruptly, and Johnny said, "Yeah."

"We'll start there, then," Officer Weil said. "We'll just ask you to stay down here with Officer Parks for a few minutes."

In the living room, we sat stiffly side by side on the furniture we'd had for my entire life, but which now felt unfamiliar and strange. Upstairs, the men traipsed from room to room. Officer Parks sat in the recliner we always reserved for Grandpa, awkward as an uninvited guest.

"So, tell me," Dad blurted abruptly. "This is Bill Lemke's idea, isn't it?"

Officer Parks furrowed his eyebrows. "What's Bill Lemke's idea?"

Dad let out a short puff of air through his nose and said nothing.

Overhead, feet crossed the hall. I imagined the officers entering our bedrooms, recording the details of our lives: the unmade beds, Mom's negligee hanging from a hook next to her closet, Johnny's heaps of dirty clothes. I tried to think like Nancy Drew; what kind of clues were they hoping to find—diamond earrings or an envelope full of money or a signed confession? I wondered if they were searching Stacy's bedroom, too, finding her perfectly made bed, her bare walls, the picture of the boy with his face etched out, someone who wasn't Johnny at all.

The back door opened, and we all flinched, startled. Aunt Julia called, "It's just me. Should I make more coffee?"

Mom looked to Officer Parks, who said, "That would be fine."

"Please," Mom answered her weakly.

We listened to Aunt Julia clattering around in our kitchen, rinsing the pot, filling it with water, setting mugs on the counter with a delicate clink. Meanwhile, we sat stiffly, prisoners in our own living room.

Outside, somewhere, was Stacy and a whole troop of men looking for her. I couldn't wrap my mind around it, Stacy fumbling, snow-blind. Upstairs, men we barely knew were sorting through our possessions, trying to determine Johnny's involvement. I remembered how those police dramas on TV always said, "Innocent until proven guilty"—and that's where Johnny was, then, dangling in limbo between those two worlds. I tried to read his face, so I could decide for myself. But his face was blank, his mouth slack, his eyes boring into the carpet, into nothing.

Mom cleared her throat. "What happens next?"

Officer Parks looked up from his notes. "That depends on what they find upstairs, and how the search is going outside. But I'm guessing that within the hour a detective will be here with some more questions."

"What else is there to ask? Haven't you heard everything already?"

"It's sometimes surprising what turns up in an interview. Things you wouldn't even guess would be important turn out to be crucial." Officer Parks said this calmly, his eyes shifting from face to face. I almost choked when he looked at me. I knew what might be crucial: the fight between Johnny and Stacy five days ago. But his eyes settled firmly on Johnny. "If you have anything new to add, anything that would help the guys out in the field… Right now, time is of the essence."

"She just started walking," Johnny said. "I mean, she was mad at me—"

"Why was she mad at you?"

We all stared at Johnny, who looked terribly nervous.

"Because I'd crashed the truck, and it was so cold, and I guess she thought…"

Officer Parks tapped his pen impatiently.

Johnny swallowed, and the next part came out in a whisper. "I think maybe she thought I would follow her."

I could see Stacy then, looking over her shoulder, stamping her pretty leather boots in annoyance. A few more steps, a glance back into the night. Was she still there, expecting Johnny to rescue her? I thought of the men in the search party, tramping through snowdrifted fields. The way it was coming down, the snow would blur their vision, make every figure Stacy's, every movement that of a wandering teenage girl. The wind would make them unable to call to each other, unable to hear Stacy's voice.

"The thing is," Officer Parks said, resettling his bulk in Grandpa's recliner, "it always looks better if you tell everything you know, right off the bat."

Mom abandoned the diligent chewing of her thumbnail, leaving a ragged edge exposed. "Looks better to who?"

"There's nothing else," Johnny insisted, ignoring Mom. "Stacy left the car, she was walking. She's out there somewhere."

Heavy footsteps came down the stairs, and we all

swiveled to see Officer Weil in the doorway. Officer Merrill followed him, carrying a small white garbage bag in one hand.

"What's that?" Mom demanded.

"We've identified a few things that may be important to the investigation," Officer Weil explained. "We have some correspondence here that looks like it's come from the victim."

"Our letters?" Johnny asked, his face reddening.

Mom groaned, leaning her head against her palm. It seemed like a lifetime ago that she had confronted Johnny with Stacy's desperate note. *It's like you're the best drug in the world and I need you in me all the time, pulsing through my veins.... If I can't see you every day, I'll kill myself.*

"What else do you have in there?" Dad demanded, and Officer Merrill held up a small white plastic bag.

Johnny jumped up. "You can't just take that, can you?"

"What is it?" Mom asked.

Officer Merrill exchanged a glance with Officer Parks, who nodded, and Officer Merrill gently lifted up a rectangular pink-and-white box between his gloved fingers.

"What the—" Dad began at the same time Mom said, "Johnny, how could you be so—" And Johnny, who had looked for a second as if he might charge the officer, sank back onto the couch.

"A pregnancy test," Officer Weil clarified. "Just the box, looks like the contents have been removed."

We were all holding our breath then, the meaning of the empty pregnancy kit clear to all of us. Aunt Julia, standing behind the officers in the doorway to our kitchen, leaned heavily against the door frame.

Johnny stuttered helplessly, "I just don't see…that doesn't have anything to do with…"

"The search warrant explains all of that for you," Officer Parks said crisply. "Also, I'll need to ask you to change your clothes, Johnny. We need to take what you're wearing now, as well as the coat you were wearing earlier."

It had seemed insignificant in the face of everything else, but took on a new importance now. The blood on Johnny's sleeve. Johnny's blood—or Stacy's? Or some of both? My mind spun so hard I felt sick to my stomach, dizzy like the time I'd inched onto a ledge off the hayloft to reach a kitten who had wandered too far. The height hadn't bothered me at all until I'd looked down. That's what it felt like now, as if we were all standing on a ledge, a gulf opening underneath us.

Dad and Mom looked at each other in wordless conversation. "Go on, Johnny," Dad said, and Johnny stood. In the kitchen he stripped out of his sweatshirt, T-shirt, jeans and socks, until he was down to his boxers. The further he stripped down, the younger he looked to me—in the beginning a man, at the end a boy.

"All right, Johnny," Officer Merrill said and placed Johnny's clothes carefully in a white garbage bag with his gloved hands.

"Are you finished, then?" Mom asked, her voice tight.

Officer Weil nodded. "For now. The truck has already been towed to the station, so this should about cover it. We appreciate your cooperation."

Under her breath, Mom muttered, "We haven't had much of a choice."

Dad put a hand on her arm. "Go on upstairs, Johnny. Get some clothes on."

And yet Johnny stood there for a minute, pale and skinny, his collar bones prominent, as if they might break through his skin with any movement. Although I knew his strength, had seen him hoist bags of feed and wrestle a pig to the ground, he didn't look like much of an athlete standing in front of us. He didn't look like someone who could execute a pin in a matter of seconds, or even take on a teenage girl.

At that moment, he really didn't look like much of anything.

seventeen

Aunt Julia had removed our stained tablecloth and set coffee mugs and napkins directly on the scuffed wood surface. She poured Johnny a cup when he came downstairs, fully dressed again, but he didn't take it. Instead, he headed back to the living room. "I could make some hot chocolate for the girls," Aunt Julia suggested.

"They're going back upstairs," Mom said firmly. She ran a hand over my hair. "Change into fresh clothes and get some sleep. We'll wake you when we know something."

Emilie nudged me, and I followed her upstairs, my feet heavy as a zombie's. I caught a glimpse of the clock at the top of the stairwell: nearly four in the morning.

Downstairs, Mom hissed, "Of course everything was normal. What are you saying?"

"I'm only asking. I don't know what to think." Aunt Julia's voice was defensive.

"Don't you do it, Julia. Don't you look at me that way," Mom said.

Aunt Julia must have stepped away from her, because a moment later the only sound was the splash of water in the kitchen sink.

Emilie flopped onto her bed, her face toward the wall. I slipped out of my dirty pajamas and into sweatpants and a T-shirt and lay on my bed, too, although it didn't seem as if this would be a night to get any sleep. I wondered if we would ever sleep again if Stacy Lemke didn't make it home.

My mind kept snagging on the officer's words—the *victim.* Stacy was a victim, just like girls in after-school specials, like the kids in grainy black-and-white images on the backs of milk cartons. I was too keyed up to sleep, and my own bed felt strange, different from the place where I'd slept my entire life. I fluffed my pillow and straightened my quilt, trying to figure out what was different. Maybe I'd been a different person before—just last night—when I'd changed into my pajamas and cuddled up with a book. I'd only been a child then. Or maybe it was the thought of the officers raiding our house, rummaging in our closets, in our laundry hampers and drawers. As if Stacy were hiding in here…a pocket-size Stacy Lemke, fitting into the old shoebox under my bed…not missing at all.

I woke, not realizing I'd been sleeping, to voices downstairs.

"I think the detective is here," Emilie told me. She was sitting up now, leaning against the wall. "That means they're going to question Johnny again."

Again? I rubbed my eyes and looked at her. It seemed very important, suddenly, that I ask the question. "Do you think Johnny hurt her?"

Emilie glared at me. "How the hell should I know?"

Downstairs, I peeked into the living room. Dad and Johnny sat side by side on the couch. Dad looked exhausted; Johnny looked pitiful. With the months of weight loss and the stress of the past few hours, his skin was sallow, stretched tight across his cheekbones. His pulse seemed to thump from his Adam's apple.

The detective loomed over them, as solid and powerful as a linebacker. He had a green folder clutched in one hand. "I'm Detective Halliday," he announced. "I know you've already talked to Officer Parks, but, unfortunately, I have more questions."

Mom and Aunt Julia carried in two wingback chairs, salvaged from an estate sale a few years back but never refinished according to Mom's original plan. Detective Halliday settled into one chair, and Officer Parks took the other. Lined up across from each other that way, it was two against two, but somehow Dad and Johnny seemed woefully outnumbered.

Aunt Julia excused herself and came back to the kitchen. We stood in the doorway as she ran a bony hand back and forth over my head.

"We've already told the officers everything we know," Dad protested, his hand resting on Johnny's leg. "We've been talking for hours."

"If I could just go out there—" Johnny said, his voice almost a whimper. He pounded his left fist against his thigh. His right hand, bandaged and useless, lay at his side.

Detective Halliday opened the green folder. It already contained papers, handwritten responses on typed forms. "Let's get through these questions first." His voice was quiet, but with an edge. "We'll start from the beginning."

Johnny breathed hard through his nose. "I already told Officer Parks, we were driving home—"

"No," Detective Halliday interrupted. "Let's start with Saturday morning."

Johnny leaned back a few inches. I saw him struggling to understand the question. Saturday morning? What did that have to do with anything?

I thought about Saturday morning. It was only yesterday, but it felt like a million years ago. I'd been at the kitchen table reading the comics when Johnny had come in from milking the cows. "Colder than a witch's tit out there," he'd said, once he was sure Mom wasn't in earshot. It had been too cold for a run, but I'd heard him later in the garage, jumping rope for minutes at a time, stopping to catch his breath, and starting up again. That's where he'd been when Mom had sent me outside for a can of orange juice from the extra freezer. I'd heard his breathy count: "One seventy-five…one seventy-six…"

Yesterday morning he had been my brother. Now, things had happened so fast that I couldn't be sure who he was.

Mom walked past into the kitchen, giving me a look, *the* look, the one that told me I was too young to be part of an adult conversation, even if it was the most important conversation of my life. We left Johnny to mumble his answers for Detective Halliday and assembled around the kitchen table. Aunt Julia pulled me onto her lap, and I breathed in her musky cigarette smell.

"I hope Stacy's okay," I whispered to no one in particular. Aunt Julia hugged me a little more tightly.

From the doorway, Emilie said, "She's not okay, you idiot." Her hair was mussed on one side from sleep, her face wrinkled from being pressed against a pillow.

"Emilie!" Mom snapped.

"She's not okay," Emilie repeated quietly.

I stared at her. "What do you mean? How do you know?"

"Are you kidding me?" she scoffed. "She's been out in the cold for hours now. It's got to be ten degrees out there. Think about it."

"That's enough, Emilie," Mom hissed, but of course Emilie was right. I tried to picture Stacy in her appliquéd jeans and her Ships sweatshirt, or maybe her red sweater with a row of white hearts across the chest. She would have been wearing her new boots, a Christmas gift from her parents. Emilie and I had both idolized those boots: soft brown leather, with laces that went all the way up her shin bones. Not boots for walking in the snow. Her winter coat was Kelly-green with big toggle clasps, which she topped with a knitted hat with dangling pom-poms. For some reason I couldn't imagine her whole face at once: strands of red hair, green-gray eyes, the crease of skin on her cheek when she smiled. Already I had lost a clear vision of her; already I was seeing her in pieces.

Stacy's boots would be ruined by now, soaked through, her toes freezing inside. Her face would be rubbed raw from the cold, snowflakes sticking to her eyelashes. The cold would have seeped inside her coat, through her jeans, down her sweater.

I imagined her coming up the steps to our back door, her fingers and toes brittle with frostbite, snapping off like autumn branches. I'd read about the Titanic, how the people who went into the water froze to death before they could be scooped out. I felt a sob rise in my throat and tried to disguise it with a cough.

Emilie glared at me.

Mom said, "We've just got to pray for her. We've just got to pray that God keeps her safe."

Emilie folded her arms across her chest. "Might be too late for that."

Mom hissed across the table, "Now you listen to me—"

But just then a police radio sputtered to life in the living room, and our phone rang. Mom lunged for it, picking up on the second ring.

She's alive! She's safe! Emilie was wrong, the detectives were wrong, I was wrong for thinking what I had thought. Stacy was alive and everything would be okay.

"Oh, my God." Mom's face was flushed. "It's Uncle Paul. Says he just heard on the scanner..."

The men filled the doorway, led by Detective Halliday.

"What's going on?" Emilie demanded.

"We've got a report of someone matching Stacy's description at a gas station up north, near Highway 10," Officer Parks said. "We're heading up to check it out."

Johnny, eager, reached for his coat.

"Can we go, too?" I asked, squirming in Aunt Julia's lap.

"No, baby. They've got a whole team out there," Dad said, and I could tell from his voice that he was hopeful, too. He and Mom exchanged a long look, and then the men headed out the door. I wrestled free of Aunt Julia's grasp and watched from the window as Officer Parks opened the back door of his patrol car and Johnny and Dad piled in. Their faces were lit for a moment until the light inside the car faded, and they vanished into the dark. A knot of fear stuck in my throat, thinking of Dad and Johnny behind the protective screen, riding along like a pair of criminals. The patrol car did a quick turn in the driveway before heading off into the night. The digital clock on the microwave read 4:37. Was it possible that this was still the same, long night?

"Highway 10? That's a long way to walk," Emilie said from the door. She had pulled one of Dad's hooded sweatshirts over her pajamas, its sleeves flopping beyond her fingertips. With the hood cinched tight, only a small oval of her face showed—the inside corners of her eyes, her nose, the sad set of her lips. "How would she even get there?"

"Shush," Mom said, but the house was already quiet, absent the police officers. "We're going to wait and see." We shushed obediently and listened to the silence, which wasn't really silent at all. We were breathing, the coffee was percolating, the wind was smacking snow against the windows. Stacy was missing, and now Dad and Johnny were gone, too.

I took a deep, ragged breath. "They're coming back, aren't they? Dad and Johnny, I mean?"

Mom was chewing on her thumbnail again, worrying the ragged edge. "Of course," she said. "Of course they're coming back."

I waited for them on the couch, tucking a crocheted afghan around my body. How long would it take to get there, up to the juncture with Highway 10? Was Emilie right, or would Stacy be waiting for them, as if she'd been there all along? I heard the grandfather clock chime five before I fell asleep. It was almost morning, then. It would be morning by the time I woke up. And in the morning, everything had to be better.

eighteen

Dad called later, when the sky was changing from black to blue and the snowfall had slowed. It was maddening to wait for Mom to hang up the phone and tell us the news. A lifetime seemed to pass in those seconds.

"Did they find her?" I demanded the second the receiver was back in its cradle.

Mom shook her head. "Nothing. A false report."

So Stacy Lemke wasn't near Highway 10; she wasn't headed north to anywhere. I didn't understand how there could be a false report; either there was a frostbitten teenage girl wandering in the area at 4:00 a.m., or there wasn't. It didn't seem like the sort of thing that could be mistaken.

Aunt Julia stretched in the doorway. "They're coming back, then?"

Mom fidgeted uneasily. "They're taking Johnny in to look at his cut."

"It's that bad?" Aunt Julia asked.

"His hand will be fine. The police need to, you know, examine the cut in case there are…well, you know. Fibers and things."

We let this sink in. Outside, Kennel began to bark.

"Is Johnny a suspect?" I demanded.

Mom swallowed. "I don't know if that's the word—"

Emilie asked, "What other word is there?"

The knock at the back door made us jump. I craned my neck around Emilie and Aunt Julia—hoping for what? Stacy? Dad and Johnny? It was Jerry Warczak, stamping to clear the snow from his shoulders and boots.

"I've been out with the search team," he explained, peeling his hands out of his gloves. "Heard all the commotion and wondered if I could be of any help here."

Mom started to her feet. "Oh, thank you, Jerry. Thank you. But I'm not sure—"

He flexed and tightened his fingers, working the cold out of them. "I thought maybe I could help out with the milking."

The milking. We'd all forgotten, in the chaos of things, that we lived on a farm, that there were a hundred cows to milk. Dad usually took this early shift, heading out to the barn long before the rest of us were awake, returning to doze while Mom got breakfast going. Weekdays, he and Jerry worked together, sometimes with Grandpa's interference. Weekends, the job mainly belonged to Johnny. It might have felt like a million years since last night, but it was only Sunday, after all—time for Johnny to begin his shift.

"Yes—that would be wonderful," Mom gushed. "I'm sure John would be so appreciative. And I know he'll want to thank you somehow—"

"He'd do the same for me," Jerry said, brushing her off. Maybe he felt awkward to stand in our kitchen without Dad or Johnny there. "Well, then," he said after a moment. "I'll just go ahead and get started, I think."

"Thank you again, Jerry," Mom called as he left.

For what seemed like the first time in my life, none of us went to church that Sunday. Mom suggested we all shower and get dressed, I guess to be prepared for whatever else the day might bring. Meanwhile, she set out bread and butter and jam, just to keep busy. Aunt Julia went to her house to "freshen up," promising to return the second we needed her. *Right now!* I thought, watching her Buick head down the driveway. *Right now, we need you.*

Grandpa came over with a dozen questions Mom couldn't answer, then wandered out to the barn to help Jerry. It was nearly eight when Dad and Johnny arrived, blurry-eyed. We reassembled around the kitchen table, exhausted. Johnny's hand was rewrapped in a thick bandage. He slumped into his chair at the table and immediately fell asleep leaning on one arm. He'd been awake for more than twenty-four hours at this point.

"I don't think I've ever been so tired," Dad said, forcing down a few bites of toast. He looked as if he'd been gone for a year instead of a few hours. Give him some gray hair and he'd look as old as Grandpa. "And Johnny—they've really been putting him through the wringer." He glanced at Mom pointedly, a glance that said he would talk to her later, without Emilie and me listening.

Mom nodded, understanding. "Hopefully he can just rest for a bit. Take a shower, sleep a little."

"They'll want us back at the station later, you and me, and Johnny," Dad said. "Detective Halliday said he would send a car for us."

"Okay," Mom said carefully. "I'll see if Julia can stay with the girls."

"We can stay here by ourselves," Emilie protested, but Dad's look shut her down.

Dad and Mom went upstairs, closing the door to the stairwell firmly behind them. Emilie and I cleared away the breakfast dishes, most of which were untouched, and walked carefully around a sleeping Johnny. Wordlessly we finished the tasks Mom had started and abandoned: the heap of laundry to be folded, the dishes that lurked in the sink under a few inches of soapy water.

The phone rang and Johnny bolted upright. Emilie and I stared at it as if it was a grenade about to explode.

"Think we should answer it?" Emilie asked, but someone intercepted the call on the upstairs receiver.

The morning wore on, with the entire town of Watankee checking in by phone or traipsing through our kitchen. "It's all over the news," Aunt Julia reported when she returned, her hair blow-dried and curled, her makeup carefully applied. Grandpa came by to tell us what he'd seen on Channel 10; Uncle Paul drifted in and out; a friend of Mom's from the hospital stopped by with a pot of soup. Mom and Aunt Julia stood in the driveway talking for a long time. When they came inside Mom had tears in her eyes. Jerry Warczak must have finished the milking; he left without coming inside.

After church let out, Pastor and Mrs. Ziegler came over, refusing the offer of coffee. "We don't want to cause any additional trouble," Mrs. Ziegler said. Pastor said a prayer in his booming voice that seemed too loud for our kitchen; afterward, Mrs. Ziegler clasped us, one by one, in an uncomfortable hug. It was as if we were having a funeral service, as if Stacy was buried and gone already. Or maybe the funeral was for Johnny; he might as well have been dead, too.

"Now you hang in there, son," Pastor Ziegler said, putting his hand heavily on Johnny's shoulder.

By now, I realized, everyone in Watankee must have known, from the butcher to the librarian to the kids in my fourth-grade class. Had my Sunday School class prayed about this? Was everyone staring at our empty pew and whispering, speculating, gossiping? In their minds, had they already buried Stacy, and tried and convicted Johnny?

Detective Halliday came over just before noon, his large frame filling our doorway. "We're going to have a little meeting down at the station with the Lemkes," he announced. "Just to get a few things out in the open."

Dad said, "Yes, sir."

Mom nodded, running her hands through her hair to tuck in a few stray curls. "Do you want us to follow you?"

Detective Halliday shook his head slightly. "If it's all the same, I'll just take you in my car."

"Let's go, then," Johnny said. He swished past me and banged out the door, his coat tucked under one arm.

"Listen to your aunt, now," Dad commanded, giving Emilie a pointed glance and me a kiss on the cheek as he went. The three of them clambered into the back of the detective's navy sedan and left.

"Okay, then," Aunt Julia said brightly, as the car pulled away. "Should we get some lunch together?"

In response, Emilie wandered into the living room and snapped on the television. Aunt Julia and I followed, perching mutely on the couch. We watched a string of commercials about heater repairs and used car sales before the news came on. A perky blonde woman informed us that the local area had been hit hard by snow, with the Manitowoc area receiving nearly thirteen inches in the past twenty-four hours. The roof of the Toys "R" Us in Sheboygan had collapsed. I half tuned out, picturing thousands of toys buried in the snow, when suddenly I heard Stacy's name.

"Turn it up!" I yelped, and Emilie obliged.

"...vanished last night during the snowstorm after some car trouble in rural Manitowoc County."

"Vanished?" I repeated, the word salty on my tongue. People didn't just vanish. They fell into holes or got into cars, but they didn't vanish.

"Shut up!" Emilie snapped.

"Throughout the night, volunteers from all across the county searched the neighboring fields for any sign of the missing girl."

There was a shot then, of a field I recognized farther down Rural Route 4, and a group of men walking across it, about an arm's length apart.

"Early this morning there was a report of a teenage girl spotted up north, close to Whitelaw, but authorities have dismissed the lead. Anyone with information about the disappearance of Stacy Lemke is asked to call—"

Emilie turned down the volume, and the reporter's voice dissolved.

"It's not going to help to hear any of this," Aunt Julia said gently, touching her palm to Emilie's shoulder. Emilie had put on Dad's sweatshirt again; it was big enough that she could disappear inside it. Maybe she wanted to vanish herself.

"Maybe she was hurt in the crash," I suggested, trying out the idea. "That must be what happened. She was hurt, and then she—"

Emilie waved the floppy cuff of the sweatshirt at

me. "If she was hurt, she wouldn't have left the truck. And Johnny would have said something, wouldn't he?"

"I don't know," I admitted. "I'm just thinking."

"Well, try to use some sense when you think."

"Okay, let's come away from the television," Aunt Julia suggested, helping me to my feet.

"And do what? Play some checkers or something?" Emilie sniffed. "I mean, what's the point? He's fucking ruined everything."

Aunt Julia frowned. "We don't know that your brother has done anything."

"I'll tell you what he's done," Emilie huffed. "He took his girlfriend out on a date, and he didn't bring her back. That's all anyone is going to need to know."

As much as I hated her for saying it, I knew she was right. All the regular things from our regular lives were pretty useless now.

Everything *was* fucking ruined.

nineteen

Aunt Julia made macaroni and cheese from a box; in between haphazard stirs of the noodles on the stove, she went out for at least two smokes. "There's no point trying to quit during a time of stress," she explained. The noodles ended up overcooked, limp, coated in a sticky paste of orange cheese. Emilie took one look and excused herself to lie down in front of the television again. I moved the macaroni around my plate and scraped the rest into Kennel's bowl by the door.

"Did you tell my mom what I told you?" I asked Aunt Julia. "About the fight and everything else?"

Aunt Julia closed her eyes. "You know, I'm just not sure it's the right time."

"What do you mean?"

She opened her eyes, rubbing one hand across her temple. "Well, I don't think it necessarily proves anything. They might have had an argument, but that doesn't mean that Johnny..."

Her voice trailed off, but mine filled in the blank.

"Killed her?" I prompted, then clapped my hand over my mouth. It was a horrible thing to think, let alone to say. I had a woozy feeling that by saying the words, I'd made them true.

Aunt Julia swallowed. "Well, right. There's a big jump between arguing with someone and hurting them. I mean, Lord knows your uncle Paul and I have had our disagreements." She gave me a crooked smile. "And if we mentioned it right now, it might make Johnny look guilty of something he's not."

"But he might be," I said, my voice small. Aunt Julia's eyes narrowed.

Just then the phone rang, and Aunt Julia grabbed for it. She listened, then pursed her lips tightly. "The family has no comment at this time," she announced, and placed the receiver back in its cradle. She looked at me. "That was a reporter from the Green Bay paper."

So Johnny's name was out there, and people all the way in Green Bay had heard about it.

I spent much of the afternoon watching our driveway, like a sentry at a fortress, on the alert for all visitors. I was alone with my uncomfortable thoughts—Emilie slept away the afternoon, Aunt Julia disappeared to talk with Grandpa for an hour, and Jerry Warczak came once to check on the cows, this time without stopping by the house. Throughout the day, the phone rang, as if it was a living thing on its own.

Detective Halliday's car didn't turn down our driveway until nearly seven. Aunt Julia had made us peanut butter and jelly sandwiches, but I hadn't been able to take more than a bite. Dad and Mom, climbing out of the backseat, didn't look at each other. Dad went straight to the barn, and Johnny, more like a ghost than a person, headed upstairs before I could say anything to him. But what would I have said?

"I'm so exhausted," Mom groaned, collapsing into a chair. "I feel like I could sleep for days."

"So there's still no word?" Aunt Julia asked.

Mom shook her head, her eyes closed. "There are still people out there, searching." She went quiet, letting her sentence hang in the room. There was an odd choking noise in her throat, and I realized she was trying not to cry.

"Oh, Alicia," Aunt Julia said. "Oh, you poor thing."

"You should have seen the Lemkes, Julia. For God's sake, she's only sixteen years old. If it was Emilie or Kirsten, I don't know what I would do." Mom looked directly at me, and I squirmed under her glance. Suddenly I felt guilty that I was safe and Stacy wasn't, that Johnny was safe but Stacy wasn't.

"Bill kept saying these awful things, like how he knew Johnny wasn't ever good enough for his daughter. And the pregnancy test—my God. Johnny just sat there the whole time and took it, and Bill and John ended up screaming at each other. And Sharon Lemke couldn't even stay in the room during the questioning, she was so hysterical." Mom bit her lip. "I tried to comfort her, but what could I say? If they don't find her, Julia—"

I swallowed hard, trying to imagine Mrs. Lemke as anything less than perfectly poised, her hair coiffed, her linen dress starched wrinkle-free. I thought of Mr. Lemke at the party, singing happy birthday in a big, showy voice. He'd orchestrated the whole show that day, from the tour through his house to the grand unveiling of Stacy's Camaro, as if the day had been as much about him as about Stacy. He was someone who liked to call the shots, but where did that leave him now?

Aunt Julia put her hand on top of Mom's. Her skin

was still somehow dark, although it had been months since she'd tanned on her deck. "We can't think like that, Alicia," she said, rubbing her thumb back and forth in an oval across Mom's pale skin.

"What about Johnny? What's going to happen to him?" I asked, but Mom kept talking to Aunt Julia as if I wasn't even there.

"I don't know what to think," Mom whispered, her voice strained with exhaustion. "There's really no proof of anything from that night, one way or another. Johnny says they went to a movie in Sheboygan, but he didn't keep the stubs. He told them all about the movie, but admitted that they'd seen it once before, so that didn't prove anything. The officers have interviewed the employees from the theater, and no one remembers seeing them."

"But Sheboygan is a bigger city than Watankee," Aunt Julia said. "So there wouldn't necessarily—"

Mom continued, not listening. "And the detective asked him why he went all the way to Sheboygan, twenty-some miles away, when Manitowoc had a perfectly good theater, and snow was coming?"

I'd wondered the same thing.

Aunt Julia nodded. "What did Johnny say?"

Mom shrugged, smiling grimly. "That they wanted to get away from everything for the night, just be by themselves."

"Well, that's understandable." A hint of a smile had crept into Aunt Julia's voice. "They're teenagers, after all."

"No one remembers them at dinner, either," Mom continued, still whispering. Maybe, I realized, she didn't want Johnny to hear. "Johnny says they went to The Humble Bee in Cleveland. He described exactly what they ordered. The waitress remembered some young couples in there, but the officers showed her a picture of them and she said they didn't look familiar."

"Hmm," Aunt Julia said. "It doesn't prove anything either way, does it?"

I pictured the inside of The Humble Bee, where we'd stopped a few times coming back from Sheboygan, all of us piling into one of the round corner booths. Dad had described the decor as "fussy"—with bright yellow curtains and bumblebees printed on the menus. It wasn't Johnny's kind of place, either, but I could see how Stacy would like it.

"And no receipt?" Aunt Julia prompted.

"He thought it might have fallen out of his pocket sometime last night, while he was trying to push his truck out of the ditch, or later, with all the running around we were doing."

"Of course," Aunt Julia murmured. She was still touching Mom's hand, her thumb kneading Mom's skin.

"I don't see how I have any choice but to believe him." Mom slid her hand from Julia's grasp and leaned wearily against her. "But it doesn't look good."

We heard Dad's boots on the stairs and froze. He came in, still wearing the mask of a hundred-year-old man.

"John—" Aunt Julia began, rising.

"I've got to get some sleep," he mumbled, shuffling past us, a ghost, just like Johnny. His footsteps clumped heavily on the stairs. I listened to him walk down the hallway, pause at Johnny's door, and continue on.

"What about tomorrow?" I asked, my throat suddenly tight. "It's Monday. We have school."

Mom seemed startled, as if she hadn't realized I'd been sitting there the whole time. "For now, we're all just going to stay right here."

I nodded, thinking of Kevin and the spelling bee, of my desk at the front of the room with my textbooks waiting inside. School would go right on along without me, without Emilie and Johnny, without Stacy.

"I think that's a good idea," said Aunt Julia. She smiled at me, bright and false. "I'm going to go check on Dad and then head home for the night. I'll be over first thing tomorrow morning...."

Mom gave a crooked, thankful smile.

"But what's next?" I demanded. "What's going to happen to Johnny? Is he under arrest?"

"Of course he's not," Mom said immediately, reflexively. "But...we don't know what's going to happen next."

At the doorway, Aunt Julia looped a scarf around her neck several times and pulled on her coat. "Want to walk me out, Kirsten? You've been cooped up all day."

I looked to Mom, who nodded absentmindedly. "Wear your coat," she said.

The chill was surprising, even in my too-big hand-me-down winter coat and snow boots. We crunched our way around the side of the house, past Grandpa's house. A light was on in his living room; he was sitting in one of the matching recliners with his heating pad. He did this every night after dinner, but tonight he was leaning forward, his head in his hands.

"This is going to kill him," Aunt Julia murmured.

"What?" I asked, not sure I'd heard right, but she shook her head.

It was dark but clear, the wind calm, the snow settled into stiff peaks like meringue. If it had been like this yesterday, I thought, Johnny wouldn't have driven off the road. If it had been like this yesterday, Stacy would have made it home. Only twenty-four hours ago, Johnny and Stacy had been driving back through a storm. Only twenty-four hours ago, Johnny had watched Stacy walk away, her red hair and green coat visible for a few moments, before being sucked away into the night. Except… except. I kept thinking of what Mom had said, that no one had seen Johnny and Stacy on their date, not at the movies and not at dinner, which meant that maybe they hadn't been on a date at all. My stomach churned, thinking this. If that was true, what had they been doing? How had Johnny come home safe and Stacy not at all?

We passed the long rectangle of Grandma's old garden, which Grandpa tended haphazardly in the years since her death. Deep furrows of new footprints, partially hidden by new snow, trailed across the boundaries of our property, to the outbuildings and the farm itself. The men must have been out here, crisscrossing our property in their search.

"Doesn't this feel good, to be out of the house for a minute?" Aunt Julia asked. Her words came out in a thick puff of air.

"I guess." Suddenly I worried that I was missing something important that was happening inside our house, the phone call that said Stacy Lemke was okay or Johnny's confession of what had really happened that night. "How far are we walking?"

"Let's head over to see the fence," she suggested, her gloved hand gesturing to the place where our property met up with the Wegners' property.

We approached the line of firs at the front of the yard, the moon bright and the stiff branches in dark relief against the snow. It was the sort of winter night you'd find on a Currier and Ives cookie tin, where the cold looked harmless. At the side of the yard I paused and looked back at our house. The kitchen light was still on; Mom, I imagined, was still at the table, too exhausted to move. It was dark upstairs, except for a light in Johnny's room. For a moment his shadow darkened the window, passed, then returned. He was pacing back and forth, his back hunched. What was he thinking? Was he going over every moment he'd ever had with Stacy? I shivered, and not just from the cold.

We picked our way across the field, which for three short seasons of the year was dotted with dandelions and clover and other weeds Dad cut back with the riding mower. The snow was deeper here, and I fell behind, my footsteps landing in the deep depressions where Aunt Julia's feet had been. I wasn't wearing snow pants—under ordinary circumstances, Mom would have killed me for wandering through thigh-high snow with nothing more substantial than a pair of jeans to protect my legs from the chill. But these weren't ordinary circumstances; I realized sharply that the rules I'd followed my whole life were no longer important. Who cared about snow pants or eating dinner on time? Maybe there would be no more ordinary circumstances, ever.

The snowdrifts were deeper close to the fence, and Aunt Julia took my hand, hoisting me onto the bottom slat. She was much taller than me, of course; the snow barely came to the top of her boots. In the middle of the pasture, the snow was flat and smooth; at the fence line it had gathered in curved ridges. I wondered if they had searched this field, too—if men had walked arm's-length apart through the Wegners' horse pasture, scanning the snow for the slightest clue—fresh footprints, a dropped glove.

"Kirsten, listen to me," Aunt Julia said suddenly, as

if she'd been chewing over the words for some time. "Things are going to get tricky from here on out."

I nodded, a movement so slight that Aunt Julia couldn't have seen it, but she continued anyway.

"People are going to be saying things and speculating—making assumptions—about Stacy and your brother. Do you understand?"

The cold caught in my throat. "Yes."

"I've lived in Watankee my whole life," she continued. "I've seen that it can be the best place in the world. When Paul's mother had cancer, I swear to you that everyone in town must have stopped by with a casserole for us. But it can also be the kind of place where people gossip, where people turn against each other…."

"I know," I said, leaning back from the fence, letting the weight of my body swing free while my hands gripped the top slat. Even the people we knew, friends of my parents, members of our church, stared at me curiously, whispering to each other: *She's so small!* "I've lived here my whole life, too."

"Of course you have," she chuckled, then continued seriously. "Our family has been in a tight spot before, when your parents were first together. It takes a lot of courage to go on living your life when everyone's watching you."

For once I knew what she was talking about without having to ask, although try as I might, I couldn't imagine a younger version of Mom, pregnant with Johnny. I knew there had been some bitterness between Mom and her parents, who had retired to Arizona and only called on Christmas, and between Mom and Dad's parents—particularly Grandpa, who was critical of her every move.

"Why can't people just…" I shook my shoulders helplessly.

She sighed. “I don’t know, sugar. I don’t know what it is in people that we like to find something to pick on. I guess we want someone to take the blame when things go wrong. This is something so big…bigger than Stacy and Johnny, you know. It’s bigger than Hammarstroms and Lemkes. The whole town is going to take sides. It won’t be hard to find someone to blame. I think you should know that, because it’s going to be tough for Johnny, and for your mom and dad, and for you and Emilie, too.”

I looked at her sharply. It hadn’t fully occurred to me that I would be involved, guilty merely because Johnny Hammarstrom was my brother and Stacy Lemke had been his girlfriend.

Her voice was gentle, continuing. “At this point, it’s looking like—even if they do find Stacy, she’s not going to be okay. I just think—I think you should know all of this.”

I nodded slowly, taking it all in. Really, I was grateful; this felt like the first real conversation of my life. Wasn’t this what I had always wanted, not to be treated like a little girl, the youngest kid, the runt of the litter? But I was terrified, too. Maybe it was easier to be too young to know anything.

“So, look—I just want to say that you can come to me for anything. Whenever things get tough, you just give me a call. Or come over. You could even stay with us for a while.”

“Okay,” I said woodenly.

“No matter what happens—and it can get worse, maybe a lot worse—we’ll just have to weather the storm. We can do that together, okay?”

I swallowed, remembering a video I’d seen in school of a tornado. In slow motion, the wind had picked the shingles off a roof, one by one, as if they were nothing but scraps of loose-leaf paper. Now I imagined it being our house, our barn, our lives, caught up in a wind and blowing away piece by piece. And there would be the Hammarstroms, hanging on to whatever we could, weathering the storm.

Aunt Julia put her arm around my shoulders. "You okay?"

I stared at the field, barren and lifeless in the snow. "I wish the horses were out," I said finally. "During the summer, I feed them apples right out of my hand."

"Maybe we could call them?" Aunt Julia suggested.

So that's what we did. We called them, even though they were tucked away in their stable for the night, acres away, deaf to our voices.

"King Henry!" I screamed. And then, again and again, "Come out here, King Henry!"

Beside me, Aunt Julia bellowed, "Queen Anne!"

The air was icy, burning my lungs, but at the same time it felt wonderful. I put everything I had into those screams. I turned to look back at our house, but no other lights came on, even though I was screaming loud enough to wake the dead.

And then it occurred to me, and I screamed, *"Stacy! Stacy Lynne Lemke!"*

My voice seemed to echo off the snow, off the treetops and the farm buildings, off the dark ceiling of the sky itself. If she were anywhere in the world, I thought, she had to hear me. She had to know someone was calling her name.

When my throat felt raw and I couldn't scream anymore, Aunt Julia wrapped my body in a hug from behind and helped me down from the fence.

twenty

I dreamed of snowstorms, of frostbite, of being a toddler and losing Mom's hand in the middle of a department store. I dreamed I was following Stacy through a maze, always one turn behind, just catching sight of her green coat. I had almost reached her, almost grabbed that bit of fabric when I jolted awake. Salty tears slithered down my cheeks, and I licked them away. In the dream, I'd felt I almost had her, that it was almost over. Awake, I knew that wherever she was, it was out of my reach.

The darkness outside was blue-black, and there was an eerie quiet to our house. I could almost believe that each member of my family was suddenly missing, scooped out of their beds by a giant, godlike hand. Listening to the predawn silence, unbroken by breath or voice, I thought: these are the mourning hours. And this is only the beginning.

Coach Zajac was our first visitor on Monday morning, rapping with his big fist against our back door just after seven o'clock. He explained he'd been in Milwaukee all weekend at a meeting with WIAA officials and learned about Stacy only last night.

There was an awkward silence, and Mom said, "Johnny hasn't been down yet."

I knew Johnny was awake, though. The first sounds I'd heard that morning had been from Johnny, throwing up in the bathroom.

Dad gestured Coach Zajac to a chair, and Mom offered a cup of coffee.

"He's pretty low right now," Dad explained. "He's got a lot on his mind. I tried to talk to him last night, but..."

"Maybe I can help?" Coach asked, pouring a dollop of milk into his coffee and swirling the cup slowly in his big paw. "I could talk to him, see where his head's at."

Mom glanced at Dad, and Dad shook his head. "I appreciate the offer, but not right now."

"Of course," Coach said, rising, his coffee untouched. "Will you tell Johnny I stopped by?"

I wandered into the living room, climbing carefully onto the arm of the couch to avoid Emilie, who had spent the night there, covered by a heavy quilt. Her face was buried in the crook where the top cushion met the bottom cushion, and she groaned as I approached. I watched Coach Zajac's car stop at the end of the driveway, signal and turn left. A minute later, at 7:15 exactly, the yellow Manitowoc County School bus approached down Rural Route 4, slowed at our driveway and then resumed speed as it headed to its next stop, without me.

"Wake up," I said, nudging Emilie's foot. "It's Monday morning."

"So?" She rolled over, pulling the quilt over her face.

In the kitchen, the phone rang. I slid off the couch.

"Hello?" Mom asked. A half-million phone calls between Saturday night and this morning, and still she was hopeful with each one. She cupped the receiver to her shoulder and whispered, "It's someone from the *Journal-Sentinel,* out of Milwaukee. He says he wants our side of the story for his article. What do I say?"

"We don't say anything," Dad said. "We have nothing to say."

Mom cleared her throat. "I'm afraid we have nothing to say at this time," she said into the receiver. She listened for a moment, then said, "No, thank you. I appreciate the phone call, but, no, thank you.... No, I'm sure. Thank you." When she replaced the receiver, her hand was shaking, her face pale. "But don't you think we should speak up and defend Johnny? It makes sense to tell his side of the story—"

Dad shook his head. "Anything we say could be taken out of context, spun in a dozen different directions."

"But Bill Lemke will be all over this—"

"Let him be all over it, then. We can't beat him at this game."

The *Manitowoc Herald Times Reporter* was next, then a reporter from a radio station in Green Bay, then someone from the *Journal Times* in Racine.

"Racine," Mom marveled. "That's four hours away—"

"The story is everywhere by now," Dad said.

"What are we going to do?" Mom asked, but this time I knew for sure it was a rhetorical question, one that we weren't supposed to answer, and one that we couldn't.

Johnny came down the stairs after nine, freshly showered. "Where's Dad?" he grunted.

I gestured to the barn. Where else?

"Are you doing okay, Johnny?" Mom asked. "I mean, of course you're not okay, I know that, but are you feeling okay?"

Johnny sat heavily at the table, silent. He looked straight ahead, as if she hadn't spoken.

"He was sick earlier," I volunteered. "I heard him throwing up in the bathroom."

Johnny didn't react, didn't confirm or deny, didn't shoot me a look that told me to mind my own business.

Mom reached over to touch her palm to his forehead. "Let me see," she said, but Johnny pulled away.

"Come on, Johnny," she said. When she reached for him this time, he jerked completely out of her reach, and they stayed like that for a moment, his head leaning to one side and her empty hand extended.

Mom sighed. "Suit yourself, then." She went to the refrigerator and started pulling out ingredients. The whole world might be falling apart around us, but there were meals to be made. There were cows to be milked and calves to be fed.

I sat at the other end of the table, watching Johnny carefully out of the corner of my eye. In the space of twenty-four hours, he had split into two people, or at least two halves of his former self. He was my seventeen-year-old brother still, who could be a grump or a sweetheart, depending on when you caught him. He had slammed the front door more than his share of times; he had been known to peel out of the driveway in a spray of gravel. But I knew the other Johnny, too, the one who had sneaked into my bedroom late at night, shaken me awake and carried me piggyback down the stairs, across the lawn and into the barn to see a new litter of kittens, the one who hoisted me onto his back for a run around the bases. He had been in love with Stacy Lemke. Had been? Was still, I told myself. He was still in love with Stacy Lemke. Didn't these things add up, somehow, to proof? Wasn't this more convincing than finding movie stubs or a receipt from a dinner?

"What do you want?" he asked, his voice sharp.

Caught staring, I blushed. "Nothing."

"Then knock it off."

I looked away, embarrassed. It was hard to say what Johnny was. All his individual parts added up to a pack of contradictions. True, he struggled to maintain a C average, but he could strategize on the mats with the best of them. He could get angry, plunk plates on countertops, pound his fist on the table, slam doors behind him. And he was strong as anything. Did anyone know what he was really capable of doing?

Somewhere between the night of March fourth and this morning, Johnny had become an adult, a man. For the first time, I realized he was taller than Dad, broader and stronger, if not heavier. His steps on the stairs, I knew suddenly, were a man's steps. His hands were a man's hands. He had been shaving for more than a year, but it wasn't until right now, sitting across from him, that I saw the pale brown hairs on his chin, sprouting down his cheeks.

Later that morning, Detective Halliday and Officer Parks returned, walking purposefully from their cars and then standing in our open doorway to deliver the news: with the snow cleared, a fresh batch of patrolmen and volunteers from all over Watankee had gone through the fields near the site of Johnny's crash. Police dogs had been sent into the surrounding woods.

"What did they find?" Mom asked sharply.

They shook their heads in tandem. Nothing.

"We'd like to take Johnny back to the scene," said

Detective Halliday. "To go through his story one more time. The district attorney is going to meet us there."

Johnny agreed immediately, reaching for his boots.

"The district attorney? My husband should go with you," Mom said.

Dad, seeing the patrol car, was already halfway back from the barn. "More questions?" he asked flatly as the screen door tapped shut behind him. "What are you hoping for, a different story this time?"

"John—" Mom shook her head.

"We're just trying to get some answers. There's a girl missing here," Officer Parks said.

"They're involving the district attorney," Mom told Dad.

Dad's face registered surprise. "The district attorney? I thought you said yesterday… Does this mean Johnny is going to need a lawyer or something?

"It's his right to have a lawyer present during questioning, although he hasn't been formally charged with anything," Officer Parks clarified.

Detective Halliday added, "But if he waives his right to speak with an attorney, we can proceed without any of these technical holdups."

"I've got nothing to hide," Johnny said, looking from Dad to Mom. "Let's go."

Dad nodded. "Okay. Let's roll."

"I don't know about this. I'm going to make some phone calls," Mom said. The men ignored her, heading outside. "John!" Mom called after Dad from the doorway, her voice rising dangerously. "John!"

Emilie came in, most of her hair having escaped its droopy ponytail. "What now?" she demanded. "Where are they going?"

By this time, I was getting used to seeing Dad and Johnny duck into the back of a patrol car. It no longer surprised me.

Mom shut the door, hard. "Back to the accident site."

"Jesus," Emilie said.

"Emilie Janine!"

"They said they were sending search dogs into the woods," I repeated, thinking aloud. "But why would Stacy go into the woods? Do they think she was trying to take a shortcut or something?"

Neither of them answered, not even Emilie, who could normally be counted on to tell when I was being stupid. It didn't make any sense; the Lemkes' house was a mile and a half from the ditch where Johnny's truck had been found, a straight shot from Passaqua Road to Center Road to the Lemkes' long, paved driveway. Even walking without her heaviest coat, even in the pretty brown leather boots she got for Christmas, Stacy should have been home in twenty minutes.

"I'm going to take a shower," Emilie announced disgustedly, heading upstairs.

The oven timer dinged, and Mom took out three loaves of bread, which she would later punch down with flour-coated fingers. "Do you want to help?" she asked me.

"Am I going to school tomorrow?" I asked back.

"I don't know. No, I guess."

"What about Wednesday?"

"Kirsten! Enough."

I thought about the district spelling bee this Thursday night. Mom had forgotten, of course; it was tucked away with everything else that didn't matter anymore.

Upstairs, Johnny's door was ajar. I peeked inside,

expecting to see a crime scene, rather than a collection of dingy T-shirts and the piles of jeans he'd stepped out of, half holding his form. I sat on his unmade bed, pulling my knees to my chest.

What was it Stacy had said, that day I'd overheard them from my hall closet hideout? *I'll be quiet. I could camp right here for a week or two, and no one would even notice.*

Johnny's room was as big a mess as I'd ever seen it, the five drawers of his dresser each pulled out, clothes spilling over the sides. His desk, never actually used for studying, was heaped with wrestling gear, the source of the room's biting, sour smell. A history textbook was visible, buried under a heap of crumpled binder paper. She'd wanted to stay here, amid the cache of sports equipment—the deflated basketballs, a dozen tennis balls rolled loose, the bats and gloves we'd used in our brief time as the Hammarstrom Hitters.

It was creepy being in this room, where my brother slept night after night, dreaming his hidden dreams. Stacy had been in here, too, in this filth that was so different from the crisp clean of her room. I remembered how her bedspread had felt, the little white pills of cotton that would be bumpy if you laid down on it, that would leave the imprint of the spread on your skin. She must have sat on her bed night after night, writing those long letters to Johnny; he must have sat right here, writing her back.

I remembered the photo in Stacy's dresser drawer, the boyfriend before Johnny whose face had been blotted out, as if he'd never existed. The same thing, I realized, could have happened to Johnny, if he'd left her behind, accepted a scholarship to Iowa or gone off to find a job. It was strange to think this, but in a way it was Stacy who had been blotted out, Stacy who was so far gone she might never have existed at all.

"What are you doing in here?"

I turned. Emilie stood in the doorway, her wet hair streaked with neat rows from a comb.

"Nothing," I said.

We stared at each other.

"Nothing," I said again, more loudly, as if that would clear it up. "I mean, I was just thinking."

Emilie looked at me for a long time. Her hair left a wet stain on her shirt. Finally she said, "What's there to think about? Johnny was in a car accident. Stacy tried to walk home and got lost on the way."

"Right," I said. "I know."

She laughed, and I gasped, because I didn't know it was possible to laugh anymore, as if it was an unwritten moral code: we don't laugh anymore, because Stacy is missing.

"So, you believe that?" Emilie asked.

I sucked in my breath. "Don't you believe that?"

Emilie narrowed her eyes, the blue of her irises disappearing into a dark line. "We shouldn't be in here," she said finally. She gestured with her right arm, and I marched out the door like an obedient soldier.

twenty-one

That night, I dreamed I was Stacy Lemke. I was tall and lean, wearing my new boots, my red-tipped fingernails tucked into a pair of knitted gloves. Wind was swirling around me, snow slapping against my face, blinding me. Everything was white—the ground, the sky, my breath as I called for Johnny. Where was he? I burrowed my hands into the pockets of my green coat and screamed for him. My lips froze, stung by the cold. "Johnny!" I screamed, the wind erasing my words. I spun around and suddenly he was behind me. But something was wrong. His eyes were blue and hard, unblinking, as if they were frozen in his face. He reached for me, but I pulled away. I tried to run, but my feet were stuck, buried in a mound of snow. I tried again, and this time I lost my balance, falling backward—

"Hey, wake up." Emilie was shaking me, her hair hanging in my face. "Are you okay?"

I sat up, trembling.

"You kept calling for Johnny."

"I had a bad dream." I closed my eyes, and it came

back instantly—I was Stacy, and Johnny was standing over me, his hands reaching for my neck.

Emilie gave me a long look.

At breakfast, Mom felt my forehead, dosed me with medicine and ordered me back to bed. The day passed in a cold, dull blur. Propped up on one elbow, I read in *Myths and Half-True Tales* about strange appearances and disappearances—a Roman soldier in full dress who was found wandering in a Nebraska cornfield; ships found unmanned, their crews nowhere to be found. I drifted in and out of sleep, imagining once that Stacy had suddenly appeared in an African village and another time that she had fallen, Alice-like, down a rabbit hole. Downstairs, life went on without me.

Wednesday morning I woke up feeling refreshed. There was a long, peaceful moment before I remembered that Stacy Lemke was missing, and everything in my entire life had changed. When I came down to breakfast, Grandpa was just coming in the back door. "I've been chasing reporters off the property all morning," he announced.

"What reporters?" Mom asked, peeking out the window.

"The ones in the white vans parked at the end of the driveway." Grandpa gestured over his head with a heavy arm.

"We're going to be on TV?" I asked.

"Well, actually—" Mom took a deep breath "—we are going to be on television later this morning."

I swallowed, imagining myself in front of a bulky video camera. "We are?"

"Not you, honey." Mom ran her hand up and down

my back. “Your dad and Johnny and me. There’s going to be a press conference this morning.”

“Oh.” I waited, but she didn’t continue. “What does that mean?”

“Stacy’s parents are going to talk about what’s happened. They asked us to be there, too.”

“Damn fool idea, if you ask me,” Grandpa commented.

“It’s not your decision to make,” Mom told him, and he let the screen door slam into place behind him. “Everyone’s just upset,” Mom continued, giving me a tight smile.

This was a terrifying development. My family on television? For the past couple of days, I’d been able to convince myself that only a few people knew about our situation. Now everyone would know, for sure.

For the first time in days, we moved as if we had purpose. Emilie, grumpy, ironed Dad’s and Johnny’s dress shirts, and Aunt Julia came over to help Mom pick out her clothes. I sat on the bed, watching them reject item after item in Mom’s wardrobe. Ninety percent of Mom’s wardrobe consisted of white pants with elastic waistbands and baggy pastel-colored smocks, her nursing uniform.

“Not this—it’s going to wash you out too much,” Aunt Julia said, tossing away a light brown cardigan. “You basically disappear in this sweater.”

“I do?” Mom held up the red pullover Dad had bought her for Christmas, the one she’d worn all through the holidays. “What about this sweater? I like this one.”

Aunt Julia shook her head. “Too festive. You don’t want to look like you’re having a good time.”

“I should go with something conservative.”

Aunt Julia snorted. "All of your clothes are conservative."

"I mean, tasteful," Mom clarified. "I don't want us to look like country bumpkins next to the Lemkes."

This was a real possibility, I feared—remembering the Lemkes in their starched linen at Stacy's birthday party.

Aunt Julia smiled. "Then tell John to leave his rope belt at home." Her smile was just a flash and then gone, a guilty pleasure that couldn't be indulged.

"I just hope— I mean, they told us we wouldn't have to say anything. We'll just be there to present a united front. I can't imagine what I would say, anyway…."

Aunt Julia dug out a navy blazer from the recesses of Mom's closet. "What about this?"

Mom slipped it over a white turtleneck. It was a little tight at the shoulders and looked as though, if she flexed too hard, it would tear at the seams.

"Not bad," Aunt Julia judged.

Mom turned to face the mirror, grimacing at her reflection. "All this damn food," she said. "That's all I've been doing, sitting and eating."

"It's fine. It's conservative. Reserved. Tasteful. And here—" Aunt Julia dipped her head to one side and then the other, removing her gold studs. "These will help."

Mom poked the earrings into place and turned from side to side, viewing herself from all angles. "I just don't know if I trust them—the Lemkes, I mean. The other night they were determined to hang Johnny right there. And now, today…" She slipped into the seat at her vanity table, and Aunt Julia hovered over her with various little tubes of makeup.

"But this is to help find Stacy," Aunt Julia reminded

her. "That's all it is. Get the word out, see if anyone knows something and can come forward. Now, hold still." When she was finished, Mom looked like a costumed version of herself, as if she was dressing as a school board member for Halloween.

"Perfect," Aunt Julia pronounced. When she left the room to help Johnny with his tie, Mom blotted half her lipstick onto a tissue.

She must have forgotten that I was still there, lying across her bed propped up by one elbow. I watched as she looked at herself in the mirror, fussing with her makeup and smoothing flyaway strands of blond hair. Then she sank her chin into the palm of one hand and stared straight ahead, directly into her own eyes in the mirror, although she didn't seem to really see herself. But I saw both of them, the Mom in real life, exhausted and haggard, trying to hold it all together, and the Mom in the mirror, who seemed to be plotting her next move.

twenty-two

They left in Mom's Caprice, as solemn as if they were headed off to a funeral. Johnny sat in the middle of the backseat, hunched and awkward, like an overgrown child. We promised to watch on TV—what else could we have done?—and Emilie pulled out a new tape and set the VCR to record. While we waited, I flipped idly back and forth from the news station to *The Price Is Right.*

"God, this makes me so nervous," Aunt Julia said. "I'm just going to pop outside for a quick second. Call me when it starts?"

A dark-haired woman was trying to guess the prices of household items from least to most expensive, while Bob Barker wagged the microphone in front of her impatiently. Helpless, she looked to the audience, throwing up her arms.

Emilie flipped back to the news station, which had a school picture of Stacy Lemke on the screen.

"Aunt Julia!" I hollered.

"Stacy was last seen by Johnny Hammarstrom, her boyfriend, also of Watankee, when she set out to walk home in Saturday's snowstorm. Although police have questioned Hammarstrom, they have not yet identified him as a suspect," reported the announcer. An 800 number appeared across the screen, and then the news flashed to the brick exterior of the Manitowoc Police Department.

Last seen by Johnny Hammarstrom, her boyfriend… Emilie and I looked at each other. It was strange and shameful to hear Johnny's name on the news, which of course was our name, too. *They have not yet identified him as a suspect.* Not *yet.* But it didn't matter—I suddenly thought. People were going to think Johnny was guilty, whether he was or not. Wasn't that what I thought every time I saw someone on the evening news, mentioned in connection with a crime?

Detective Halliday's face appeared on the screen. He stood at a podium flanked by Mr. and Mrs. Lemke on one side and Dad, Mom and Johnny on the other. I felt like pinching myself. My parents were on TV. My brother. Their faces occupied the space on the screen where Bob Barker had been only moments before. Dad was frowning; Mom's face was grim. Johnny looked as if he was about to be sick.

"Oh, dear God," Emilie said, and Aunt Julia dashed inside, reeking of smoke.

Mr. Lemke, on his side of the podium, had his arm tightly around his wife's shoulders. He wore a black suit; she wore a blue dress with a cowl-neck, and, when the camera pulled back, I saw that she had matching shoes in the exact same brilliant blue. They might have been headed out to a fancy dinner. Behind them stood a handful of officers, anonymous in their crisp navy uniforms. On the far left side was an American flag, and on the far right, the blue flag of Wisconsin.

"Here we go," Aunt Julia breathed, crouching onto her haunches in front of the TV.

"This is the most embarrassing thing in the world," Emilie murmured, clutching a pillow from the couch to her chest. "I could die right here, right now."

Detective Halliday was already speaking in his gravelly voice, although it took a moment for us to register his words. Flashbulbs were popping; Johnny, after a few giant blinks of surprise, looked down at his feet. The camera zoomed in on Detective Halliday's face, and Aunt Julia leaned forward, adjusting the volume.

"The community of Watankee has been investigating the disappearance of one of our own, Stacy Lemke. Stacy is a sixteen-year-old junior at Lincoln High School. On Saturday night, Stacy was involved in a car accident and attempted to walk home. As you know, she never made it. We are scouring the fields, interviewing witnesses and conducting a thorough investigation. And at this point, we are seeking the public's help."

More flashbulbs; a few questions called from the crowd simultaneously.

Detective Halliday held up his hand. "I'll take questions in a moment. The Lemkes have asked to make a statement first."

It was shocking to see the Lemkes in their close-up. They didn't look like the glamorous couple I'd met only last summer. Now their eyes were red-rimmed, their expressions drawn with grief. Mrs. Lemke's lips were downturned and trembling.

Mr. Lemke cleared his throat, waited for the reporters to settle down, and began. "As you can imagine, the past four days have been a nightmare for our family. We would like to thank the police department and volunteers for their diligent searches. We would like to thank—" His voice caught, and Mrs. Lemke leaned her head against his shoulder. "We would like to thank the people who know and love Stacy and the strangers who have generously donated their time and energy to help us find her." He paused, looking down. The camera flashes doubled in intensity, and the screen zoomed in on Mr. Lemke's face, wet with tears. Then it zoomed out to include our family again—Dad standing stiff, staring straight ahead with his eyes unfocused, Mom in her too-tight blazer, Johnny awkward in his green dress shirt.

"We would also like to—" Mr. Lemke continued, fighting for control of his words. "We would like to make a special plea to anyone with any information about Stacy's whereabouts. If you have any information at all about our daughter, please contact local law enforcement immediately. We are prepared to offer a $15,000 reward for any information that leads us to Stacy."

Mrs. Lemke's shoulders heaved; the camera zoomed in on her downcast face. The lines around her mouth were deep and hard, like someone had taken an Etch A Sketch and given her a permanent frown. Mr. Lemke tightened his grip around his wife's shoulders, the fingers of his left hand clenched tightly.

"Oh, that poor woman," Aunt Julia breathed.

"Please," Mr. Lemke continued. "Please help us find Stacy. Please bring her back to us." He stepped back from the microphone, pulling his wife to his chest. An officer stepped forward to guide them to the side, and Detective Halliday came to the podium again.

"Fifteen thousand dollars?" Emilie repeated, whistling. It was funny how the world worked. Fifteen thousand dollars was more money than we had ever had all at once, I was sure. Fifteen thousand dollars would have paid for a good chunk of Johnny's college or zillions of private music lessons for Emilie or a fancy vacation for Mom and Dad, the kind that involved airplane tickets and sandy beaches.

"At this point," Detective Halliday said, "we'll take questions."

There was a volley of voices at once, unintelligible and excited. Detective Halliday held up one hand, and the reporters obeyed, settling into order. The television camera panned the room, and we saw for the first time dozens of reporters, holding cameras and microphones and little pads of paper. The questions came, disembodied, male and female, terse and eager.

"Can you tell us how far Stacy was from home when she started walking?"

Detective Halliday nodded. "We estimate just under a mile."

"What was the cause of the accident?"

Johnny reacted slightly at this, his head jerking to one side.

"It appears that the tires lost traction in the heavy snow and veered off to one side. When we located the truck, it was wedged into a ditch."

"Was the driver speeding?"

Again, Johnny flinched.

"We're examining the possibility that speed may have been a factor, especially with the road conditions Saturday night."

"And Johnny Hammarstrom was driving the truck?"

An explosion of flashbulbs, a close-up of Johnny. His face was stony, yellowish under the fluorescent lights. A faint sheen of sweat shone on his forehead.

"That is correct," Detective Halliday confirmed.

"What kind of search has been conducted?"

"At this point we've involved members of the Watankee Police Department, a volunteer force and a K-9 unit from Manitowoc. We've searched the fields surrounding the accident site several times and private properties throughout the area."

"Does that include the Hammarstroms' property?"

"Yes, it does."

"Does this mean you consider Johnny Hammarstrom a suspect?"

I was holding my breath, a million oxygen molecules slamming around in my lungs.

Detective Halliday cleared his throat. "From the beginning, we have considered Johnny Hammarstrom a person of interest, since he was the last person to see Stacy alive and had a personal relationship with her. However, he has not been named as a suspect."

The buzz intensified.

"Will that change? Will he be named as a suspect?"

"Are there any other possible suspects?"

"Doesn't it seem likely that the last person to see her alive—"

"Is it possible that there's some sort of madman on the loose, driving up and down the streets of our town?"

Detective Halliday's voice was steady. "The investigation is ongoing, and it's too soon for me to speculate on these questions. But at this time we have no reason to believe that we are looking for a random assailant."

Another barrage of flashbulbs, rapid-fire questions from reporters.

"When will you speculate?" a man sneered. "When there's been a spring thaw?"

The detective's lips settled into a straight line, and

his jaw nudged ever so slightly forward. Mrs. Lemke let out a small, sharp cry.

"What exactly was the relationship between Johnny Hammarstrom and the victim?"

"They were dating. They were boyfriend and girlfriend," Detective Halliday said firmly, back on solid footing.

Johnny, the camera full on his face, moistened his lips nervously. Yes, I thought. They were dating. They were *boyfriend* and *girlfriend.* But it was more than that. They wrote love letters, they had sex, they talked about the future, they fought the way people who are really in love fight.

"How long were they dating? Were they serious?"

"They were not serious," Bill Lemke announced suddenly, away from the microphone, but loud enough for the reporters to pick up his words. Johnny's head snapped in their direction, as if he'd been slapped from the other side. Mom glanced at Johnny, and Dad glanced at Mom, like a chain reaction. Mr. Lemke was standing up straighter now, his chest puffed forward. Was he saying that Johnny Hammarstrom wasn't good enough for his girl, that Stacy was too smart for such a fool?

"Was she also dating other people?" the same voice asked, clearly puzzled at Mr. Lemke's reaction.

Mom put a hand on Johnny's arm, but it was too late to stop him from speaking. "We were serious. We loved each other," he announced, looking from Mr. Lemke to the reporters and back. "We were—" Mom's grip tightened on his arm, and he stopped.

Emilie sucked in her breath, then let it out. She had heard, too, what I'd heard: *loved,* not *love.*

Detective Halliday raised his hand, trying to regain control of the situation. "We know they had a dating relationship. I can only reiterate to you that Johnny Hammarstrom has been cooperative with this investigation."

"You have to 'iterate' something in the first place in order to 'reiterate' it," Aunt Julia huffed. "He failed to mention that Johnny had been cooperating."

"At this point, if there are no other questions dealing specifically with the investigation," Detective Halliday continued, "then we'll close this press conference."

This would have been the end of it if it wasn't for Mrs. Lemke, who slid downward, suddenly weak in the knees. Mr. Lemke grabbed for her—unnecessarily dramatic, it seemed to me—and the flashbulbs went wild again, capturing her unsteadiness, his heroics. "Look what you've done," he yelled, to no one in particular, it seemed at first, and then, throwing his head like a mad horse, to my family. "Look what you've done to us."

Dad and Johnny were frozen, uncertain, but Mom was trembling.

"I can't watch," Emilie said, her hands in front of her face.

"What we've done?" Mom said, and repeated, more loudly. She leaned across Johnny, in front of Detective Halliday. The blazer did look tight on her, her arms like encased sausages, especially as she raised one hand to point directly at the Lemkes with an outstretched finger. "What do you mean, what we've done? It was *your* daughter who was obsessed with *our* son. She was the one who—"

And then Dad, no longer a prop in this setting, gave her arm a good yank and pulled her off the stage, away from the podium. Cameras followed them as they retreated toward an exit at the far end of the auditorium, Johnny only a few steps behind.

"Well, shit," Aunt Julia said, and snapped off the TV.

twenty-three

After the press conference, things only got worse. It felt as if we were in the middle of our own tiny volcano with the pressure building and building, and we were waiting for it to blow. I watched from the kitchen window as Dad and Johnny emerged from the Caprice followed by Mom, already in midargument. Johnny pushed past me at the door and pounded up the stairs.

"Tricked us into it," Mom was saying. Her face was red, the flush of a deep, public embarrassment.

"It's probably not as bad as it seemed," Aunt Julia said, trying to be kind.

Mom huffed. "You saw it, didn't you?"

Aunt Julia nodded and started to speak, but Mom silenced her with a look that said she didn't want to be babied, or pitied, or consoled. "I need to see it for myself," she decided. "But we were set up! Come to the press conference, everyone said. Present a united front with the Lemkes..." Suddenly uncomfortable in her clothes, she began to wriggle her arms out of the navy blazer. Normally Dad would have stepped forward to assist—he was always on hand to help Mom with a necklace clasp or a back zipper—but this time he held back, keeping his distance. We all held back, watching her squirm.

The phone rang, and Mom grabbed for it, one arm still tangled in the blazer, the other sleeve flapping loose. "Hello?" she demanded, listened for a second, and slammed the receiver into the cradle. "Those damn reporters!"

"Alicia," Dad began, tiredly, "if we don't work with them—"

"They don't want to work *with* us! Don't you see that? They just want a story, and the story is us. The story is Johnny, the murderer." Mom finally freed herself from her blazer and stood panting and triumphant before us. Aunt Julia took the blazer from Mom's arms and hung it over the back of a chair.

"I should have known, I should have seen it," Mom continued. "You get mixed up with a family like that, with a man like that..." She was moving around the kitchen like a madwoman, touching things haphazardly, not caring when she dragged the sleeve of her white turtleneck through a smear of strawberry jam on the counter, left over from breakfast. "Look what *we've* done, he says. What *we've* done! We! When all along I tried to discourage them.... And it was her! She was the one pushing him into a relationship!"

Dad tried to steady Mom with a hand on her shoulder, the pressure of his fingers on her arm. "Okay now, okay," he kept repeating. "We just need to think this through."

Mom picked up a bread knife, glanced around as if she were trying to find a loaf of bread, and set it down. "What does anything matter anymore? You heard the man. Johnny might as well just turn himself in this second for daring to touch his daughter. But that probably won't be enough to satisfy him. Maybe we'll get lucky and they'll only want to crucify the rest of us in the public square." Her eyes flashed dangerously around the room, not settling on any of us.

"No one wants to crucify you—" Aunt Julia began.

The phone rang again, and Mom reached for it, but Dad was faster. "We have no comment at this time," he said firmly, then held down the switch hook and set the receiver on the table. We stared at it, listening to the faint beeping sound of the busy signal.

Emilie came in from the living room, her face pale. "They're going to replay it."

We raced into the living room in time to see a montage of photos of Stacy flash silently across the screen: as a sticky-faced toddler on a summer day, holding a Popsicle; as a little girl in pigtails, about to dive into her birthday cake; as a sixth grader in front of her science project. I imagined Mrs. Lemke sobbing, pulling back the protective plastic sheet on a neatly organized photo album to remove these pictures.

Mom gasped as another photo appeared, one of Stacy sitting on the hood of Johnny's truck, laughing. There were precise, towering rows of corn in the background, the tops foaming with tassels. A slant of late-afternoon sunlight hit her backside, lighting up her loose red hair like a halo of fire, the way it had been the first time I met her. Johnny must have taken the picture, I realized, not only because she was sitting on the Green Machine, but because she was flirting with the camera, her lips slightly parted, her expression teasing, *Come here.* She was still the most beautiful girl I had ever seen.

The last picture, the one that lingered longest on the screen, was of Johnny and Stacy at their Winter Formal in December. They were standing in front of a black backdrop with thousands of sparkly stars, Johnny's right arm wrapped around her shoulder, Stacy's left arm tucked around his waist. We had a wallet-sized version of this photo stuck to the front of our refrigerator, but blown up like this, I noticed things I hadn't seen before. Johnny was in his rented tux, broad-chested and strong-armed, and Stacy was in her sea-green chiffon dress with the cinched waist. They were smiling, but it was a smile-on-demand kind of situation, and both of them looked as if they were smiling only with their mouths. They stood close together—so close that Johnny's arm looked too tight across Stacy's shoulders, as if he wasn't going to let her go without a fight. Somehow, I noticed, Stacy wasn't looking directly at the camera. It was as if someone off to the side, out of range, had called her name and at any moment she was going to squirm free of Johnny's stiff grasp.

The whole situation made me feel light-headed—my own brother on the television screen and the tiny picture from our refrigerator, such a small, personal thing, broadcast now to the greater Wisconsin area.

"I've had about enough," Mom said, but we couldn't drag ourselves away. All of a sudden Bill Lemke was on the screen again, standing on his front porch. While we'd been telling the reporters we had no comment, the Lemkes had apparently been inviting the world inside their house. There was Stacy's bedroom, with its crisp and sterile white linens. There was a shot of the Lemkes sitting down to dinner at a table set for five, with one place conspicuously empty.

"What, no shot of the billiard table?" Dad murmured, his voice biting.

Then there was a video of Joanie and Heather taping up a Missing poster at the Chevron station off 151 and the announcer's sober voice-over: "Missing the sister they might never see again." Were the Lemkes watching this? Were Joanie and Heather gathered around a television set, too?

We all gasped when our property came into view, courtesy of the television crews parked at the end of our driveway that morning. This was our snow-covered lawn, the thick branches of our leafless oak trees. There was Grandpa's house with its faded yellow curtains out in front, and our house tucked behind it, as if we had something to hide. Farther back was the barn, gleaming red from a new coat of paint last summer. At least we looked like respectable people—or, in the menacing way things looked on the news, bad people hiding behind a respectable facade.

The reporter, who had been rehashing the details of the search for Stacy Lemke, suddenly caught my attention again: "According to police reports, Stacy was a regular fixture at the Hammarstroms' home in rural Watankee. Here her boyfriend, Johnny, helped on the family's struggling dairy farm."

"Now that's going too far," Aunt Julia protested.

Struggling dairy farm? I peeked at Dad, whose head was very still. Somehow, even though I'd overheard snatches of late-night conversations about finances—the mortgage, the renovations to the barn, milk prices—it had never occurred to me that we might be *poor.* Dad was always trading one good or service for another, sure, but it seemed smart, not cheap, when he delivered a load of firewood to Ted Nagel after Ted fixed the thermostat on our milk tank. And mostly Dad could fix things himself, at least temporarily. Mom referred to his homemade fixes as "Okie innovations," and until it was pointed out to me, I'd believed Okie was some kind of Swedish slang for genius. It had simply never occurred to me that finances kept Dad from buying the part, hiring a repairman, or scrapping the whole thing for a new machine.

"Tensions continue to run high between the Lemkes and the Hammarstroms," the reporter said smartly, and the screen cut to that morning's press conference—Mrs. Lemke nearly toppling, Mr. Lemke pointing at my parents, Mom firing back.

I watched Mom watch herself from between her spread fingers, as if she was peeping at a horror show. "Oh, God," she sobbed into her hands. "I shouldn't have, I know. I just couldn't stand there and…"

Watching Mom cry gave me this funny feeling all over, as if something was inside my skin, crawling up and down my body, alerting every nerve ending all at once.

In two steps Dad was at the television, and with one flick of his wrist the set was darkened. We sat that way for a long time, with Mom crying and none of us sure what to do.

Then Aunt Julia cleared her throat, murmuring something about having to run a few errands. "Anyone want to come with me?" she asked, but Emilie and I shook our heads.

What was worse, staying in the house where we only had to face each other, or heading into town, after everyone in Watankee had watched the Hammarstrom family drama, tangled and juicy as any soap opera, unfold on their television sets? Aunt Julia gave our hands a quick squeeze and left, the screen door flapping quietly into place behind her.

Emilie walked slowly to the stairs, but instead of following her, I slipped out through the back door. Kennel trotted over, his pink tongue wagging, and we sat on the steps near the kitchen window, which Aunt Julia had opened just a crack.

Dad was saying, "It won't help anything if we don't calm down. We just need to get hold of ourselves. Maybe what we need to do is to talk to someone."

Mom's laugh was so harsh and unfunny, it made my skin tingle. "Oh, yes, I can see it now. Pastor Ziegler, what does the Bible say we should do when our son is a suspect in a criminal investigation, and the whole town—"

"Quiet down now," Dad said firmly. "I wasn't talking about Pastor Ziegler. I was thinking, maybe, you know, some kind of an attorney."

"A lawyer?" Mom shrieked. "We haven't done anything, and we should get a lawyer?"

"Damn it, Alicia," Dad said, losing his patience. "I'm not saying we need a lawyer. But it wouldn't be a bad idea to talk to someone, see all our options. Bill Lemke knows the law—this is his world. We've got to be able to keep up with him."

"A lawyer," Mom repeated more quietly. "Even if we did need one, we couldn't afford it. What does something like that cost? There would be a retainer fee—that's hundreds of dollars right there, maybe more."

There was a silence, and the word *lawyer* rang in my ears. Wouldn't we be admitting that Johnny was guilty if Mom and Dad talked to a lawyer? Regular people didn't have lawyers, did they? On television, lawyers were reserved for criminals, thieves and well… murderers.

Dad said, "Maybe we could ask my dad."

"Are you kidding me? Because he's been so supportive up to this point, hasn't he? I bet right now he's sitting in front of that TV, rewinding the video of the press conference and shaking his head, ashamed he even knows us."

"That's not fair." Dad's voice was wounded. "He doesn't know how to handle this any better than we do."

Mom sputtered, "I'm sorry it's been so hard on *him!*"

"Well, maybe it won't even cost anything just to talk to someone. Those television ads always say that new clients are entitled to a free thirty-minute consultation."

"I don't think we want the kind of help we can get for free." Mom sighed. "Can't you just imagine everyone in town whispering about us? *Those Hammarstroms, hiding behind their lawyer.* We've been completely honest and cooperative."

I shivered suddenly, although the afternoon was warming and Kennel's body was draped over my legs like a heavy blanket. Maybe Dad and Mom had been completely honest, but I hadn't. Telling Aunt Julia about the fight between Stacy and Johnny that night wasn't exactly the same as telling it to Detective Halliday.

"You worry too much about that," Dad said sharply. "It doesn't matter what anyone else thinks. This is about our family." He stressed the word—*family.* That was always how Dad saw things, as if our 160 acres was its own tiny kingdom, removed from everyone and everything else.

Mom cried then, unable to find her words.

"Okay," Dad said. "Let's just play it by ear. No lawyer, no press conferences, no reporters—"

"And we'll avoid the Lemkes at all costs."

Dad's voice was quiet, considering. "I don't think that he… I mean, deep down, I'm not sure that Bill believes what he said back there. It's just grief and frustration talking. How would we react if…well, if the unthinkable happened?"

"The unthinkable has happened," Mom pointed out, which is just what I was thinking, too. We were always planning for what came next—the plowing, the planting, the harvest, not enough rain or too much, the heifers birthing, the calves being vaccinated. But this hadn't been on our radar, hadn't been anywhere near our map of the world. It was unthinkable that a person could just go missing, that Stacy Lemke could disappear from the face of the earth. And it was unthinkable—wasn't it?—that my brother could have been the reason she disappeared.

Mom continued, calmly now, "But this didn't just happen to Bill Lemke, or Johnny, or Stacy. It's happened to all of us."

twenty-four

After their conversation, I waited for Mom or Dad to come out onto the porch, to scold me for sitting outside without a coat, to ask if I was hungry or even if I could help with the laundry. I wondered if anyone cared about how I felt, knowing that the world was watching my family on TV, how it felt to miss the district spelling bee I'd studied hard for, how it felt to be so insignificant that no one even noticed where I was. The longer I waited, the more I convinced myself that I wasn't important anymore. I wasn't forgotten, exactly—just no longer an essential variable of the Hammarstrom equation. If I went missing, no one would even notice.

I hopped to my feet, nudging Kennel off my lap, and took off at a sprint, as if I could outrun my thoughts. I was only wearing tennis shoes, but I didn't care when the half-melted snow seeped through my jeans and ankle socks. I passed the dark windows of Grandpa's workshop and entered the barn through the door nearest the calf pen, my chest heaving. Dozens of heads swiveled in my direction, huge cow eyes studying me uncertainly. "It's okay, it's okay," I soothed, but my voice was cracked and anxious, and the calves drew back as I passed down the center aisle, their heads out of reach of my outstretched hand. That was all I wanted—for someone to tell me everything was okay, and mean it, too.

In the hayloft, I let the kittens climb all over me, mewling and licking. They were still tiny, crawling, blind things. Their mama, half-wild, lay on her side, licking her raw nipples. I would just stay here, then, I told myself, the one place where none of the rest of it mattered.

Alone, it was easy to torture myself with my thoughts. What if I had said something or done something—would Stacy still be here? If I had said "Johnny, I saw you and Stacy fighting" right when he came in that night, with Mom pulling a casserole out of the oven and Emilie setting the table, what then? If I had told Mom that they'd been in his bedroom, the doors shut, the bedsprings creaking—what then? If I could go back in time, to the softball game, to the moment when Stacy Lemke's shadow had fallen over me, what then?

I couldn't undo anything, not even a single second. If this were one of the novels I'd read, I would disappear into a time machine and travel backward until I could set things straight. But this wasn't a novel. This was my real life, and there was no time machine. I couldn't change Stacy and Johnny meeting or their first kiss or the desperate way she'd clung to him. The past was the past.

One of the kittens settled into the crook of my neck and I sobbed quietly. If I sobbed louder, would someone from the house hear me and come running? I tried it, letting my breath come in exaggerated, ugly gasps until I'd worked myself into a true fit.

What would Nancy Drew do, I wondered? Sit by herself and cry until the tears dripped one by one, salty, into her mouth? No. She would gather together her crew—George, Bess and Ned, and if she was desperate, her lawyer father, Carson—and she would work the case.

I sat, tipping the kitten into a soft pile of straw, and took a deep breath. I didn't have a crew, so I would have to work the case alone. It was hard to focus at first, to allow myself to replay the possibilities in my mind.

Maybe—I considered first—Stacy had just wandered off and gotten lost in the snowstorm. Maybe she had sat down to rest for a minute, to get her bearings. She would have been sleepy, too tired to move on. Maybe she'd given up wandering and figured she'd just wait it out, and eventually someone would come along. But instead she'd frozen to death—it'd been about twenty degrees that night, cold enough so that even inside the house, I'd been bundled up in bed beneath several quilts. Then her body had been buried under the new snow. I wanted this to be true—the simple, sad explanation where no one was guilty. But it didn't really seem possible—not for someone who had spent sixteen winters in Wisconsin, who had driven these roads every day of her life and had probably known every farm, telephone pole and fence post. She would have known where she was, how to make it home.

Or else—

Stacy might have been nearly home, around the bend on Passaqua Road, when a truck pulled up. I could picture it, one of those massive trucks that barreled past when I walked to Aunt Julia's on summer days, crossing the divider bumps of the middle lane as a courtesy but still engulfing me briefly in its downdraft. These trucks were always driven by men, but none of their faces stood out in my memory; they were just pale flashes, there and gone, a mile down the road before I registered their presence. I imagined this driver shooting down Passaqua Road toward 151, his last load delivered, when he spotted Stacy. She would have been bundled up against the stinging cold, her face down. He would have rolled down his snow-crusted window, asked, "Can I take you somewhere?" I couldn't give him a face, only a baseball cap pulled down to his eyebrows and a jacket collar pulled up to his chin. And Stacy, sweet, trusting Stacy who didn't watch detective shows where cold-blooded killers were always afoot, would have smiled and said, "Sure! Thanks." He would have had to hand her up into the cab of his truck, noticing only then her red hair, the brush of freckles across her face, the tears dried on her cheeks. She would have stretched out her frozen fingers in front of the heater and said, "I live just a mile or so in that direction." Maybe she thought she could get Johnny back, make him jealous, show him that a real man—a gentleman—would deposit her right at her front door.

But I couldn't imagine what was next with any clarity, only the missed turn off Passaqua, Stacy's protests. She'd been taken to God knows where. In the books I devoured, the heroines could get out of any sticky situation with a little bit of cunning and luck, and nothing was ever done that couldn't be undone. But it had been four days now, and if someone had Stacy…well, he wasn't in any hurry to return her. That was how it always played out on the opening moments of a police drama—a woman's body was found, covered over with a white sheet, and what was done couldn't be undone.

It was easier, maybe, to think that Stacy had been picked up by someone she knew, another boy from school, someone who looked friendly. Someone she trusted, like Erik Hansen or Peter Bahn from the wrestling team, or any one of a hundred junior or senior boys at Lincoln High. But it didn't make sense. I could no more imagine one of them taking Stacy than I could imagine them taking me. Who would ever want to hurt Stacy Lemke? This just wasn't the way people were in Watankee. In big cities, I knew, people kept their houses locked even when they were at home. In Watankee, you could walk right into someone's home if you wanted to return a casserole pan or drop off a half bushel of apples you'd picked only that morning; their back doors were always unlocked. If Stacy had been taken by someone she knew, then nobody was safe. We would all have to start keeping one eye behind us as we hung clothes on the line, as we walked to the bus stop, as we carted groceries to the car.

But if none of these explanations was right, then what was left? It looked bad for Johnny, I knew, but deep down I couldn't imagine that he had done something to Stacy, something horrible that ended up with Stacy dead, her body hidden. He just wasn't a mastermind like the killers on TV shows, planning and plotting and lying and sticking to his story. He would have had to run his truck off the road on purpose, to concoct the whole story. It wasn't possible. Not Johnny, not Stacy.

And yet…he was strong, a fierce competitor, stubborn as anything. I had watched him in our own living room take down full-grown men like nothing. And what if Stacy really was pregnant, like I'd thought for months, carrying Johnny's child, the grandchild that none of his grandparents would welcome. What if Johnny hadn't wanted the baby—had wanted, instead, the wrestling scholarship, the chance to leave Watankee behind once and for all? Maybe that's what they were arguing about when Stacy pushed him that Tuesday, just over a week ago. Stacy would have insisted, would have gone desperate in her attempt to keep him. *I'll die without you,* she would have said. *I'll kill myself and kill this baby, too.* Whatever she'd said, Johnny hadn't called her later that night, like usual; he'd gone to his room after dinner and avoided the phone. Once he picked her up on Saturday night, there was no other person on earth who remembered seeing them, not the cashier at the theater or the waitress at the Humble Bee. Johnny had been the last person to see Stacy alive, had been alone with her late at night, the snow falling. I understood why the police officers had grilled him over and over. What other explanation could there be?

Doubting Johnny felt like the biggest sin of my life, bigger than telling a lie or plotting revenge, bigger than even the "unforgivable sin" Pastor Ziegler was always warning against. I'd worried more than once that it was unforgivable to even think about the unforgivable sin, because if it was, then I was doomed. I felt the same sort of panic thinking that Johnny had somehow hurt Stacy Lemke. If anything was unforgivable, it was believing this.

It's not Johnny, I told myself. *It can't be Johnny.*

But deep inside, a little voice answered me back: it has to be.

twenty-five

Dad came to the barn eventually, his voice traveling through the rafters. "You up there, Kirsten?"

I wiped my eyes with the back of my hand. "Yep," I called back. Through gaps in the floorboards I watched Dad split open bags of feed and fill the troughs, then fork new hay into the stalls. The cows didn't shy away from his touch as they had from mine; they pressed up against the bars of their pens eagerly, as if they were coming toward an altar to worship their god.

"You going to come down?" he called after a while.

"Sure," I said, wondering what he would do if I didn't reply; would he charge up the creaky staircase to the hayloft two steps at a time, hurrying to check on me? Was he, like every other parent in Watankee, now charged with keeping an extra close eye on his girls?

We trudged back to the house under a dark blue sky deepening to black. The driveway was crisscrossed with muddy tire treads in snow that had melted and refrozen. Kennel met us at the edge of the lawn, his tail thumping against our legs. We paused on the back porch, while I stepped out of my tennis shoes. "I'm sorry about all of this, Kirsten," Dad said, his hand on my shoulder for balance while he wriggled out of his boots. I wanted to say something back—that I understood, or that I was sorry, too—but the words got clogged in my throat. Maybe Dad wanted to say something to me, too, because he kept his hand on my shoulder, kneading my wool sweater with the tips of his fingers.

What could he say? Make some empty promise about things being okay, and life going back to normal? I looked him straight in the eye, waiting to hear it.

"You're my good girl," he croaked finally, his voice thick.

The table was already set, and Emilie was dropping rectangular chunks of ice into each water glass when we came in. Mom ladled potato soup with chopped bits of ham into our bowls, and we sat silently. When I looked at Johnny, my chest ached as if someone had taken my heart out and put it back in upside down and backward. He was my brother, and I'd always love him, but I'd as good as pronounced him guilty. He kept his head down, eyes focused on his plate. The rest of us went through the motions, passing the salt and pepper shakers, buttering thin slices of French bread. We were trying too hard to be normal, to be the family we had always been.

I swished my spoon through the soup, loading and unloading it without bothering to bring the spoon to my mouth. "What happens next?" I asked, determined to break the silence.

Mom glanced at Dad quickly, then away. "What do you mean?"

"I mean with Johnny. With the case."

"Well, I guess we don't exactly know."

"Damn it!" Johnny snapped, looking up. He bumped

the edge of his bowl with his elbow, scattering a few milky white drops of soup across the tablecloth. "What are you trying to do, protect my feelings or something? Go ahead and tell her."

Mom flushed, glaring at Johnny. "We're waiting on the D.A. at this point. If he decides to press charges, then Johnny will be taken into custody. He'll have a bail hearing, and he'll need a lawyer. There will be a trial, and then, well, we'd have to go from there."

Johnny made a funny sound in his throat, half laugh, half groan. "Might as well say *when,* not *if.*"

I let it sink in. Johnny would be arrested. He would spend the night—many nights, maybe—in jail, go before a judge. He would have a chance to say what he knew in court before God and everybody.

Mom, ignoring him, said, "It seems unlikely that will happen, though. Very unlikely."

"Why are we pretending?" Johnny demanded. "The police have been here. They've taken my truck, searched my room, questioned me..."

Mom picked up her untouched bowl and headed for the sink. She turned the water on full force, spraying the front of her shirt.

"Isn't it obvious that I'm the number-one suspect?" Johnny continued, raising his voice over the noise at the sink. "I mean, I'll tell you one thing, it would be a relief to be arrested. It really would. A relief!"

Mom whirled around, the water still going. "Are you kidding me? Are you determined to throw your life away?"

Dad held up a hand suddenly, shushing her.

"No, I'm going to say this!"

“Quiet,” Dad ordered suddenly, his expression alert. “I thought I heard something outside.”

Stacy, I thought suddenly. *She’s back.*

“I don’t hear anything,” Mom said, but she turned off the faucet and wiped her hands on her pants.

Dad straightened to attention, his hand still raised for quiet. Slowly, he shifted his eyes to the back window. The shades were still open, but now it was fully dark, the world dissolving into inky blackness after a few feet. Someone outside, however, could have seen us sitting at the table, turned in our chairs and staring out into the night. Right then Kennel started barking.

“Something’s definitely out there,” Dad said, standing. Johnny stood, too.

Outside, someone yelled—not close, but not far away, either. It wasn’t a friendly yell, or the cry of someone who was hurt. I instinctively knew that this was a yell that signaled trouble.

“Wait here,” Dad ordered. “Johnny, come with me.” They stood, walking deliberately to the door. Dad snapped the light switch, and the back porch came into view.

A voice called again, angry and indistinct. It came closer, splitting into two voices, then several, then more. A man yelled, clearly now, “Show your face, Hammarstrom!”

I must have let out some kind of cry, because Mom pulled me so tight against her chest that for a moment I couldn’t breathe. Leaning over, she grabbed for the phone receiver, which had been off the hook all afternoon. She clicked it into the cradle and lifted it again, listening for a dial tone. Dad whirled around from the door.

"No police," he said. "We're going to settle this on our own."

Mom pleaded, "John!"

"Don't do it!" he seethed, and swung the back door open. Mom dropped the receiver onto the table with a clatter. The night had turned bitterly cold; the chill filtered in through the screen door. A hinge creaked as Dad stepped halfway out, one foot in the kitchen and the other on our back porch. Johnny stood behind him, and their bodies blocked the doorway.

"Come out here and fight like a man!" someone called, and there were whoops of agreement, like war cries.

Whimpering, I slid from Mom's grasp and landed beneath the kitchen table. Emilie joined me, and we grabbed at each other silently, clutching wrists and shirtsleeves. Emilie muttered, "Holy shit," under her breath a half dozen times, like it was a prayer. I clapped a hand over my own mouth, terrified that I would let out a scream.

"Who's out there?" Mom demanded. "Who is it?"

With Dad and Johnny blocking the door, we couldn't make out anyone from the crowd. The men were approaching the porch steps, their voices clear now. One voice, louder than the rest, hollered, "Hammarstrom, you coward!" and I recognized it as belonging to Bill Lemke. The other voices were both familiar and unfamiliar at once. They sounded like men I might know, except their voices were wild and angry, not at all like the men who had said a polite hello to me every time we met.

"Come out and face us, Hammarstrom," Bill Lemke taunted, his voice commanding. I remembered how he had taken charge at Stacy's birthday party, leading the guests in a wild, off-key chorus.

"You've got some real explaining to do," another man echoed. "We're not letting you get away with this."

It wasn't clear to me if they were talking to Dad or Johnny.

Mom gasped. "That's Sandy Maertz," she whispered, her fingernails digging half moons into my arm with the ferocity of her grasp. I was shocked, too—Sandy went to our church. He had been here that night—one of the First Responders who sat around our kitchen table, warming himself with a mug of coffee. He'd been on our softball team, I remembered—center field.

"Now listen—" Dad began loudly, but his words were immediately drowned out.

"Let's settle this once and for all!" Bill Lemke yelled.

Someone else called, "Just admit what he did! Tell us where the girl is!"

"Don't her parents deserve to know, Johnny?" That last voice was plaintive, more pleading than angry. I recognized it as belonging to Chris Hansen, the father of Johnny's longtime friend and wrestling buddy, Erik.

Emilie recognized it, too. "Oh, my God," she said, looking at me.

"We've got to call the police," Mom mumbled, although she made no move toward the phone. "We've got to call…"

His body still half behind the screen door, Dad was trying to calm the men with a voice that quavered when he spoke. "We don't need to start more trouble than we've got already. This isn't going to help us find Stacy." He seemed determined to ignore the rest of them and addressed Bill alone. "I don't want to have to get the police out here. Think about your wife and girls. Think what this would do—"

"Don't you talk about my girls!" Mr. Lemke howled, his voice unsteady.

"He's smashed," Emilie said in my ear. She was so close to me that I could feel her heart beating through her sweater—or else it was my own. I realized she was right—they were all drunk, unreasonable and dangerous.

There was laughter, and someone called, "Go ahead and call the police. See whose side they're on!"

Sandy Maertz shouted, "You've got some nerve, Hammarstrom, talking about his girls—"

Johnny, who had been frozen in place, now pushed against Dad's back. "That's enough. Let me out there."

"Johnny, you stay put!" Mom shrieked. Dad held him back with one hand against his chest.

"Your boy's more of a man than you are," someone jeered. "Send him out here to fight if you won't."

Johnny tried to slip around Dad. He had a tight hold on the door frame, but Mom, coming around the table, gripped him around the waist.

"So you're a coward, too, Johnny? You going to hide behind your dad?" Sandy Maertz called. "Come out here and face what you've done!"

"Yeah! Get him out here!"

"I'm going out there," Johnny insisted, struggling against Mom and Dad. Mom lost her grip on Johnny's waist, but Dad had pinned one of his arms. "I've got to do something!" Johnny wailed, desperate. "I've got to say something!"

"What are you going to say, Johnny? Are you going to tell the truth about what you did to my little girl?"

Mr. Lemke's voice was closer now, and I realized he had stepped onto the porch, almost face-to-face with Dad. In the yellow pool from the overhead light, he wasn't the genial, proud Bill Lemke from Stacy's birthday party last September. Now he was reckless, balancing himself against one of the porch beams, his mouth hanging loose and sloppy. "How did you do it? How did you fucking do it?"

"I didn't—I didn't—" Johnny's voice was half scream, half sob. He stopped struggling, his legs going limp in Mom's grasp. Dad pushed Johnny back into the house, then opened the screen door the rest of the way and stepped completely onto the porch. He was only a foot from Mr. Lemke, and the contrast between them amazed me—one man sober, his jaw set in a firm line, and one man drunk, his face contorted with pain.

"That's it, John," Mom pleaded. "We're calling the police right now."

"Wait," Dad ordered. He raised both hands above his head, as if he was surrendering, and to Bill Lemke he said, "Here I am. I'm not hiding behind anything. You got something to say, here I am. You want to take a shot, you take a shot."

Emilie moaned, and I turned into her shoulder, too scared to look.

There was a low rumble, like a growl from the crowd. *Please, God, please, God,* I prayed.

"You want me to take him, Bill?" someone called. "I'd be happy to do it."

And then Mr. Lemke seemed to collapse. He tilted to one side, grabbing the porch rail to steady himself. "My girl!" he wailed, his voice quivering. "What happened to my girl?"

Dad's voice was shaky, too. "I feel sorry for her and for you, Bill, and for what's happening to your family. God knows I do. But I can't take responsibility for something that my son didn't do. And deep down I know you know it. Johnny didn't do anything to hurt your daughter."

There was a collective cry of outrage, and the men rushed onto the porch. One of them—it was impossible to tell who from my vantage point—tackled Dad, and he went down hard, his body thumping against the concrete. "Get him, Bill!" someone yelled, and Bill Lemke took a drunken swing that connected with Dad's cheekbone. Later, Mom said that Dad didn't struggle, didn't even bother to cover his head with his hands—he just took it, square on. Johnny, wild-eyed, tried to push open the screen door, but it was blocked by Dad's body. Bill Lemke raised his arm back above his head and brought it down again, and we heard another crunch as it connected with Dad's face.

Mom screamed, "Stop! Stop!"

Bill Lemke's face had broken open with grief. He reminded me—although I couldn't think this until later, until after the fact—of an animal in pain, like the time one of our steers had gotten its head stuck between two bars, and the more it writhed and tried to break free, the more desperately it was trapped. He had brought his arm up a third time, his fist tight, when the noise of a shotgun split the night.

I didn't even realize I'd been screaming until Emilie clapped both hands over my mouth.

"Next time you lay a hand on my son, I'm not going to miss," Grandpa called, his voice coming from around the corner of our house. I'd been wrong; I thought my grandfather could sleep through just about any noise in the world.

"Jesus," Mom moaned.

"I mean it now," Grandpa said, coming into view. His voice was as level as the shotgun balanced on his shoulder. "You think this is the way to settle this? A bunch of drunks attacking a man on his own property in the middle of the night?"

"Hey, now," Sandy Maertz said, backing up with his hands raised. "Calm down, old man."

"We just wanted some answers," someone else said.

"It's about justice!" Mr. Lemke was standing again, and a few men were trying to hustle him off the porch. "It's about justice for Stacy!" On the lawn again, he looked smaller, defeated. He was so drunk he could barely walk on his own; he leaned between two men as if he were using a pair of crutches.

Johnny pushed open the door finally and sidestepped Dad's body. But if he was looking for a fight, if he wanted a chance to defend his honor or Dad's, it was too late.

"Move it along now," Grandpa warned.

With his shotgun trained on them, the men moved as a group down our driveway. Just out of earshot, someone turned around to yell something unintelligible in our direction.

"They parked out on the road," Emilie said, realizing. "That's why we didn't hear their cars."

We had stepped out on the porch now, and with all five of us there, it was crowded. Johnny's chest was heaving as if he'd been the one in a fight. Mom dropped down to her knees and helped Dad to his feet, putting her palm against a wound on his temple. His lip had been split, too—when he spat, a pool of blood immediately welled up in the same spot.

"Let me have a look at that," Mom insisted, but Dad pushed her hand away.

Grandpa lowered his shotgun and came toward us. With the gun at his side, he looked like the old man he was—past seventy, gray hair sticking up in tufts.

"You shouldn't have done that, Papa," Dad said.

"I was supposed to let them kill you?"

Dad was quiet for a long moment, and then he spat more blood onto the porch steps. "We needed to let him win," he explained, letting the significance of his words hang in the night between us. "Whether Johnny had anything to do with this or not, Bill Lemke's the one who's suffering the most, and we need to remember that."

He wiped his lip again, smearing blood onto his chin. His face was beginning to swell, the lower half bloody as a cannibal's. Turning to Johnny, he said, "But this isn't done. This might be only the beginning."

twenty-six

Mom counted them off on her fingers the next morning: Sandy Maertz; Chris Hansen; Greg Fedderson, who butchered at Gaub's Meats; and the other two were brothers of Sharon Lemke, men who had helped with the barbecuing at Stacy's birthday party. And then Bill Lemke, of course, Mom said, spitting out his name like it left a bad taste in her mouth. Ten days ago, I would have said we didn't have any enemies in the whole world. Now, I wondered how many people had read the newspapers and watched the press conference and passed judgment against Johnny, and against the rest of us.

"Your father and I have been talking," Mom announced. "And we've made an appointment with a lawyer in Green Bay. I'm so sorry—we're so sorry—that you kids had to witness that last night. We're going to make sure nothing like that ever happens again."

Emilie raised her eyebrows skeptically, and I could tell what she was thinking. How could a lawyer prevent something like that? What was he going to do—set up a tent on our lawn?

I expected Johnny to make some kind of protest, about how he didn't need a lawyer and he hadn't done anything wrong, but he just sat there, staring ahead. Maybe last night had taken all the fight out of him.

"Wonder what the lawyer will make of this," Dad said, gesturing to his face. One eye was a purplish-black, and a bandage covered an inch-long cut on his cheekbone. His lower lip was swollen, the wound still raw.

"I think it speaks for itself," Mom said drily.

"Can I come with you?" I asked hopefully. I'd barely slept, which was starting to feel normal. Every noise, every breath had me sitting up in alarm. I'd looked out the window a dozen times, half expecting to see the shadows of men sneaking onto our property, or Grandpa standing sentry, the shotgun on his shoulder.

Mom shook her head. "Aunt Julia's coming over to stay with you two."

Emilie rolled her eyes, but didn't say anything. Maybe we did need a babysitter now. Maybe there were more things to worry about than who would make us lunch or make sure we weren't watching inappropriate shows on TV.

Dad, Mom and Johnny left, dressed up as if they were headed to Sunday service. Mom drove and Dad reclined in the passenger seat, holding an ice pack against his eye. Johnny stared out the window at nothing. I wondered what he would say to his lawyer. Maybe he would even confess, and this whole thing could come to an end.

"So," Aunt Julia said, too brightly. "Who wants to go to town?"

Emilie and I agreed to the trip warily. It was Thursday, and we had only missed four days of school, but it felt as if we'd been locked in the house for a month. I wondered if I would come back eventually to find that my classmates had already mastered long division, that they had finished our entire unit on the early Native Americans in Wisconsin. On the other hand, town was an intimidating place, where we were sure to bump into people we knew, people who had seen our family on the news. We piled into Aunt Julia's Buick anyway, Emilie ducking behind the passenger-side visor mirror, and me sitting directly behind her. A news bulletin was just coming on the radio, and Aunt Julia turned the dial to Alannah Myles crooning "Black Velvet."

We turned onto Rural Route 4, then Passaqua Road, passing acre after acre, farm after farm. It must have snowed again that morning, because everything we passed was dusted white. I usually loved the way snow covered things up, made every car and every house look the same, but today it looked depressing. Somewhere around here, I thought, they had looked for Stacy.

"Is that it?" Emilie cried suddenly. "Is that the spot?"

"Where?" I craned my neck, rubbing away the condensation on the window. There wasn't much to see, just the ridges of tire tracks. Snow had long submerged any footprints, any trace of Stacy Lemke or Johnny Hammarstrom.

"There—" Emilie pointed, and I followed the line of her finger to a single white cross, almost lost against the backdrop of snow.

"Shit," Aunt Julia said, pulling her car onto the shoulder. "Who put that there?"

It was the kind of cross that was planted on the graves of veterans in the memorial cemetery just outside

Watankee, and it was sort of strange, because of course Stacy wasn't a veteran, and for that matter, we didn't absolutely know she was dead. Only Johnny knew that, I thought, and instantly regretted it.

Emilie opened her door and slipped out. She crossed in front of the Buick and then jogged across the road.

"Shit," Aunt Julia said again and rolled down her window to call after Emilie. "Where are you going?"

Emilie waved with one hand over her head but didn't look back.

"This isn't a good idea," Aunt Julia said, strumming her fingers nervously on the steering wheel. She met my eye in the rearview mirror. "Not you, too. You're staying put."

I rolled down my window and watched Emilie pick her way through the snow. She was wearing her tight black jeans, the ones that had spawned an argument when she'd first brought them home from the Shopko in Manitowoc. She knelt in front of the cross, and for a second I thought she was going to yank it out of the ground.

"What's she doing?" I asked. Aunt Julia shook her head, watching the road nervously. Emilie pulled on her jacket, and then I realized she was unwinding her red scarf from her neck, and rewinding it around the cross. When she stepped back, we could see the cross clearly. It looked more purposeful now, more permanent somehow, draped in her scarf.

Emilie loped back to us, wrapping her coat around her body. I wondered how she would explain her missing scarf to Mom, or if it would be just one more thing nobody noticed, now that there were bigger things to care about.

"All right, then?" Aunt Julia asked, looking somewhat peeved. Once Emilie's seat belt was clasped, Aunt Julia pulled back onto the road. None of us mentioned what Emilie had done.

We were in town a couple of minutes later, heading straight down Main Street, as if we didn't have a thing to hide. It was strange to see that the town hadn't changed without us in it. A few sedans were parked at the bank, and a Volkswagen Bug idled outside the library. I held my breath when we passed Watankee Elementary School, but the playground was deserted.

"I'm going to run in for a couple of things," Aunt Julia said when we got to the Stop 'N' Go at the edge of town. "You want to come in?" We both opted to stay in the car, and Emilie fiddled with the radio station. Looking up, I saw that the marquee, which had boasted congratulations and good luck wishes after the big wrestling match, now said, Missing: Stacy Lynne Lemke, 5'7", 130 pounds.

Aunt Julia came out of the store gripping two plastic bags. "Here you go," she said, handing each of us a can of Coke and a couple of tiny bags of candy, the ones you could pick up at the register for fifty cents.

"This was what you needed to buy?" I asked, confused.

"Thanks," Emilie said simply, and ripped into a package.

On the way home, we passed the roadside memorial again. Emilie's scarf was the single dot of color on the landscape. I'd been straining to see it, leaning my head forward so that my chin rested on the middle of the front seat between Aunt Julia and Emilie. But even so, the splash of color surprised me for a moment. It looked for all the world like a smear of blood across the snow.

twenty-seven

Mom's spirits seemed buoyed by the meeting with the lawyer. "Mr. Gibson says it's a good sign that the district attorney hasn't pressed charges yet," she reported, dropping her purse on the kitchen counter and easing her feet out of her gray pumps. Dad, his face even more puffy and swollen, immediately headed to the barn. "If they had even the slightest bit of evidence, Johnny would have been arrested. Mr. Gibson seems to think that Johnny is in the clear, barring any new developments."

It was hard to know how to react to this news. Be thankful that he was free, that he hadn't been found out? I turned to Emilie, who was looking deliberately at the floor. Aunt Julia stepped forward, giving Johnny a hug that, for once, he didn't back away from. I stepped forward toward Johnny. I was the right height to throw my arms around his waist, to bury my face in his stomach with a hug, and I'd done that before.... Now, all I could manage was a clumsy one-armed embrace.

"Thanks, shorty."

"It's good news," Mom continued, with such conviction that it almost sounded true.

But I doubted that the men from last night would see this as a positive sign. It might not make any difference in the world to them that Johnny hadn't been arrested. This made me think about the rest of Watankee—everyone from Pastor Ziegler to my teachers at school. Everyone must be talking about it—all the kids in my class, their parents. It was hard to imagine that they weren't talking about it every night at dinner. *We* would be talking about it—if the circumstances were different.

"And what about last night?" Aunt Julia asked.

Mom looked confident when she said, "They're absolutely not allowed on our property. In fact, we could even apply for a restraining order against them, which we still might do. John doesn't think that's such a good idea for right now."

Although Mom seemed certain that we had nothing to worry about, that other people would start to see Johnny was innocent, not everyone had received the memo. More television vans appeared at the end of our driveway by early afternoon. Grandpa, against Mom's protests, went down to shoo them away and succeeded at least in moving them across the road, where they camped out as if they had no intention of leaving.

We flipped back and forth between television stations, catching snatches of soap operas and the occasional update on the case—although as far as I could tell, there were no real updates. At one point, a camera shot showed "live footage" of our house. Way in the background, Dad walked from the shed to the barn. In the foreground, Grandpa stood in front of his porch, as if he was one-half of the American Gothic painting, minus a pitchfork.

"Doesn't this get old?" Mom sighed. "What are they

waiting for? Do they think Johnny is going to run across the street and offer up a confession?"

In the absence of real news, however, the media found plenty of people who were eager to comment on the case. An older woman, describing herself as a "friend and confidante" of the Lemke family, said that Stacy had been a sweet, innocent girl, as all-American as they come. "She never gave her parents a minute of trouble," the woman said, tearing up. Mom rolled her eyes.

Next, the announcer introduced Stacy's former boyfriend, now a freshman at UW–La Crosse. I sat up suddenly, paying attention. This was the boy whose face Stacy had methodically scratched out in the photo I'd found in her bedroom. He was dark-haired, broad-shouldered. "You hear something like this on the news, and you just can't believe it," he said, shaking his head. "Stacy was so loving and trusting—those were her biggest strengths as a person. But I could see her loving and trusting the wrong person, and getting into trouble that way."

"That's practically slander," Mom commented.

The special report concluded with one more testimonial, and this one a clincher. The reporter intoned dramatically, "Although the district attorney has declined to press charges against Johnny Hammarstrom at this time, there are quite a few people in Watankee who feel this is a mistake."

We gasped when the screen cut to Mrs. Keithley, the children's Sunday School teacher at St. John's for the past twenty years, who had sat on a tiny little stool in one of the church classrooms each Sunday, listening as a line of kids recited their catechism. She was standing in front of the bank downtown, where a little crowd had gathered, eager to be part of the excitement. During the long focus on Mrs. Keithley, other people from the community—parents with their toddlers, a few teenagers—stepped into the background.

"It sure is such a tragedy for our community," Mrs. Keithley began, the camera glinting strangely off her thick glasses. "But it goes to show you that you never can know the heart of another person. You take that Susan Smith who has been in the news, the one who concocted that crazy story about her kids being taken, when all along they were lying at the bottom of a lake." She paused for a moment, indignant, and continued in a louder voice, "Now maybe Johnny Hammarstrom is telling the truth when he says that she just got out of his car and wandered off into the snowstorm, but I tell you, it doesn't seem likely. Johnny can hide the truth from us, but God knows. God always knows."

Behind her, the small crowd erupted into a cheer.

The reporter said, "Certainly a lot of tension in this community right now. We'll come back to this story later, with an update about the search of a local forest."

We sat too stunned to move, as if we'd been punched in the gut and couldn't get our wind back. Finally Mom said, "I'm calling Mr. Gibson right now," and disappeared to use the phone upstairs.

Not long after, Coach Zajac's rusted-out Subaru passed the bank of TV vans on Rural Route 4 and pulled into our driveway. It surprised me to see him, because with everything else going on, I'd completely forgotten about wrestling. Also—it suddenly occurred to me—no one else had been stopping by to visit, or calling to see how we were doing, or making any of the polite gestures that were pretty much ingrained in the fabric of Watankee. Not one single other person who wasn't family had reached out to us since the press conference.

Dad and Coach Zajac had a long, man-to-man conversation at the kitchen table, too quiet for me to overhear. After a while, Dad called for Johnny, and he came downstairs and joined them.

"What do you think they're saying?" I asked Emilie, who was lying on her bed staring at the ceiling. It seemed unfair that I was old enough to witness a group of drunk men attack my father but wasn't allowed to listen in on other adult conversations.

"Oh, you know, the usual." She leaned on her elbow and delivered her next lines in a pretty good imitation of Coach Zajac's voice. "Bad luck, chum. Girlfriend goes missing. But life goes on. You can't just give up because of one loss."

I giggled in spite of myself. "But Johnny's not going to wrestle anymore."

Emilie raised an eyebrow. "The last I checked, he's still on the schedule at state."

"There's no way," I said at the same time Dad called for Mom. Emilie and I followed Mom down the stairs.

"It's not going to look good," Mom said, shaking her head.

Dad said, "Coach has a point, you know. Someday soon, the truth is going to come out that Johnny had nothing to do with any of that mess. He shouldn't have to miss out on the one thing he's worked so hard for these past four years."

"It's going to seem like we're running away," Mom said, touching Johnny on the shoulder. "How are you feeling about this?"

Johnny shrugged miserably. "I think I should be here, in case something happens."

Dad asked, "Like what?"

"I don't know. Like maybe they find Stacy. I want to be here when that happens."

"If there's any news, we'll come back instantly," Dad promised. "If you don't go, Johnny, you're always going to wonder what would have happened."

Johnny shrugged again.

I thought maybe it was Dad—and Coach Zajac, too—who would always wonder.

Surprisingly, it didn't take much convincing for Mom to go along with the plan. "I suppose people have made up their minds anyway, no matter what we do," she said finally. "Especially if they've been listening to the news."

In the end, the decision was made by Mr. Gibson, who acknowledged that Johnny had the legal right to represent his school, since no charges had been filed against him. He even agreed with Mom that getting out of town might not be a bad idea, at least for a few days, until things settled.

Mom made arrangements for a hotel in Madison, and Dad called Jerry Warczak to see if he could help Grandpa with the milking, since Grandpa couldn't be persuaded to go. I imagined him falling asleep in his recliner, the shotgun stretched across his lap.

It felt almost like a vacation, the sort we were always planning but never actually ended up taking, since it was nearly impossible for Dad to take time off from the farm and Mom's three shifts a week often included weekends and school holidays, too. Eagerly, I pulled out the suitcase I'd gotten for Christmas from

Aunt Julia and hadn't had a chance to use. I'd loved it only a few months ago, but now it was too babyish—Tinker Bell–themed and impossibly pink. Had I grown up without realizing it?

We set out on Thursday evening in Mom's Caprice, as soon as the last television van had moved for the night. Coach Zajac was going separately, on the team bus. For every other wrestling match of his career, Johnny had traveled with the team, too. It was telling that no one from the team had stopped by, not even Peter Bahn or Erik Hansen. Of course, Erik's dad had stopped by—and it was easy to figure that he had spoken for all of them.

Johnny took a window seat in our car, his head leaning sleepily against the glass. Every so often he would wake with a jump and a wild look around, like he wasn't sure where we were going or why. I kept watching him out of the corner of my eye and caught Dad watching him, too, in the rearview mirror. If I couldn't sleep without dreaming about Stacy, then I imagined Johnny couldn't, either.

We stopped at a Denny's outside Madison, and Dad steered Johnny toward the endless stack of pancakes, plus eggs, sausage and hash browns for good measure. "Eat, eat," he urged, worried that Johnny would be underweight for his class. Johnny ate everything put in front of him—including half of my ham-and-cheese omelet—but without seeming to enjoy a single bite.

We packed into a hotel room with two double beds—Mom and Emilie in one, Dad and Johnny in another, me in a green folding cot that Dad said looked like surplus from World War II. We took turns with the bathroom, carrying our pajamas in and our jeans out, then settling into our spots quietly. Dad watched a movie on television with the sound muted. Absent the sound, it became nothing more than one bright flash of color after another. With one elbow propped against the frame of my cot, I watched two actors in a heated conversation, their mouths literally inches apart.

"Are you feeling okay about tomorrow, Johnny?" Mom asked, and Johnny gave a grunt that could have been yes or no.

"I just wanted to say—" Mom continued, and although her voice was soft, it was distinct against the quiet of the room "—with everything else going on, I think we've forgotten to say that we're proud of you."

After this statement, the quiet was even more obvious. On TV, there was some sort of silent explosion, and a car went wheeling through the air, its tires catching on nothing. I was waiting for someone else to chime in—Dad, at least—to echo Mom's feelings. But listening to the silence, I realized that it didn't matter anymore. No matter what, we would never escape what happened that night.

I think that's when it hit me that no matter what else Johnny Hammarstrom ever did with his life, he would always be Stacy Lemke's boyfriend, the boy who killed his girlfriend and somehow got away with it.

twenty-eight

Early Friday morning, Dad and Johnny left to get Johnny checked in, and I crawled into their empty bed and flipped between morning news shows with the volume on low for an hour before Mom or Emilie stirred. There was nothing about Stacy Lemke, no news bulletins about a missing Watankee girl. We were three hours away from our lives. If we stayed here, I wondered, would we always be three hours removed from all our troubles?

The plan was that Dad would pick us up at the hotel later, when Johnny was weighed in and warmed up, and the real wrestling was starting. The state championship worked on a double elimination basis, which meant that every wrestler had at least two matches today, with the championship rounds tomorrow. Mom, toweling off her blond curls, suggested that we "take it easy"—something we hardly ever did. Emilie and I rose to the challenge, making numerous trips from the complimentary breakfast suite with glasses of cold orange juice, oversize muffins, bear claws and toasted bagels. Mom ate along with us, sitting cross-legged on the bedspread.

The food didn't seem particularly tasteful or fresh, but I was suddenly starving.

Emilie finished a bear claw and lay back, crossing one long leg over the opposite knee. "This is nice," she said, and gave Mom a quick, apologetic glance.

"It does feel good to get away," Mom admitted. "I thought I was going to burst if I stayed in that house for one more minute."

"Are we going back to school on Monday?" I asked, biting the crunchy top off a muffin.

Mom's face registered surprise, and I realized I had blown our peaceful moment. "We'll see," she said tightly, which meant "no" more often than it meant "yes." It surprised me to think that she might be winging it, that she hadn't concocted a new master plan for our lives. "Things need to settle down a bit more first," she added.

I was glad. As much as I'd missed school, it seemed so far away from our lives now, so inconsequential. "What about Johnny? Will he go back to school?"

Mom frowned. "He's so close to graduation… I can't imagine how hard it's going to be for him, but—"

Emilie sat up again, a spray of crumbs falling from her shirt onto the bedspread. "What about me?"

"You'll go back, too."

"I don't think so."

"What else would you do?"

Emilie stared at her. "No one is going to want us back there, Mom," she said carefully, as if she was speaking to someone who was slow to understand. "It's going to be awful."

As uncomfortable as I was about the whole idea, it would probably be even worse for Emilie, who went to the same high school as Johnny and Stacy, and was in the same class as Stacy's sister Joanie. It wasn't hard to imagine Emilie eating lunch alone for the rest of her life, walking down a hallway amid jeers and taunts.

"We're going to figure this out like we've figured out everything else, one day at a time," Mom said, a hint of annoyance creeping into her voice.

Emilie expelled air through her nose and lay down again. "And if we don't figure it out? What then?"

Instead of answering, Mom stood, gathering together our napkins and plastic cups and dumping them in the room's tiny trash can. I was wrong—we weren't three hours away from our problems, after all.

Dad came back to the hotel to pick us up around noon, and one look at his face told us it hadn't gone well for Johnny that morning. One loss and he was out of the championship, although he could still vie for third. "The thing is," Dad reported, not taking his eyes from the road, "the rest of those kids have been non-stop practicing. Johnny's been through hell this week, and it showed. He looked pretty rough out there, gave away too many easy points."

"Maybe this was a mistake," Mom suggested quietly. "Maybe it's too soon for him to—"

Dad brushed this off. "He can still take third. He's got another match coming up. Maybe he'll be more warmed up by then."

But a blind man could have seen that there was something wrong with Johnny. Instead of waiting near the mats with the competitors or sitting with the members of his team—who had gathered around Dirk Bauer as if he was a celebrity—Johnny sat in the bleachers like a spectator. His face shadowed by the hood of his sweatshirt, he looked way too old to be a high school senior.

Dad went over to sit with Johnny, but Mom, Emilie and I took seats as far away as we could, about ten rows up. There were other people from Watankee there, but none of them approached us. I stiffened when I saw Chris Hansen, Erik's dad, in the crowd.

They called for the 160s, and Johnny came lumbering down the stands, led by Coach Zajac. He sloughed off his sweatshirt, pulled the straps of his singlet up over his shoulders and stood, arms crossed.

"This isn't going to be good," Emilie whispered.

When Johnny stepped into the circle, he already looked defeated. His opponent was a few inches shorter and a little stockier, but he looked young and healthy, as if he could run circles around Johnny. He looked like someone who was thinking only about a state title. Johnny had far more on his mind, and it showed.

The ref blew the whistle, and in a half-second Johnny was down, as if his opponent had rushed nothing more than a massive sack of flour.

"Do something, do something," Mom whispered.

I flinched, looking away from Johnny's body twisted under his opponent's grasp. Dad was standing with his hands clenched into fists at his sides, not daring to look away himself. Maybe it was all flashing before his eyes, the way it was before mine: Johnny wrestling in the living room on summer nights, lifting weights in the barn, strategizing on the mats, taking down his opponent while everyone in the stands cheered, while Stacy Lemke called his name, louder than anyone else. Or maybe Dad was seeing his own wrestling career, which had ended early, too, around the time Mom became pregnant.

It took only twenty-five seconds for Johnny to be pinned. He walked off the mat, grabbed his sweatshirt and kept going, straight for the doors of the gymnasium. Coach didn't try to stop him or offer words of encouragement this time. Johnny was beyond that now, and no one could reach him.

"That kid bottomed out in the first round, too," someone behind us said. "That's what you call an oh-and-two barbecue."

We stood up, making our way through the stands. From farther back, someone yelled, "That's what he deserves! How dare you come here like this!" None of us turned around. We did the march of shame across our row in the stands, then down to the next level and around to the exit.

"His heart just wasn't in it," Mom said, touching Dad on the arm. Johnny had gone ahead of us and was standing at the entrance to the parking garage, as if he wasn't an athlete at all; he'd been here simply to view the matches, not contend.

"He didn't even put up a fight," Dad said, shaking his head. "That's worse than not competing. We might as well have stayed home."

"Maybe he just wanted to be beat," Emilie commented.

Dad scoffed as if this didn't make a bit of sense, but I thought she was probably right. When I'd done things that were really bad—like letting the caterpillars shrivel up in that shoebox underneath my bed—I'd wanted to be punished. I'd needed it, like some kind of penance, like Hercules punishing himself with twelve impossible tasks. Was it the same with Johnny? If the criminal justice system didn't punish him, how far would he go to punish himself?

We were quiet in the Caprice, letting the car take silent turns onto unfamiliar streets. We were getting very good at avoiding the elephant in the room.

"I could run out and pick up some burgers," Dad offered as we pulled into the parking lot. "Anyone hungry?" When no one answered, he muttered, "Later, then."

There have been times in my life where I thought that things couldn't get worse, that no new set of bad circumstances could possibly compound the bad set of circumstances I was already in. I felt that way coming back to our hotel room that night, with the mystery of Stacy unsolved, our collective nerves still unsettled from the confrontation on our back porch steps, and now Johnny going down in what could only be described as a public disgrace. *An oh-and-two barbecue.* That's what I was thinking when we walked into the darkened hotel room. *Things are bad, really bad, but they can't possibly get worse.*

And then I saw the red light on the phone blinking soundlessly, steadily, and I knew deep down that I was wrong.

twenty-nine

Dad listened to the message, hung up and lifted the phone to dial. "It was Julia," he said, as we sat on the edges of the beds, waiting. "It's Papa, he fell off a ladder."

Mom gasped. "My God. Is he okay?"

But Dad was busy with the phone call, which left us to decipher the facts based on his side of the conversation. Aunt Julia had received a call from Jerry Warczak, who found Grandpa during the morning milking. She'd called an ambulance and ridden along to the hospital, where Grandpa had gone through all sorts of X-rays and scans. He was alert, but had a possible concussion and a broken hip.

"What in the world was he doing on a ladder early in the morning?" Mom asked, but Dad shook his head, tight-lipped. "What's going on? There's something you're not saying."

Dad stood. "We're heading back," he announced, and just like that, our vacation-that-wasn't-really-a-vacation was over. Johnny changed clothes in the bathroom and carried his duffel bag to the car, the first one ready to go. I shoved my clothes and books back into my Tinker Bell suitcase while Emilie visited the vending machine down the hall one last time, and Mom haggled with the front desk clerk over the details of our checkout.

"It doesn't seem fair to be charged for the night if we aren't actually staying the night," she huffed, meeting us at the car.

We must have driven for half an hour before Mom turned to Dad and said, "John, I'm sorry." I couldn't tell if she was talking about Grandpa or about something else.

"I'm sorry, too," I piped up from the backseat, and Emilie echoed me. Johnny, locked in his own private pain, stared out the window at the muddy landscape that was beginning to emerge next to banks of melting snow.

Dad grunted in acknowledgment. He drove faster, the suggestion of burgers forgotten, and none of us daring to mention it now.

I stared out the window as night descended like a giant hand being lowered from the sky, trapping us in its shadow. One week, I thought. Everything in the world had changed in only one single week.

Mom looked surprised when Dad took the turnoff for Watankee, instead of heading straight into Manitowoc. "We've still got about a half hour before visiting hours end," she pointed out. "If we stop off at home first…"

Dad didn't flinch. "There's business at home to attend to," he said, and I assumed he meant the night's milking, or something to do with one animal or another, but when he pulled into our driveway, he didn't slow to park in front of our house, but headed instead toward the barn, turning the steering wheel sharply at the last minute to pull the Caprice up onto the lawn.

"John, what in the—"

Our barn, built by Grandpa's dad more than a hundred years ago, had been repainted a beautiful red last year by

Johnny. It had been a month-long process that had started when school was out and ended around the time of the softball tournament, involving ladders and scaffolding and, at one point, Johnny dangling from a harness in his paint-blotched jeans. We'd been proud of the result, standing back to admire it all the way from the main road. Best-looking barn for miles around, Dad had said.

Now he flicked on the high beams, and we all saw it at the same time.

Emilie gasped, and Mom cried, "Oh, dear Lord!"

Dad jerked the car into Park and hopped out, Johnny close behind him. Mom and Emilie followed, but I stayed put, still belted into the middle, as they inspected the damage. I didn't need to be any closer—I could see it perfectly from where I sat. The headlights had illuminated the cheerful red of the barn, but also an ugly smear of white sprayed across it, in letters at least eight feet tall. *FUCK YOU ILLER,* it said. A tipped-over ladder lay sprawled on its side, probably right where Jerry Warczak had found it. At first glance, the ladder seemed to be covered in blood. But then I spotted the five-gallon bucket of red paint, which Grandpa must have dragged out of the shed that morning to paint over the giant *K.*

KILLER.

Even before I emerged from the car, I could hear Mom and Dad yelling at each other—Mom insisting that they should have called the police the moment Bill Lemke stepped onto our property the other night, Dad saying it wouldn't have mattered, that calling the police on Wednesday wouldn't have prevented Bill Lemke and his cronies from coming back onto our property later.

Mom's voice bit through the night. "Well, we'll never know, now! If we had done something to stand up for ourselves—"

"I'm telling you, that wouldn't have made a bit of difference! Look at the situation we're in. They need someone to blame, and here we are—"

"Yes, here we are! A bunch of cowards, afraid to stand up for ourselves, afraid of what people will think of us! Maybe your dad had the right idea with that shotgun. Or maybe I should have had it, because I don't know if I would have fired into the air!"

The strange bubbling noise beneath their yells, I realized, was Emilie sobbing. I don't know if I'd ever heard her cry before. I was the one who cried when a calf didn't make it or when I got in trouble, and Emilie was the one who rolled her eyes, scornful of my reaction. Now she stood in front of the barn with tears streaming down her cheeks, her lower lip quivering.

I looked at Johnny, who was staring at the barn, his hands shoved in his jeans pockets. I wonder if I was the only one who heard Johnny say, over and over beneath his breath: "It's all my fault."

"What are you doing?" Dad called, and I realized that Mom was crossing the lawn, already halfway to our house. He charged after her, catching her by the elbow, and she pushed him away. "You need to think about this," he hissed.

"What's there to think about? Bill Lemke and his cronies vandalized our property, and I'm not going to let them get away with it!"

"You need to cool down first," he said as she pushed against his chest. I was crying now, too, the tears hot on my cheeks.

"You know what? I've had enough! I don't care how it looks, or what people might say. We haven't done anything wrong!" She looked at each one of us in turn, her gaze lingering unsteadily on Johnny. That look seemed to say everything we hadn't been saying—that some of us in particular were innocent, that one of us in particular wasn't. Mom seemed to catch this slip herself, because she changed focus. "What do they want from us? Are we just supposed to take it and take it and take it—"

Dad whirled around on us, barking sharply, "Inside! Now!" His voice was angrier than I'd ever heard it, and his face was ugly with fury, too, as if he had morphed into some monster version of his human self. There was nothing to do but obey this voice, so Emilie and I walked carefully around them, past Kennel, who was straining at the edge of his chain. Inside, Emilie put her arm around me, and we stared out the window together, as if we were watching some kind of horrible storm blow through and hoping against hope that our house would survive. Johnny came inside a minute later, but Dad and Mom stayed outside for a long time. Even with the door closed behind us, we could hear them yelling.

This was worse, somehow, than drunken men showing up at our door late at night, or someone sneaking onto our property overnight to paint *FUCK YOU KILLER* on our barn. It hurt worse than anything Bill Lemke might say, or anything that might show up in print about us in the newspaper. Watching them from an upstairs window, I realized that when Stacy Lemke went missing, something had broken within us—not like a chip off a piece of china, which could be superglued back together, and not like a broken pipe that could be mended, at least temporarily, with a strip of duct tape. This was no clean break; it was as if something had shattered and splintered into a million little pieces. Even if there was a way to get it all back together somehow, it would never be exactly the same.

thirty

Mom called Dennis Gibson first thing in the morning, and he drove down from Green Bay to be with her when the police arrived. The deputy on duty looked like a teenager, with a thin face and a knobby Adam's apple. He snapped a photo of the barn with his Polaroid and waggled the print back and forth while he waited for the picture to develop. Mom watched this scornfully, as if she had absolutely no trust that this flimsy photo would ever do her or anyone else a bit of good.

"Nice of them to send Barney Fife along," Mom said, coming into the house with Mr. Gibson in tow. "Dennis is going to help us get started on a restraining order."

Dad folded his arms across his chest and leaned back against the countertop. "We don't even know for sure who it was, Alicia. You're reacting without thinking things through." From his tone I knew that their argument from the night before wasn't finished.

Mom ignored this and smiled icily at Mr. Gibson. "You see, my husband thinks that we shouldn't do anything, and somehow it will all go away."

Mr. Gibson, in his fancy pin-striped suit, said, "Now,

sir, I would have to disagree with you there…." He reached into his briefcase and pulled out a stack of papers.

"Kirsten," Mom said pointedly, gesturing toward the stairs. I took each step slowly, letting my foot drag across the carpeting. It seemed funny that Mom was intent on keeping people away from us. I had begun to realize that people wanted to keep *us* away from them.

The adults-only conversation halted only when a nurse from the hospital returned Mom's call. Grandpa was in pain, but he was alert and had been asking for us. After Mr. Gibson left, we piled into the Caprice again, minus Johnny.

"Aren't you coming?" Mom called, spotting Johnny on the steps.

He shook his head.

"Your grandfather is in the hospital," Mom said coldly.

He only stared at her, so we piled into the car and headed out. It was impossible to tell what Johnny was thinking, as if he was locked in his body without a means of communication.

"Why should he get to stay?" Mom demanded. "Isn't he going to take some responsibility for this situation?"

Dad looked at her sharply. "He's not responsible for this situation."

Mom seethed all the way into Manitowoc, getting a grip on her anger only when we entered the lobby of Holy Cross Hospital and it was time to smile at her coworkers. "I'm coming back next week," she promised, and a few of the women stepped forward to hug her.

In the hallway, a compact man in a white coat introduced himself as Dr. DeGuzman. He explained there would be surgery, some kind of pin inserted, recovery time in a rehabilitation unit. "The concussion appears to be minor, although he was disoriented yesterday when he was brought in," he continued, opening the door to Grandpa's room.

The man lying in bed didn't look much like Grandpa; he looked smaller, somehow, with an IV hooked to his arm and an oxygen tube trailing from his nose. The pale blue hospital gown was nearly translucent; where the sleeve ended, his arm was covered in a purplish bruise up to the point where it disappeared beneath the bed sheet.

"How are you holding up, Papa?" Mom asked.

Dad went right over to Grandpa, smoothing back the wisps of hair that lay against his forehead. He gave his shoulder a little tap. "Papa?" Grandpa didn't respond. His body was limp, the way people looked in cartoons sometimes, but never in real life. When Dad touched him again, Grandpa's head flopped over like a Raggedy Ann doll.

"Is that normal?" There were tears in Dad's voice.

Dr. DeGuzman said, "He was awake only a few minutes ago. The medicine must have tired him out."

Suddenly Grandpa's eyes fluttered open, and he shifted in the bed. The movement was obviously painful; he winced and looked around wildly.

"Now, you just stay still, Papa," Mom said.

Grandpa looked back and forth, taking everything in. "Where—"

"You're in the hospital," Dad said. "You fell yesterday. Do you remember?"

Grandpa's eyes focused on Dad's face for a moment,

then darted to Emilie and me, who had crammed together into the room's single chair, our legs overlapping.

"You're in good hands now," Mom said, close to his face. "Dr. DeGuzman is one of the absolute best."

Grandpa closed his eyes, exhaled painfully. "The barn..."

"We saw it, Papa. We're going to take care of it right away," Dad said. "I'm sorry that it happened when you were by yourself."

Grandpa wanted to say something but only gasped.

The doctor cleared his throat. "Maybe that's enough for now. We should let him sleep. You can always come back before visiting hours end tonight."

Emilie and I, taking this as a cue, stepped forward and gave Grandpa twin pecks on his cheek.

"I still wish you hadn't tried to take care of that yourself, Papa," Mom said, helping him lean back against his pillows. "You could have been hurt much, much worse."

Grandpa struggled to come to a sitting position once again, but the jostling motion caused him to howl with a primal, animal-like pain.

Dad sprang back, but Mom leaned over Grandpa, settling him. "Just take it easy now, okay," she said.

Grandpa shook his head, trying to move out of her reach. "Don't you tell me..."

"He still seems to be in pain," Dad complained. "Can't you give him something else?"

"Don't you..."

"What's he trying to say?" Mom asked, inclining her ear toward his head. "Papa? Is there something you want to tell us?"

"Don't you...touch me...you...bitch." His voice came more clearly now, his blue eyes alert.

Mom recoiled as if she'd been slapped.

"You're nothing but a…dirty…whore." The words out, Grandpa collapsed onto the pillow, his chest heaving with the effort.

Mom took a step backward, and then another, holding her hands out in front of her body, palms up. She gave a short, nervous bark of a laugh and looked from the doctor to Dad and back. All of our eyes were on Mom, as if she was a bomb that might go off if we didn't focus our full attention on her. "This is what I get for trying to help!"

Dr. DeGuzman cleared his throat again, clearly uncomfortable. "You know, sometimes with a concussion…" he began, and launched into medical-speak about head injuries and temporary memory loss.

Mom smiled tightly. We left a few minutes later, when a nurse arrived with a syringe to be emptied into Grandpa's IV.

"Nice of you to come to my defense," Mom said when we were back in the Caprice. She was driving this time, taking the turns a little too fast.

Dad, looking out the window, closed his eyes. "Oh, come on. He was delirious. There's no point in getting all worked up about it."

Mom's laugh was biting. "He was not delirious! You know what it was? For once in his life he was actually saying what he meant. He's felt that way for eighteen years!"

Mom took the turn onto Passaqua Road particularly fast, and I had to hold on to the door handle not to go flying.

"We don't need this on top of everything else now, Alicia."

"You're right—we don't need this," Mom agreed, but she seemed to mean something else entirely.

A stony silence persisted between them, until we pulled into our driveway and saw that Johnny was nearly finished painting over the graffiti on the barn. Dad joined him for a second coat, and I stayed outside, too, brushing out Kennel's fur. But I kept sneaking peeks at Dad and Johnny, at the easy way they worked together. I could hear their voices, although not their exact words. I wondered what they were saying to each other that they wouldn't say to the rest of us—was Johnny confessing something? Was he saying he was sorry for throwing his wrestling match, or was Dad saying that it didn't matter, that he was the one who was sorry, that Johnny's losing mattered less than anything else in the world?

When Dad and Johnny came in later that afternoon to grab something from the refrigerator, it was obvious to me that they had some new understanding, as if they were on one team, and Mom, Emilie and I were on the other. They'd worked shoulder to shoulder in their private male kingdom while we women only meddled, only complicated matters by saying the wrong things and placing blame and getting emotional. After that day, I felt a divide between us, and when Dad went outside for one last check on the animals, I simply didn't follow.

thirty-one

On Sunday, I read in the *Manitowoc Herald Times Reporter* that Dirk Bauer had won the state title in the 121-pound division. His photo was on the front page, with the ref holding Dirk's triumphant, skinny arm over his head. Colleges, the article implied, were jumping over themselves with offers for him. There was no mention of Johnny Hammarstrom. It was as though he'd never even existed.

None of us mentioned church, especially now that Mrs. Keithley had as good as condemned Johnny on television. Although he had called several times last week to see how we were holding up, Pastor Ziegler didn't stop by again to see us. I wondered if it were possible to pray against someone, and if that's what the St. John's prayer chain was doing now, praying that Johnny Hammarstrom come clean about what he'd done to Stacy Lemke and face the music once and for all. If I was being honest with myself, that's what I was praying for, too.

Mom went to get groceries and returned twenty minutes later, shaken. "The way they were staring at me… It was like I had the plague or something."

On Monday Detective Halliday stopped by to say

that the blood analysis had come back. It turned out that the blood inside the truck and on Johnny's clothes belonged to Johnny.

"I told you it was mine," Johnny complained. "That's what I said from the beginning."

Detective Halliday explained, not unkindly, "We can't ignore any kind of physical evidence, especially in a case like this. We have a responsibility to follow up on everything."

"What about finding the people who vandalized our barn?" Mom insisted. "Are you following up on that?"

Detective Halliday frowned. "With all due respect, ma'am, my efforts have been concentrated on the missing girl who is presumed to be the victim of foul play."

Stacy. Sometimes, in the middle of everything, I almost forgot that she was at the center of all of this.

Detective Halliday also reported that Johnny's truck, now that it had been processed for blood and fingerprints and fibers, was ready to be picked up. Dad drove Johnny to the police station and Johnny returned in the Green Machine, its front right fender bent at the passenger side—the last place where Stacy Lemke was known to have sat. He spent an afternoon with a hammer, crudely banging the metal back into place. It looked wounded but it still ran, and Johnny still drove it, much to my envy. I wished I had a truck of my own, so I could escape for a few hours.

Later that week, we invited Jerry Warczak over for dinner; he was one of the few people in town who was still speaking with us, it seemed. Dad thanked him repeatedly for finding Grandpa. "If it hadn't been for you…"

"I was just coming over for the milking," Jerry said, both cheeks dotted with a red circle of embarrassment.

"Still, we're grateful."

Jerry ducked his head, accepting Dad's appreciation. "How's he doing?"

Dad reported what he knew, which was that Grandpa had made it through surgery, that when he had his strength back he was going to begin a stint in the rehabilitation center. It was Mom who called each morning for the report, slicing through the red tape that would otherwise have entangled Grandpa's records, but it was Dad who visited in the evenings to help Grandpa with his dinner. "I'll go," Mom had huffed, "when he's ready to apologize." Dad had thrown up his hands as though he was giving up.

For the first few weeks after Stacy's disappearance, Mom dutifully retrieved our homework packets from school on Mondays and returned them on Fridays. I had always loved school, but when learning was reduced to a stack of worksheets, I became bored quickly. To occupy my free time, I volunteered to help out around Grandpa's house. There seemed to be a delicate balance between overwatering and underwatering his ferns; one day they looked limp and waterlogged, the next day the leaves were crispy, breaking off in my fingers. But taking care of Grandpa's house—as badly as I'm sure I did it—was a wonderful reason not to be in my own house, where a desperate silence had taken hold, punctuated occasionally by heated arguments. It seemed lately that none of us could do anything right.

True to her word, Mom went back to work right away, jumping at the chance to pick up an extra shift here and there. The transition back to work was awkward for her, though. I overheard her confide to Aunt Julia that few of her patients seemed to realize or care who she was, but the other nurses treated her differently, mostly talking in hushed whispers and avoiding direct contact with her.

Still, she believed that life had to go on. Sitting Emilie and me down one night, she said, "It's going to be difficult for you both, but this has to be done." She compared it to pulling off a Band-Aid; there wasn't much pain after the initial sting. "In no time, you'll be back in the swing of things, going places with your friends...." Her voice was too upbeat, propelled by a false cheer, and Emilie and I knew it.

Mom notified our schools that we would be back the following Monday. She was working that day, so Dad would bring Emilie and Johnny would bring me, on his way to who-knows-where. Johnny wouldn't be going back to school—he refused to go, and the school district didn't want him, anyway. Mom supplied him with a stack of GED review books, still seeming to believe that Johnny had a future in front of him, including—if not college on a wrestling scholarship—at least a decent job. I wondered who in all of Wisconsin was going to hire him, with his picture plastered all over the evening news.

Johnny's life was a mystery to me then. Each morning he shoved his feet into work boots and tramped out to the barn for chores. Later, when the rest of us assembled loosely in the kitchen for breakfast, his truck wheezed to life, the ignition caught, and he rumbled away from us. Much later he returned, heralded by the crunch of tires on gravel and the *whack* of his boots against the porch steps. He entered the house, sloughing off his jacket and hanging it on the peg that was, and had always been, his. We didn't ask where he went, and he didn't tell us. Sometimes the only proof of his physical presence was in the bathroom, in the puddles of his jeans and flannel shirts on the floor, or the smeared handprints against the fog of the bathroom mirror. No one called for him, no one stopped by to see how he was doing.

When he took me to school that Monday, it was the first time we'd been alone in weeks. He turned up the radio, a Pearl Jam song at a numbing volume that prevented conversation. That was fine with me. We had nothing to say to each other, and my stomach was a nervous mess. Would I pick up with my classmates right where we'd left off, or would I have to start all over again, forming new alliances? If Mom had been driving, I might have asked her to pull over, but with Johnny I had no choice but to force my nerves to quiet down.

We mostly rode in silence, with Johnny drumming his fingers against the steering wheel each time we came to a stop sign. *Stacy sat here,* I suddenly reminded myself, running my fingers over the cracked leather seat. She had buckled herself in with this very buckle, had rested her arm against this very armrest. Adjusting the sun visor, she had seen her own reflection in this very mirror—her wide gray-green eyes, the freckles on her cheeks.

"Where do you go, Johnny?" I asked him suddenly, my voice rising as loud as the music as we hit the single blinking red light that led into town. "Do you go looking for her?"

His glance shot to me, and I saw that his mouth hung open slightly in surprise. Of course he didn't go looking for her, I rebuked myself. No amount of driving around was going to do a thing for Stacy Lemke. He didn't need to look for her, since he knew exactly where she was.

"Never mind," I said quickly. "Don't tell me where you go."

"Kirsten, I don't even—"

"No! Don't tell me!" I screeched, afraid that in this moment, our one moment alone together in weeks, he would suddenly say things that he could never unsay and that I could never unknow.

It was a huge mistake to take a ride from Johnny, I realized the instant his Green Machine pulled into the parking lot. The teacher on yard duty stopped reprimanding a little boy to stare at us; some kids I recognized as sixth graders pointed at Johnny's truck as they walked past. Suddenly I knew I couldn't just go back to class, quietly learn my multiplication facts and my Wisconsin history. I couldn't blend in with my classmates as if I was one of them, after all that had happened. For a moment I wished I could take back what I'd asked him, so that he would bring me with him, wherever it was he went.

"I guess I'll see you," he grunted, the truck idling.

I slammed the dented, hammered door of the Green Machine behind me just a touch too hard, and Johnny swerved back onto the road, leaving me on the curb. I watched as his truck shot forward, away from Watankee, away from Manitowoc. I guessed that he wasn't going anywhere in particular. He was driving the countryside in widening loops, taking roads he hadn't taken before, just to end up somewhere he hadn't ever been.

Miss Swanson welcomed me with a little hug and pointed me to my desk, which was in the same place, with the same pens and pencils and crayons inside my plastic zippered pouch. Like a shrine, I thought, to the girl I was a month ago. It seemed that my classmates had been instructed not to say anything to me about Johnny or Stacy or missing girls or murderers. That was fine, except as the day wore on from the morning bell to the Pledge of Allegiance to the first recess, I realized that this meant that no one was going to say anything at all to me, period. Boys who used to tease me for being so small ignored me completely. Katie and Kari, who I used to sit with at lunch, linked arms and moved in the opposite direction when I approached. The other girls stopped talking when I came within earshot and resumed when I left. I felt like a hot potato—get too close for too long, and you might get burned.

Kevin Coulie passed me a note during our math lesson that said *I'm sorry.* He didn't need to say what he was sorry for; I understood he was sorry that I missed the spelling bee, that my brother was a murderer, that neither he nor any of my classmates was ever going to speak to me again.

When the bell for lunch rang, I lingered in the room until Miss Swanson said she needed to head up to the teacher's lounge. She smiled at me kindly, but I couldn't take anything at face value anymore. Maybe she was simply a good actress, too.

As soon as I rounded the corner onto the playground, my brown lunch bag clenched in my hand, I was swarmed with kids. "There she is!" someone called, and a few others took up the chant, "Kir-sten! Kir-sten!"

"What is it?" I asked, terrified. If their silence before had been painful, their enthusiasm for me now was simply alarming.

"Tetherball match!" someone yelled, and it was instantly echoed as a chant. "Teth-er-ball! Teth-er-ball!" I shook my head, looking around for Kevin or another friendly face in the group of twenty or so. I didn't see him, but every other kid in the fourth grade was there, even the ones who went to my church, even the ones who had invited me to their birthday parties.

"You have to!" another person yelled. "You don't have a choice!"

"No!" I yelled, but someone gave me a push from behind, and I found myself propelled forward onto the tetherball court, where Heather Lemke was waiting. She looked even bigger than the last time I'd seen her. Stacy had been slim, but Heather was muscular, her thick legs planted on the court like tree trunks. If I just focused on her face, though, she could have been a miniature Stacy. Curls of reddish hair escaped her braid, framing her face. She had more freckles and her eyes were farther apart, but she was undeniably Stacy's sister.

"Well, hello, Kirsten," she said, her voice icy and dangerous. If the yellow ball hadn't been strung to the pole, I think she might have clobbered me with it right off the bat. The crowd, after a few cries of "oooh," was suddenly quiet, not wanting to miss anything. Someone gave me another shove from behind, and I landed inside the half-circle of the tetherball court across from Heather. In the confusion, I dropped my brown lunch bag and looked over to see it trampled beneath the feet of some sixth grade boys.

"I don't want to fight," I said, and everyone laughed as if I'd said something hysterical. I strained my neck to look for the teacher on duty but couldn't see over my classmates' heads.

"It's not a fight, you dummy," Heather Lemke said. "It's a game."

"I don't want to play," I said, my heart smashing into the walls of my chest cavity like a billiard ball. "You know I'll lose."

"Are you chicken, Hammarstrom?" she asked, and the crowd took it up like a mantra: *"Bawk! Bawk!"*

Yes, I thought. As a matter of fact, I was a chicken. I knew that Heather Lemke was the biggest and toughest of the sixth graders; I'd seen her beat just about every boy in the school into submission on this very court. I remembered the way she'd galloped around the yard at Stacy's birthday party, with kids bouncing up and down on her back. I could barely carry my own backpack without tipping over.

"No," I said, my voice wavering with the obvious lie. "I'm not chicken. I just don't want to play."

"Bawk! Bawk!"

Heather snickered and tossed me the ball, lightly. I lunged forward, almost missing it. "I'll even let you start."

I'd read enough books and seen enough after-school specials to know that the underdog could sometimes be victorious, through courage or wits or some previously untapped source of superhuman strength—but the second that tetherball was in my hands, I knew it wouldn't be the case with me. I was short on courage, wits and strength. It wasn't going to be the sort of match my classmates remembered for years to come because I had pulled off some amazing feat. Standing in front of Heather Lemke, I felt like David confronting Goliath without even a slingshot at his side.

"Take your best shot," Heather sneered, crouching down into playing position.

I prayed right then for something to happen, like an earthquake or a tornado or a crack of lightning to split the sky in two. I prayed for a teacher to come, or my mother, or even Johnny, who could have lifted me onto his shoulder and carried me straight out to the parking lot. But nothing happened and no one came, and I had to throw the ball. *"Bawk! Bawk!"* someone clucked behind me. *I'm not a chicken,* I thought, my eyes narrowing. Heather, catching the expression on my face at that moment, opened her eyes wide in surprise. I wound my right arm back behind my head, gathered all my strength and let it fly.

The best part of what happened next was that I'd caught Heather Lemke slightly off guard, and she missed my first throw, which flew through the air with more height and speed than I would have thought possible, the ball just missing Heather's outstretched hand, the cord wrapping itself once around the pole. The crowd yelled, "Whoa!" as one. But the worst part was that the ball continued with too much height, so that I had to jump for my own throw, slapping the air with my hand as the ball whizzed by. Heather was ready this time, stopping the ball firmly in her hands.

With an easy lob, she reversed the direction of the ball and unwound the rope. I jumped for it and missed, and then jumped and missed again with her second throw. I willed myself to stay put, to not even try, but I couldn't resist reaching for the ball each time it passed. With each swipe and miss, the crowd cheered louder, the rope wrapping hopelessly tight around the pole out of my reach. Finally, she was left with one more throw.

"This one," Heather Lemke announced, in a voice I would remember forever, it was so full of rage and tears, "this one is for my sister."

And one final time the ball soared overhead, wrapping tightly against the pole until there was no rope left.

Heather Lemke held her arms to the sky as if she'd just won an Olympic medal. Our classmates swarmed her, pushing me to the outside of the circle now to give her hugs and high fives.

"Heath-er! Heath-er!" they chanted.

If she had been any smaller, they might have hoisted her onto their shoulders and taken a victory lap around our blacktop, but at this point one of the fifth-grade teachers wandered over, smiling curiously, and the crowd dispersed.

"Are you okay, honey?" the teacher asked, bending down to me. I hadn't realized that I was crying until then, but at the sound of her voice I felt the full shame of hot tears trickling down my face.

"No," I said, wiping away the tears. It was stupid to come back, to pretend that no one held anything against me. I was guilty just because I was Kirsten Hammarstrom, and my brother was Johnny Hammarstrom, and his girlfriend had been Stacy Lemke. If my life was an after-school special, I would turn the other cheek and keep coming back, day after day, until I convinced my classmates that I was the same Kirsten Hammarstrom I had been and would always be, despite the circumstances. But life wasn't a television show, and no screenwriter was going to be able to write me the courage and the smooth dialogue I would need to make it through the rest of fourth grade.

"No," I repeated loudly. "I want to go home."

thirty-two

"Was someone mean to you?" Mom asked that night as we sat on my bed, smoothing my hair back from my forehead. I'd spent the entire afternoon there, refusing to get up for dinner. "Did someone say something?"

I shook my head miserably. It wasn't *someone* who was mean; it wasn't just *anyone* who had said something. I couldn't bring myself to tell her about Heather Lemke and the tetherball match.

Instead I asked, "Do I have to go back? Maybe I could just start fifth grade this fall."

Mom sighed. "Honey..."

"I'm not going back, either," Emilie announced from the doorway. She had made it through the whole day at Lincoln High School but afterward collapsed on the couch with an afghan, refusing to talk to anyone. I remembered the phone calls Emilie used to make each night, the giddy weekend sleepovers with her friends. Maybe it had been even worse for her than a humiliating tetherball match.

"Emilie," Mom scolded. "It was only the first day back...."

"My last day back," Emilie said firmly, crossing her thin arms over her chest.

"It can't be that bad," Mom said, but the end of her words rose up in a question. "Is it that bad?" She looked from Emilie to me. My tears, which had dried by the time Dad had picked me up from the school office, started again under her scrutiny.

"Mom," Emilie said. "You don't get it. It's not just Johnny that they hate. It's us, too."

There was a long silence. I leaned against Mom's chest, pushing my head beneath her chin. Everything felt different all of a sudden. We were the same people, in the same house, in the same small town, but I could tell that we didn't belong anymore. The place that I'd always felt was reserved for me—the little corner of the universe where I had lived every minute of my life—had disappeared. Maybe it had vanished right along with Stacy Lemke, and I was only now noticing it.

"Okay, then," Mom said softly, wiping my tears with her index fingers. Her own eyes were moist and red-rimmed. "We'll see."

After Mom left, I rolled over on the bed to face Emilie. She had reached into the drawer of her nightstand and was now applying purple polish to her toes with fierce concentration. "Thanks," I whispered.

Emilie scowled. "What are you thanking me for? I just made it possible for you to be a fourth-grade drop-out. At least I made it all the way to ninth grade."

It might have been the first time I'd laughed in weeks.

That year, the snow lingered late, still falling off and on into April, when it was followed by blustery days of wind and rain. Dad and Jerry talked about planting, about the price of corn per bushel. It was the first hint that life might go on, that the cycle of birth and death and renewal was about to begin all over again. Stacy Lemke was only a tiny glitch in the overall rotation of the world.

We settled into a new routine: Dad worked in the barn or visited Grandpa in the rehab center; Mom picked up extra hours, arriving home late at night to flop onto the couch in her scrubs. Johnny's truck peeled out of the driveway after the first milking, and Emilie and I sighed with relief. Mostly, on lonely afternoons, we found ourselves in front of the television, drawn to it like mosquitoes to fresh blood. We watched reruns of *The Cosby Show* and *The Brady Bunch* and new episodes of *Boy Meets World*. Emilie held every strand of her hair up to the light, checking for split ends. I finished the books in my Nancy Drew collection and started them again from the beginning.

The investigation had tapered off, due to a lack of *credible evidence,* but Stacy was still everywhere, her picture plastered to public surfaces. Volunteers had diligently posted signs that stretched throughout the countryside, papering every telephone pole. There was even a sign at the end of our driveway, put there on purpose, I was sure, by the Lemkes themselves or one of their friends, someone who wanted to make sure we didn't forget. Every day when I walked down the driveway to check our mail, Stacy's black-and-white face stared back at me. I made it part of my daily ritual to touch the palm of my hand to her grainy gray cheek, as if I was offering her a blessing or checking for fever.

Candlelight vigils for Stacy continued outside Lincoln High School, attended by nearly a hundred people each weekend. The news stations ran short videos of Stacy's friends—girls with tear-stained, rosy cheeks and tapered candles clenched in their fists. Someone had printed a giant banner that served as a backdrop to these events: *STACY LYNNE LEMKE, LAST SEEN MARCH 4, 1995.*

I desperately wanted to go, to light a candle for Stacy, to say a prayer—but it was unthinkable. I imagined the good people of Watankee, the people I'd known for my entire life, the people who'd known my parents before I was even born, chasing me away from the vigil with pitchforks. This was the sort of thing I'd begun to dream when I fell asleep—of a pack of armed men charging through our back door, taking over our house room by room, while I listened, terrified, from my bathroom hideout, of waking to find that every inch of my bedroom wall had been covered by hideous graffiti.

"We can't keep up like this," Mom said, a daily mantra. "We can't just be hermits for the rest of our lives."

But that didn't seem fair—she herself spent every waking moment at the hospital, clocking in early, clocking out late. It wasn't exactly clear where she expected us to go, anyway—back to our pew in church, under the watchful eyes of Mrs. Keithley and Sandy Maertz? To birthday parties at the homes of our former friends, who barely acknowledged our existence?

If Stacy was everywhere, then Johnny was nowhere, as if he were the one who was missing. He continued the lonely drives in his beat-up truck, often missing dinner, never calling to report when he'd be home. We set a place at the table for him as if everything was normal and left it out for him, for whenever he returned. All night we kept an ear cocked for the sound of Johnny's truck coming down the driveway. We listened, braced for his boots on the back steps. We were ready for his icy silences, the sudden, angry way he now had of dismissing everyone.

Once Aunt Julia reported that she'd seen Johnny in a café in Two Rivers, between Manitowoc and Green Bay, and another time Uncle Paul passed his truck outside Port Washington, nearly an hour and a half away. Dad shared this with us at yet another meal where Johnny was missing in action.

"I don't understand," Mom said. "What does he do out there? Where does he go?"

Dad shrugged. "He's just getting away. I don't really think he does anything."

Mom scraped a helping of leftovers from dinner into the bowl by the door, which I would later bring out to Kennel. "Well, isn't that nice," she said, facing out the window to where RR4 gently unfolded for miles to the north. "How *nice* for him that he just gets to go away whenever he wants, while the rest of us are stuck—" She stopped short, and I wondered how she meant to finish the sentence. Stuck in this stupid little town? Stuck here with each other?

One night, only halfway through Mom's ham-and-Swiss bowtie pasta casserole, Johnny's truck pulled into the driveway. Mom raised an eyebrow dramatically. Dad ignored her, focusing instead on the tiny black-and-white TV he'd borrowed from Grandpa's house and hooked up in our kitchen. Most nights during dinner he found something to watch on TV with the volume down low, so he only had to half listen to our conversation.

"Well, look who's here," Mom said. "Have a seat, Johnny."

Dad's eyes flickered briefly from the television to Johnny and then, pointedly, to his empty chair. Johnny slumped into his seat, grunting thanks when Mom gave him two giant scoops of pasta and I passed the milk. I watched as he ate and ate, bringing silent spoonfuls to his mouth, the days of cutting weight behind him for good. His body looked healthier than it had in months. This was a weird contrast with his eyes, which were dead in his face.

Mom folded her arms across her chest and cleared her throat. "Well, as long as we have you here, Johnny, your father and I are wondering if you've made any plans for next year."

Johnny let out a hollow sound, half a laugh. "Now that I'm no longer going to college on a wrestling scholarship, you mean?"

I watched Mom's face. Her lips had tightened into a thin line, and she seemed to be chewing her lower lip with her upper teeth, as if she were holding in her words.

Dad said, "All right, Johnny," without glancing up.

Johnny took a bite of casserole and reloaded his fork.

"There are other things you can do. If you want, we can help you start looking for a job."

"I know," Johnny said, fork halfway to his mouth. "I hear there's an opening for the position of town asshole."

Mom stiffened.

"Watch your language," Dad scolded.

"You know, Mom, maybe it would be better if you just said it." Johnny took a bite, chewed, swallowed and opened his mouth in a deliberate smack of satisfaction.

"I don't know what you mean," Mom said, working the edge of her placemat with nervous fingers. We had all stopped eating by now, Emilie and I carefully watching the others as if we were minor actors in the drama, left out of the script.

"I want to hear it. I want you to say it."

"Johnny, you just simmer down," Dad said, glancing back at the TV. I followed his eyes—it was a commercial for dish detergent.

"I don't know what you want to hear, Johnny. I'm not saying anything." Mom stabbed a hunk of ham with her fork, then swished it through a mound of cream sauce.

"Fine." Johnny slammed down his fork and stood up. A few drops of white sauce splattered against the blue tablecloth. "Fine. I'll say it. I'm the screwup son no one wants to talk to, the brother no one wants to acknowledge. I don't need to apply for the position—I'm already the town asshole. I get it. Believe me, I get it. So, what do you want from me, then? You want me to confess to something—"

I had this funny feeling in the back of my throat, as if something was caught there. Yes, I thought. *Confess.* Come clean, cough it up, make things right.

"Sit down," Mom ordered.

"Really, you think I should sit down? Should I finish my casserole? Should I eat my peas and carrots, too? Should I just be the good boy while you all stare at me like I'm some kind of killer?"

"Maybe you should have thought of that before," Emilie muttered. Our heads all snapped in her direction. "I mean, before you decided to ruin all our lives."

"Emilie! That's enough out of you," Dad threatened, his face suddenly red. "Down," he repeated to Johnny. "Sit down now."

Johnny half obeyed, leaning backward into his chair, one leg folded beneath him as if ready again to pounce.

No one said anything for a long time. The theme song for *Jeopardy* began faintly in the background. In our previous lives, Mom would have snapped off the TV, forcing us into conversation. But now, the distraction was a relief. Maybe when it came down to it, no one really wanted to know what Johnny had to say. Maybe we didn't want to know the truth. Instead, we all strained to hear Alex Trebek introduce the contestants, their accomplishments, their weird obsessions.

Without warning, Johnny stood again. We all watched him, even Dad, our mouths open. This was further than any of us had ever gone in defiance. Even Emilie, who toed every boundary, would have backed down at this point.

"I can't do this anymore," he said.

What did he mean: Eat dinner? Talk to the people who had known him for his entire life?

Dad stood, too, but Johnny was faster. He was out the door in a second, digging in his pocket for his keys. We heard the whine of the ignition and then the catch. Dad sat back down, and I was still gripping my fork when Johnny's truck roared by. Although they'd worked on it a few times, Johnny hadn't had anything professionally fixed. One headlight flashed across the window, and the other pointed slightly upward, as if it was searching the stars.

thirty-three

On the most humid Memorial Day any of us could remember, we celebrated Johnny's eighteenth birthday with a barbecue at Aunt Julia and Uncle Paul's. Johnny had been more or less absent since his blowup, and it looked as if he might bolt from this gathering, too. We ate bratwurst and potato salad and a lemon cake I had helped to frost, licking my fingers carefully in between swoops of the knife. Emilie conducted our pitiful performance of "Happy Birthday" with a fork in one hand and a flyswatter in the other. Stacy had been missing for nearly three months, and we were all trying way too hard to be happy.

Johnny blew out eighteen candles in a single breath—no girlfriends. After the cake, there was a stack of carefully chosen gifts—T-shirts, blue jeans, a pair of boots. I couldn't help thinking how his eighteenth birthday party should have been, with Stacy sitting on his lap, sneaking a kiss at every opportunity, and his friends stopping by, slipping some alcohol into the punch. Now we were the only people in the world who loved Johnny Hammarstrom—and that love was tinged by a thousand doubts.

Afterward, Emilie and I changed into our swimsuits while the adults—Johnny now legally one of them—lounged in chairs on the deck. It was already past dusk, the sky tinkling with the lights of hundreds of fireflies. Aunt Julia lit a cigarette over Uncle Paul's protests.

"Please," she said, twin lines of smoke dribbling out of her nostrils. "I'm quitting again tomorrow. I'm just finishing this pack."

"Sure you are," Mom said, winking at me.

I floated on my back, watching stars appear in the sky.

"Mosquitoes," Emilie announced suddenly. Despite about a gallon of bug spray, they had begun to appear, hovering over the water like tiny, buzzing vultures.

"It's because you're so sweet," Aunt Julia said. "See? They don't even bother with an old woman like me."

In just a few minutes the sky went from indigo to black, each star glowing more and more visible above us. I knew that you could take a picture of the night sky, and it would look tiny and silly in your hand, just a black canvas with a few tiny white dots. But lying beneath it, the sky seemed immense, powerful and protective. Lying beneath it, it was easy to forget that anything bad had ever happened to anyone. I could almost make myself believe that nothing bad would ever happen again.

And then Johnny sat up in his deck chair, looking around. "What was that?"

I flipped right-side up in the pool and made a few clumsy strokes toward the edge.

"Quiet!" Johnny ordered, and I froze. Straining, I heard a low rumbling sound, not far away.

Uncle Paul took a long swig and set down his Budweiser. "Sounds like a car stopping out in front."

"Shouldn't be anyone out there," Johnny said, getting to his feet.

Although we'd only come from down the road, we'd taken two cars—Dad, Mom, Emilie and me in the Caprice, with me carefully balancing the cake plate on my lap, and Johnny just behind us in his truck. It was understood that he would want to leave early, to go off by himself.

Johnny was already around the side of the house, in front of Dad and Uncle Paul, by the time I hoisted my body out of the pool and ran dripping behind them. I heard Johnny yell something and suddenly, shattering the night, some loud popping sounds, staccato and uneven. Mom was ahead of me, too—she held out both hands to stop Emilie and me from running past.

"Oh, my God, they've shot him!" Aunt Julia rasped, bringing up the rear, and that's what I thought, too—that someone had shot Johnny dead, at point-blank range, maybe a dozen times.

But I could still hear Johnny yelling, joined by Dad and Uncle Paul and a chorus of other voices, and I broke free from Mom's grasp and ran barefoot through a planting bed to end up on the front lawn. Water from my swimsuit dripped down my legs.

There were two pickup trucks in the road, just pulling away when I arrived, and each truck had a half-dozen people in the back. Mostly boys, but girls, too—kids about Johnny's age. One girl was standing in the bed, and for some reason it was her voice I heard the loudest. "We know what you did, you murderer!" she screamed, her otherwise pretty face twisted in anger, her blond curls shaking with indignation. "We're never going to forget!"

Somehow it was even more terrifying that I didn't know her, that she was essentially a stranger, bearing this massive weight of righteous anger against my brother, as if she was angry not just for Stacy, and not just for the Lemkes, but on behalf of everyone in the whole community. Dad ran toward the truck, and someone yelled, "Let's get out of here!" The blonde girl was nearly thrown off balance with the forward motion of the pickup truck as it pulled back onto Rural Route 4, but she steadied herself with one hand against someone else's shoulder. Even when the taillights disappeared over a little ridge in the road, I could still hear her voice: "Murderer!"

Then I saw that they hadn't been armed with guns, but with eggs—dozens of cracked shells had been pelted against the side of Johnny's truck, and at least one had struck him in the chest.

"I'm calling the police," Uncle Paul said, heading into the house. "They can't just ride around the county terrorizing people."

"It's only some eggs," Dad said. He had come around the side of the house pretty fast and was breathing hard now, long deep breaths with his hands on his knees. "I thought we were done with all this by now. It's been pretty quiet for the past month."

Johnny was staring at his truck, and all at once we seemed to notice that it was parked a little funny, as if it was on an incline. Except that it wasn't—the driveway was completely level where it met with the road.

Emilie pointed. "Look at your tires!"

The two tires facing the road were flat, slit all the

way across in thick, gaping wounds. Dad stepped up for a closer look. Circling the back of the truck, he said, "Aw, shit."

The paint on Johnny's truck had long been peeling anyway, so that we called it the Green Machine more from a sense of nostalgia than anything else. Now with the dented passenger side and front fender, it looked more like a wreck on wheels. But from Dad's tone, I knew something else was wrong. We circled behind him silently and read the white paint across the tailgate: *Murder Machine.*

Mom gasped.

Uncle Paul said, "You don't think I should call the police now?"

In the midst of our seething, another sound, strangely high-pitched, broke into my consciousness. It was a sound I hadn't heard before—a shrill, almost screeching cry. We all turned to it at once, more frightened by this noise than the cracking of eggs against metal or the enraged screams of kids in the back of a pickup. It was Johnny.

He had sunk to his knees on the pavement and was leaning forward, his head between his hands. I had seen him cry off and on when Stacy had first gone missing, a few, intermittent tears of frustration and exhaustion and helplessness, but nothing like this. He'd been bottling up his feelings for months, and they came now in a heady rush. Dad stepped forward, putting a hand on his shoulder, but Johnny shook it loose. His cries rose first from his throat and then from his chest, in deep, guttural heaves, as if he was expelling something trapped deep inside him, like his heart.

thirty-four

Two days later, Johnny packed his belongings into one of his old wrestling duffel bags and left Watankee. Dad had given him a ride to the bus station in Manitowoc and also slipped him $1,753 from our savings account, which just about wiped us out. In return, Johnny left us a note on a half sheet of binder paper. He didn't know where he was going, or what he would do when he got there. He only knew he couldn't stay in Watankee anymore, and that it would be better for all of us if he left. He signed it: Johnny.

Detective Halliday, somehow getting wind of this news, stopped by our house to remind us that Johnny had been asked not to leave the jurisdiction, to make himself available for any questioning that might arise. "You're kidding, right?" Mom asked, although she'd been furious, too, discovering what Dad had done—both the ride to the bus stop early in the morning and the cash. "Maybe he should just roll over at your feet, so you could give him a good kick from time to time. Would you like that?"

Dad assured Detective Halliday that Johnny was

going to be in touch with us, that he would make himself available to the police if needed. Detective Halliday reminded Dad that if Johnny didn't make himself available, a warrant could be issued for his arrest.

That first night without Johnny, I lay in bed feeling the tension releasing from my body, the slow unspooling of something that had been tightly wound within me. Guilt? I had been, in my way, responsible for getting the two of them together. Fear? I hadn't been personally scared of Johnny, but there was the fear of the unknown things he'd done. For the first time in months, I fell into a solid, dreamless sleep.

In the morning, Jerry helped Dad tow the Green Machine to our property, where it sat behind our barn, out of view. Dad thought he might fix it up—but with its list of injuries, this was a daunting task. Maybe after the harvest this fall, he said. Maybe when… But his voice trailed off. Maybe when things settled down? Maybe when Johnny returned? Maybe when Grandpa came home from rehab? It might have been as difficult for him as for me to imagine our futures. It was as if the life cycle of the Hammarstroms had somehow stalled, midrotation.

Of all of us, Dad must have missed Johnny the most. He started spending entire evenings in the barn, making the sorts of repairs he'd been talking about for years. Jerry joined him there, moving seamlessly into the role that had long been occupied by Johnny. Some evenings, when a cooling breeze came through, they opened the hatch on the hayloft and spent hours perched there, barely talking.

Mom seemed to withdraw, too. On her days off, she barricaded herself in the kitchen, speaking in hushed tones on the phone so that I couldn't hear. She worked longer and longer hours at the hospital, sometimes coming home after I went to bed. More and more often, I came downstairs in the morning to find her stretched out on the living room couch. "Couldn't sleep," she mumbled when I questioned her.

With both of our parents conveniently distracted, Emilie had started sleeping until noon, and no one cared enough to wake her up. My mere presence irritated her; if I entered the room, she sighed dramatically, turning to the wall. Once, I picked up a pillow and threw it at the back of her head, hard as I could. She rolled over, startled. "I'm miserable, too, you know!" I screamed.

Only last summer, I thought, there had been five of us in this house, and Grandpa next door, and Stacy living with her parents just down the road. I wished I could take some kind of pill that would send me back in time. When Stacy Lemke asked me if I was Johnny Hammarstrom's sister, I would say, "No. You've got the wrong girl."

In the last week of school, the newspaper ran pictures of Johnny's graduating classmates—the boys in tuxedos and the girls in black drapes with pearls around their necks. I looked for Johnny's picture, but there was no gap between Aneissa Gunner and Donald Hancock. It was as if Johnny Hammarstrom had never existed. As if he had vanished, too.

Johnny sent the occasional postcard—from Illinois, then Ohio, then Tennessee. They always said the same thing, as if he were following a template. He was fine, no need for anyone to worry, he would write or call soon. There was never a return address, maybe because he wasn't staying in one place long enough. Or maybe because he didn't want to hear back from us.

At the end of June, Mom sat down with Emilie and me at the kitchen table, while Dad leaned against the stove in the corner. I knew something big was coming. I had known it, I realized at that moment, for weeks.

Mom's tone was serious and slightly defensive from the beginning. "Your father and I have been talking, and since things have been so difficult for all of us around here, we think it might be best if we made some new arrangements. There's a hospital in Kenosha looking for an emergency room nurse, and I think I'd like to try that, for a little while."

"What does that mean?" Emilie demanded.

"Well, Dad will stay here at the farm," Mom said, with a slight nod in Dad's direction, as if he needed to be identified for us. He stood with his hands braced on the countertop behind him, not meeting our eyes.

"You're leaving us?" I squeaked. This wasn't how it happened on television—there had been no thrown plates or threats of divorce. But looking back and forth between them right then, I knew that it was over for my parents.

Mom took a deep breath. "You can decide if you want to come with me, or if you want to stay here with your dad. Either way is fine, and we won't be that far apart, so we can all still see each other regularly."

"But if we went with you, we would go to school in Kenosha," Emilie clarified. "I mean, we would be living there and everything."

Mom smiled gently. "That's right."

I looked from Mom to Dad and back again.

"I'll go. I'm sick of Watankee as it is," Emilie said.

"You don't have to decide this minute—"

"I've made up my mind."

"Okay," Mom said carefully.

Everyone looked at me next, waiting. My head felt light and empty suddenly, and I had to close my eyes to see things clearly. My whole life seemed to be swirling around behind my eyelids—mornings in the barn with Dad, letting the calves suck my fingers, luring the half-wild cats to me with a handful of dry food, untangling Kennel's fur with my fingers, walking down the road to Aunt Julia's with a clump of Queen Anne's lace in my hand, riding the bus, stopping by the library on Saturday mornings while Mom ran errands, sitting stiffly in our pew on Sundays. But that was in the past, I knew. Somehow when Stacy went missing, every bit of that changed for me. Since then, I had only been going through the motions of life.

"I want to go with you, too," I said to Mom, and then I set my head down on the table and cried. I couldn't look at Dad again, couldn't bear to see if he was looking at me.

Mom rubbed her hand along the ridge of my spine. Dad, saying nothing, pushed the screen door open quietly and stepped out onto the porch.

thirty-five

October 2011

The close encounter with the Highway Patrol officer had rattled me; I waited for his car to pull off the shoulder and disappear into the night before easing onto the road behind him. The entire experience of being here was surreal, like Dorothy falling asleep in Kansas and waking in Oz. I'd been walking past the crumbling remains on Observatory Hill, heading into class in McCone Hall, when I'd gotten the call from Aunt Julia. And now, only fourteen hours later, I was in a rented car heading north to Watankee, Wisconsin.

There had been no mistaking Aunt Julia's voice, although it was raspier now, with large, wheezy pauses between her words. She was sorry to have to be the one to tell me, she said, and I'd fought my way through a throng of students to lean against a wall, trying to focus on her words.

"Who?" I'd asked, already knowing and dreading the answer.

"He had a heart attack," she'd answered softly. "It was very sudden."

The news had sent me into a flurry of activity—contacting the dean, cancelling class for the week, packing, leaving a note for my roommate to please feed my cat. Stunned, I'd sniffed back a few tears on the plane, overwhelmed by the impersonal nature of flying, the forced solicitousness of the flight attendants, the close quarters of the strangers who were my seatmates. Even when the plane had landed, I'd been all business—listening to voice mail messages from Mom and Emilie, retrieving my suitcase from the baggage claim turnstile, finding my way to the Hertz counter. Now, at last, I gave into the sheer, overwhelming fact of it, sobbing into a handful of scratchy napkins and trying to see the road through my tears.

Dad.

I had talked to him only the week before, one of our quick, just-to-touch-base conversations about the farm, about school. "Maybe this year you'll come out for Christmas," he had suggested, and I had pretended to consider the possibility. I didn't say that I was already making other plans with my professors and a few fellow graduate students who stayed local during school breaks.

I hadn't lived in Watankee since the summer of our move, although Mom had taken us back to visit on three-day weekends and school holidays. I would spend weeks preparing for all the things I would tell Dad, all the papers and progress reports I would show him. But each time, something odd had happened on the trip back to Watankee, as if a filmmaker had inserted a giant lens into the camera, turning the world from hopeful to gloomy. By the time I spilled out of the station wagon and greeted Dad and Kennel with giant hugs, I was already anxious to leave. Watankee was equal parts homecoming and heartbreak, comfort and calamity. After the initial excitement, our conversations dwindled to long silences. We exhausted, too soon, everything we had to say.

Mom and Dad had never divorced—never even discussed it, as far as I could tell. They had just gone their separate ways, which for Mom meant moves around the Midwest to bigger, newer hospitals. Dad had come to visit us a few times—to my high school graduation in 2004 and my college graduation from the University of Indiana in 2008. He'd looked out of place and uncomfortable—exactly as I would have looked back home, in Watankee.

Sometimes I wondered how Dad had handled it alone, all those years. What would it have been like to be John Hammarstrom in Watankee, Wisconsin, when Johnny Hammarstrom was the unofficial suspect in an unofficial crime? We'd left Dad alone with the fallout from Stacy's disappearance.

Even now, approaching Watankee, I could feel Stacy all around me. Not her presence—not the red hair and freckles, or the ghost of her teenage body. I'd spent years looking for her, in shopping malls, in airport queues, in the raucous crowd behind Dick Clark in Times Square. It was illogical, I knew. Even if she was somehow alive, Stacy Lemke was no longer a teenage girl behind the wheel of a red Camaro. She was no longer the girl who sat in the bleachers, chanting my brother's name.

What I felt now, like a punch to the chest, was her absence. Watankee was the place where Stacy had once lived, breathed, flirted with her boyfriend, vanished without saying goodbye.

I slowed instinctively when I reached the exit for Watankee, as if it could be avoided for just a few minutes longer, as if somehow the entire trip could be prevented by not taking the correct exit. I wasn't just going home to say goodbye to Dad, who I had been saying goodbye to for years. I was going to have to reconnect with the past, with the nine-year-old girl I had been, the girl who was holding her breath, fearing discovery in her hiding spot, the girl who had been sick in the bathroom the night Stacy Lemke had gone missing.

It wasn't far now; my mind knew exactly where to go. Watankee was basically the same small town, but its differences were glaring to me. It was like visiting a *Twilight Zone* version of the world. When I was nine years old, we had literally known every car on the road. Dad could point to any farm and tell you who owned it, how long he had been on the land, how many cows he milked, how the harvest was coming along. Now everything was both too modern and unfamiliar; the SUVs parked in driveways, the IGA that had replaced Gaub's Meats, once boasting to be "Butcher to the World."

The harvest was under way, and my headlights illuminated the razed crops, the dregs of stalks that still waved spookily in the slight breeze. Something clutched in my chest, and I slowed when I passed the spot on Passaqua Road. Part of me had always been a nine-year-old girl, even when I was ten and thirteen and eighteen and twenty-four. Part of me was stuck in 1995, like a stubborn coat hanger tangled on a rack. One shoe had dropped on a snowy night sixteen years ago; ever since then, I had been waiting for the corresponding thud.

thirty-six

Aunt Julia practically threw open her door at my tentative knock, causing me to gasp. In shadow she looked the same as always—tiny, wiry, her hair dyed a dark, Jackie-O brown. Her eyes were red, shadowed by puffy pouches that told me she'd been crying. When she stepped onto the porch to give me a fierce hug, I caught a glint of light off her oxygen tube, which trailed from her nose down to a portable tank at her feet on two tiny wheels. I started sniffling the second I was in her arms.

"Now, hush," she wheezed. "Let's not have any crying tonight. Your Uncle Paul's been asleep since seven-thirty, and you just missed your mom. She'd been driving all day and I sent her to bed only half an hour ago. She's—well, I guess I don't need to tell you, but she's pretty much a wreck."

I followed her inside, wheeling my suitcase behind me. "I'll just wait until morning," I said, grateful for a few hours of relative peace before the next emotional onslaught. "What about Emilie?"

"She had a show tonight, so they're going to take the first flight out of Vegas tomorrow morning." She switched on lights as I followed behind her, carefully avoiding the oxygen tank. Aunt Julia had always had her finger on what was current—the result, no doubt, of the dozen magazines she subscribed to each year. Her house was a curious mix of old and new—travertine tile floors, a low brown leather sofa, a massive oak buffet. She led me down a short set of steps to the den.

"I put you on the pullout bed for tonight. Is that okay?"

"That's fine, thanks." I was so exhausted I could have slept in the driver's seat of the Malibu, reclined at a forty-five degree angle.

"When Emilie gets here, we'll have to figure out some other arrangements, I guess." She switched on the lamp next to the sofa. The bed was already pulled out, made up with a set of white sheets. She pointed toward a folded blanket and quilt. "In case you get cool down here."

"We could share, though. That's no bother." I hadn't slept in a bed with my mother since—well, since ever, but it wasn't a problem.

"Okay, then," Aunt Julia said, stepping back, hands on her skinny hips.

"What about…" I hesitated. It felt so strange to say his name, like claiming something that didn't belong to me.

"Your brother? I don't know. I left a message on his machine, though I can't imagine getting a message like that."

I considered this soberly. Thank God I'd had my phone on, heading to class. "So he's still in Texas."

"Last I heard."

"I wonder if he'll come." I plopped my suitcase onto the end of the pullout bed and tugged at the zipper.

"Course he'll come," Aunt Julia said, the sharpness of her voice causing me to look up. "He was close to your dad. Called a couple times a week."

She didn't say: *not like you. Not like your halfhearted monthly calls with the gaping silences.*

"I didn't realize," I said, which was true. When I'd talked to Dad, he'd rarely mentioned Johnny. Mom only spoke to him occasionally, on birthdays and holidays. He'd sent me a card for my college graduation, one of those schmaltzy cards with a long, preprinted message that implied he'd always known I would succeed, blah, blah, and signed it simply: Johnny. There had been a return address for Lubbock, Texas, but when I'd replied months later, it had come back marked Return to Sender.

"I'm sorry," I said, because in the yellowish glow of lamplight, I saw that Aunt Julia was crying. For a moment I worried I'd offended her somehow, and then I saw that she wasn't expressing a complicated, tangled sort of grief, the way I was. Hers was as uncomplicated as it comes: the plain, simple grief of someone who has lost her brother. A grief that I had never been able to summon for Johnny. I clasped her to me, feeling the sharp edges of her clavicles beneath her sweater, the prominent bones of her rib cage. "Oh, Aunt Julia. I'm so, so sorry. You were such a good sister to him, all these years."

She pulled back after a moment, the toughness of her voice contrasting with her tears. "All right, enough of that. What are we going to do, cry ourselves completely out on the first night?"

I swallowed, summoning a wobbly half smile.

"So, look, it's way past my bedtime, and I definitely need some beauty rest. There are towels in the downstairs bath, some juice and soda in the fridge, and the good stuff in the cabinet above the fridge. Nothing fancy, but—"

I wiped my eyes on my shirtsleeve. "Are you kidding me? It's the Watankee Hilton."

When she gave me a dry peck on the cheek, I caught a whiff of smoke. Some things never changed.

Left alone, I wriggled out of my clothes, pulled on an oversize T-shirt and slid between the cool sheets. My body sank into the mattress, but my mind was still going strong. After years of living in cramped dorm rooms and apartments clogged with secondhand furniture and books, the vastness of Aunt Julia's den was unsettling. The refrigerator kicked on, ran hard and suddenly clicked off. At one point there were steps walking overhead, a flush and steps walking back. The house creaked, adjusting itself. Suddenly I thought of Grandpa, who used to stand on the front lawn in the evenings, listening to the corn grow. I'd stood beside him, listening impatiently, unable to tell if he was kidding or serious, if he had a farmer's sixth sense. He had never fully recovered after his hip injury; in the rehab center, there had been a bout of pneumonia and weakened lungs, and it had seemed safer to move him into an assisted-living facility. That was probably what had killed him in the end, around the time I entered junior high—not being near the land, not hearing the corn grow.

Looking back on the kid I'd been, it didn't surprise me that I never heard what Grandpa heard. I was too distracted by the blowing of a gentle breeze through the oak trees, a bee buzzing nearby, or the low rumble of a tanker truck heading down Passaqua Road. I couldn't have separated the sound of corn growing from the steady beat of my own heart, the slow thrum of pulse through my veins.

"I'm back in Watankee," I whispered, pinching myself on the thigh. *Mom is upstairs. Emilie will be here tomorrow. And maybe, maybe... Johnny.* I felt a tiny twinge of something—anticipation, hope?

But Dad—

Dad would still be dead.

And, of course, Stacy Lemke would still be missing.

thirty-seven

I woke to a hand rubbing my back, and rolled over to see that Mom had crawled into bed next to me. Sunlight from the mini-blinds landed on her face in parallel beams. Her face was puffy from crying, but she was composed. She was already dressed in jeans, a sweater and tennis shoes.

I threw my right arm around her in a half hug. "What time is it?"

"About ten. I was going to let you sleep in longer, but pretty soon I've got to head into town to deal with some things at the funeral home. I didn't want to miss you."

I struggled into a sitting position. "I'll come, too. Just let me shower and grab some toast or something."

"There's no need for you to come."

"And there's no need for you to deal with everything alone."

She sighed. "You're stubborn as your father, that's for sure."

I grinned. "And here I always thought I took after you, that you were the stubborn one."

Half an hour later, we were buckled into my rental

car, and I was finishing the last bites of a massive blueberry muffin foisted on me by Aunt Julia.

"You know, you can't drive like you do in California," Mom reminded me. "None of those rolling stops."

"Or what? The traffic cameras at each intersection are going to catch me?" I teased, backing out of the driveway. It hit me then, what I'd been too tired to realize last night. The last time we'd all been together, it had been here, at Johnny's eighteenth birthday party, a million years ago. One minute the biggest danger had seemed to come from hordes of mosquitoes hovering above the water, and in the next minute, we'd been running around the side of the house to see what all the commotion was. The dozens of thrown eggs, the Murder Machine.

We drove slowly, since there was no one behind us on the road, and despite Mom's appointment in town, no hurry to get where we were going. I slowed where the horse pasture had been, now home to a circular driveway and a four-stall garage.

"New neighbors," Mom commented. "I think the Wegners moved down to Arizona to be closer to their grandchildren."

I stopped at the end of our driveway, next to the mailbox marked *Hammarstrom, J.*

Just seeing Dad's name sucked the wind out of me. And then seeing the house—it was as if my heart was a deflating balloon, careening in my chest cavity. At first glance, everything was the same—the fields, the barn, the silo, the long, low cattle pens, the two houses, the trees lining the driveway. At second glance, everything had changed—the barn a faded red, the house a crisper white. Grandpa's house, empty all these years, had its windows shuttered, with leaves and small twigs littering its porch.

"What about the cows?" I asked, the only question I seemed to be able to form. "Is someone taking care of them?"

"Jerry's been milking them. He said he'd help out in the short term."

I faced her. "Jerry Warczak?"

"Of course. Who else?"

"I don't know. I guess I figured… I don't know."

Mom blew her nose into a Kleenex. "We'll have to come back here later, start sorting through things."

"What's going to happen to everything—the house, the animals?"

"I guess we'll talk about all of that this weekend. There are a lot of decisions to make."

"But you won't be—?"

"Me? Moving back here?" Mom's laugh was genuine, and it was a relief, the first funny thing to break through our sorrow.

"I guess that wouldn't happen."

"No. It definitely wouldn't happen."

At the funeral home, the director informed us that Dad had already made all the arrangements, five years back. He'd picked out and paid for his coffin, his plot, his simple gray tombstone next to Grandpa and Grandma. His thoughtfulness, the quiet, uncomplaining care he'd taken, broke my heart more than anything else. Dad had known he would die alone, his wife and children scattered around the country. He'd wanted to make everything easy for us, so all we'd have to do was sign on the bottom line.

"He didn't want a visitation," the director said, showing us a note in Dad's handwriting taken from his file. "Nothing formal, at least. Just for family. As for the service, he wanted it to be graveside only."

"No fuss," Mom said softly.

"Simple," he agreed. "Your sister-in-law thought that Saturday would be fine."

Mom nodded. It was Thursday.

We had lunch in town at Sprouts, a sandwich shop that hadn't existed when we'd lived in Watankee. It surprised me that it existed here at all—the menu seemed more suited to Berkeley than a sleepy town in Wisconsin. I had an eggplant sandwich with roasted peppers and Fontina; Mom had a bowl of butternut squash soup. We didn't know the cashier or the waitress; they didn't know us. A few of the patrons stared at us curiously, but more because we were strangers than because they recognized us. Even so, I half expected to find a flat tire when we returned to my rented Malibu.

Aunt Julia, Mom and I dithered over Dad's obituary that afternoon, while Uncle Paul dozed in a recliner in front of FOX News. Aunt Julia had bought a white half sheet cake from the bakery, and we ate it with plastic forks off paper plates, making small heaps of too-sweet frosting. It was the sort of cake people purchased for baby showers and birthdays and graduations and decorated with bright lettering and balloons. Ours was plain, just a blank white canvas. It wasn't clear, exactly, what we were celebrating.

It was a relief to spot Emilie in late afternoon, pulling her rental car into Aunt Julia's driveway. I would have known her anywhere, despite the spiky black hair with blue highlights and her arching silver eye shadow. "Kiddo," she said, unfolding her lanky legs from the driver's seat. I punched her on the arm.

Darby climbed out of the passenger seat, stretching. At twelve years old, she was the spitting image of no one I knew—not Emilie or any other Hammarstrom.

She was tall and dark; her brown eyes flecked with gold peered at me from beneath side-swept bangs. Emilie never talked about Darby's father, who could have been any of a number of musician boyfriends she'd had over the years. She alternated between percussionists and bass players, keyboarders and vocalists, men she changed like accessories. "Her father," Emilie told me once, "is completely beside the point."

"Either you're getting shorter, or I'm getting taller," Darby said when we hugged. Her legs, encased in skinny jeans, reminded me of Emilie's when she was a teenager. She wore a faded Dead Kennedys T-shirt, the hem reaching almost to her knees.

"Funny girl," I said, and she smirked. I linked my arm through hers. "Let me give you the grand tour."

There were hugs all around, including from Uncle Paul, who woke long enough to say hello and ask about supper. Emilie told us about the drama on last-night's set—there had been a problem with her amplifier, a drink thrown on stage and a rowdy bachelor party that needed to be hustled out the door. Aunt Julia's eyes grew slightly wider, but if Emilie seemed to be speaking a different language, none of us let on. Over dinner we filled Emilie in on Dad's wishes and finalized our sleeping arrangements for the night—Emilie and Darby in the bed in the den, Mom and me upstairs in a spare bedroom.

"Tomorrow we'll head over to the farm," Mom said, her voice decisive, although tears betrayed her once again. "It's going to be so hard to go back there..."

Emilie raised an eyebrow at me. She wasn't the type of person to cry; she was more the type to raise her chin in defiance, to clench her jaw against the world, the situation. Whatever emotions she had stayed bottled up within her, as they had always done. "Think I'll shower tonight," she announced, heading to the bathroom with a massive shoulder bag.

Darby and I, wrapped in a couple of Grandma's old quilts, went onto the deck to look up at the stars. "I can't wait to show you all my favorite spots in the barn," I told her.

With her head tipped back, Darby's face looked even younger, more like a child and less like an adolescent poised to be a teenager. "I still can't believe you and my mom grew up here," she told me.

I tried to see Watankee through Darby's eyes, all the things that were second nature to me—the huge open spaces, the tractors making their way down the road at fifteen miles per hour, the stench of manure that rose suddenly on the wind. "Well, we did," I said. "Somewhere, I bet your grandma has photographic proof."

"But my mom especially." Darby sat up, leaning on one elbow. "What was she like back then? She never talks about it."

I chuckled. "She was a clarinetist in the Lincoln High School pep band."

"Seriously? Did she sing at all then?"

"Hymns in church, Christmas carols, that sort of thing."

Darby lay back, clutching her stomach. "That's freaking hilarious."

"Well, yeah." The last time I'd been to see Emilie in Vegas, she'd been wearing a shredded black miniskirt that had barely covered her assets, her mouth pressed so close to the microphone that her voice had been throaty and unrecognizable. They'd come to visit me twice since I moved to Berkeley, sleeping head-to-toe on the couch in my apartment. I'd been busy with school each time, so I'd shuttled them off to various landmarks and beaches during the day and met up with them at night. Emilie had asked, "Where's the nightlife around here?" and I'd had to confess I didn't really know. Somehow I'd known that the Irish pub where I gathered with my fellow graduate students wouldn't quite pass muster.

"So what happened?" Darby asked, looking out into the open field.

"Well, we moved away…and your mom got more interested in music, started playing in bands." I had to choose my words carefully, unsure whether Darby knew that Emilie had left our Joliet apartment by the time she was seventeen, to live with her boyfriend and work in his friend's record store in Cleveland. This decision had prompted a massive fight between Emilie, Mom and Dad on speakerphone, with Emilie insisting she was never going to catch up on credits anyway, even if she stayed in high school until she was twenty-one, and Dad demanding that she return to Watankee where he could keep an eye on her. Sometime after Cleveland, she'd joined up with one band or another, living out of the bus sometimes, calling home when she was desperate for money, and once, to report that she was pregnant.

No—better that Darby hear these details from Emilie, who could invent herself again, a third time, if that's what she wanted her daughter to believe. "She was popular," I recalled, "lots of friends." At least this had been true before Stacy had gone missing, when she'd spent every weeknight on the phone and Friday nights with the pep band.

As for me, I'd missed Emilie horribly during my junior high and high school years. I ticked them off on my fingers sometimes, the ones who were gone: Grandma, Stacy, Grandpa, Johnny, Dad, Emilie. For a while, I'd hugged Mom desperately when she'd left for work and fiercely when she returned. I had kept Emilie's posters of Grace Slick and Janis Joplin on the wall as mementos, even when Mom and I moved to Bloomington. On her rare visits, Emilie had been alarmingly thin. She would sit at our tiny kitchen table and light a joint for breakfast, warning me not to try it, "because it will stunt your growth." Smoking helped her voice, she'd insisted—it gave her an edge. With the faint gray cloud swirling over her head, she'd become philosophical. "I had this vision," she'd said once. "I could see it all before it happened—Johnny, Stacy, the whole bit. I knew everything."

"If you knew it would happen, why didn't you try to stop it?" I'd asked, fascinated by her ragged hems, the odor of smoke and sweat and incense that seemed to cling to her.

"It's just the way of the universe," she'd said mysteriously.

"You're full of shit."

"The only true thing in the world, little sister," she had announced, inhaling deeply, "is that we're all full of shit."

Darby's voice brought me back from my decade-old reverie. "Do you think I'll get to meet Uncle Johnny?"

"Oh—I really don't know, honey. He's, um—" But what was there to say about Johnny? Sometimes he felt like a dark secret that I would take with me to the grave, someone whose existence was impossible to explain. I'd never even owned up to him—my friends all knew I had an older sister, a singer. There didn't seem to be a way to say to a boyfriend, even the ones who were fixtures in my life for months, that I had a brother who might have been—most likely was—a killer.

Darby said, surprising me with her matter-of-factness, "I know about all the stuff with Uncle Johnny and that girl."

"Well, yeah," I swallowed hard. "Stacy. Her name was Stacy."

"It's so crazy how they never found her, isn't it? I mean, all those years, you figure her body would be somewhere."

"Mmm-hmm," I murmured.

"And no one was even arrested! It's like one of those cold case shows on TV."

"Yeah, I guess." I'd thought this myself, a million times. It always looked so easy on television. Insert specimen tube into a very cool-looking machine, wait thirty seconds and *voila!* The killer's identity suddenly appeared on a computer screen.

Darby continued excitedly, "I watch shows like that all the time, those CSI shows where they find one single hair and the whole case unravels." Darby shifted her gaze to me. "What do you think happened? Do you think Uncle Johnny really did it?"

"I don't know," I said. Over the years, I'd convinced myself that it didn't really matter what I believed. He was guilty, he was innocent—it couldn't affect me anymore. "I just don't know."

Someone laughed behind me; it was Emilie, who had stepped soundlessly onto the porch, a towel wrapped around her wet hair. I turned around and met her eye to eye.

Oh, yes, you do, her look said, as the whites of her eyes narrowed to thin, flat lines. *You know exactly what you believe.*

thirty-eight

Friday morning, I put on my sneakers and slipped outside before anyone was awake. I'd become a runner in Berkeley, if a reluctant one, the habit developed more out of necessity—the high price of gas, the tremendous difficulty of finding a parking space within walking distance of campus. Watankee was a runner's paradise, with its smooth, gently sloping hills unfolding beneath a gigantic blue sky—but I didn't meet a single other jogger on the road. I stepped onto the shoulder a few times to let vehicles pass—the large, gold family sedans, the cattle trailers with a cargo destined for the slaughterhouse. Each time, I elicited curious stares.

By heading right and negotiating four successive right turns, I figured I would end up exactly where I'd started. What I hadn't remembered, though, was the length of road between each turn. I slowed as I approached Jerry Warczak's property, my calves protesting. A pair of overalls hung over the porch railing, and several pairs of boots had been kicked off near the front door. His house was more run-down than I'd remembered.

Out of breath, I walked down the road to our house—*home,* although I'd spent most of my life away from it. I was halfway down the driveway when I noticed the truck near the garage—a black Toyota—parked next to Dad's navy Dodge. I couldn't say why, but I felt a tiny shimmer of excitement, as if the little hairs on the back of my neck were standing at attention. Without the sound of engines running, the place was eerily quiet. A few cows mooed low in the pasture, a hawk circled overhead in a nearby field. I approached from behind to read the license plate: *Texas.*

Something caught my eye at that moment—a tall, broad-shouldered man with a baseball cap pulled low over his eyes coming around the side of the barn. If I hadn't seen the license plate, I would have known him anyway, would have known him if it had been twenty years, or thirty, or fifty. There was something about his walk that was familiar, loose-limbed and easy—*like Dad's.*

He stopped short, his face registering surprise, then recognition, then—breaking my heart—wariness.

"Johnny!" I blurted. The tears were already there, stinging, and I blinked them back.

He started toward me, slowly, measuring his steps, but I couldn't wait. I ran toward him, making up the difference.

"Kirsten," he said, scooping me up in one easy movement and whirling me around, so the world was a blur of green and red and blue. It was one of those déjà vu moments, where the present melted into the past. Johnny hoisting me onto his shoulders for a run around the bases, carrying me over his shoulders, scooping me up for a gentle takedown on the living room floor.

"Hey, pip-squeak," he said, setting me on the ground. He took off his hat, messing his fingers through his blond hair. It was thinner now, set farther back on his forehead, but he was still Johnny, handsome and strong. We stood there grinning at each other like a pair of idiots.

"I never would have recognized you, you've grown so tall," he said, and I rolled my eyes. At five feet and one-half-inch, I came about even with his armpit.

"How long have you been here?"

"I just pulled in. Drove most of the day yesterday and spent the night in Racine." Johnny jerked his head to one side, gesturing. "You know Dad kept that truck all these years? He did some bodywork on it, painted it black. I figured he would have just junked it."

"The Green Machine?" I asked, then remembered. The *Murder Machine,* with a dented passenger-side door and two slashed tires.

We looked at each other, then away, awkwardly. "We're all down at Aunt Julia's," I said, suddenly shy. "Everyone is probably getting up about now. You should come over for breakfast. I mean it, you should absolutely come."

He leaned back against the Toyota, looking uneasy. "Kirsten," he began, then stopped.

"It was all a million years ago," I told him, as if I was still a kid. My eyes smarted with tears.

He smiled but shook his head. "No, it wasn't."

"Johnny—"

"Why don't you get in? I'll give you a ride, at least."

In the truck, he belted himself in, checked the rear-view mirror, and then glanced over at me. I remembered the day he'd dropped me off at school, the day

Heather Lemke had kicked my ass at tetherball. I'd been so sure, then.

"What?" Johnny demanded, glancing over at me. I couldn't stop staring at him.

I shook my head, more to clear it than anything else. I hadn't thought of it in years—the way he'd wrestled with Stacy on our living room floor, with a roughness that bordered on violence. The slammed doors, the chair he'd thrown against the wall. These were the images I'd had of Johnny over the years—my brother, the wrestling star, the lover, the *killer,* the murderer, the vagabond, and now the absent but doting son to his father. Last night Emilie had laughed when I'd said I didn't know if Johnny was guilty; today, riding in the truck next to him, I knew that he wasn't.

It came to me with sudden clarity: the snowstorm, that night. Johnny had come in, shivering with cold, blood trickling from his hand. He had been so young then, just a seventeen-year-old boy worried that he'd crashed his truck. He wasn't worried about Stacy—a fact that had made him seem callous and cruel at the time. But I saw it now for what it was: he hadn't been worried about Stacy, because he'd assumed she was already at home, peeling off her jeans and stepping into her pajamas, maybe sipping from a mug of hot chocolate. Her disappearance had been as much a shock to him as it had been to us. I had cried for Stacy, for the girl who had been in my life one day and was gone the next, but it must have been exponentially worse for Johnny, who had loved her. Yet we hadn't let him grieve properly; we had kept him—for fifteen years now—on the defensive.

We pulled up in front of Aunt Julia's house too soon.

"Johnny—" I began. *Keep driving,* I wanted to tell him. *Take me around town, through the countryside, anywhere, so that I have time to get my thoughts together.* I wanted a chance to say all the things I hadn't said to him since we'd parted, and all the things I hadn't said those last months we were together, when I'd put him on trial and found him guilty without ever giving him a chance to speak in his defense.

Instead, I said the only thing I could grasp at that moment. "Johnny, I'm so, so sorry."

He closed his eyes, and for a few beats, I thought he wasn't going to respond, that maybe he was just waiting for me to get out of the car. It would serve me right; it was a fitting punishment for being a horrible sister. But then he half turned toward me, his eyes blue and moist, and said, "I want you to know that I'm sorry right back."

thirty-nine

Dad's burial service was attended by maybe twenty-five people, some neighbors, some friends from way back. This was what life had come to for a man who was decent and hardworking, a man who kept to himself and was content not to challenge his status as a social pariah. Standing in a short row, Johnny, Emilie and I sobbed, our hands linked. Mom and Aunt Julia clung to each other, dry-eyed at last. Our cousin Brent was there from Milwaukee with his wife and two preteen daughters, perfect strangers. Darby held a red rose in her hand to be placed on Dad's coffin at the end of the service.

I didn't know if Dad believed in the resurrection of the dead and the life everlasting, or any of the other passages the funeral director read from his tiny, official-looking black book, or if he had counted on it all ending with ashes and dust. I wanted to ask; I was already formulating a list of about a million questions for the next time I saw him. Which I guess explains what I believed myself, even if I hadn't practiced that belief in years.

All day Friday, reconnecting, we'd told our favorite Dad stories, laughed and cried and said what needed to be said. Darby had warmed right up to Johnny; they'd had nothing to forgive each other for and could start with a blank slate. For the rest of us, the initial awkwardness had disappeared as the day wore on. We'd carefully avoided all mention of *that* spring, as if we were all imagining what life would have been like without Stacy, if she'd never even existed. When we'd all crammed onto the couch for an impromptu family photo, I'd thought that Dad would have been proud of us, acting like a real family. Or not acting, just *being*.

Mom was invited to deliver the message from the family, and she stepped forward, slim and strong in a dark suit. "I'm not going to make a grand speech today, because that's not what John would have wanted," she began. Only that morning she'd been a mess, slow to get herself dressed for the day. Now, I knew, she was drawing on her reserve strength, the way she must have done during her shifts in the E.R., facing one family's tragedy after another. "John Hammarstrom was a loyal man, a good father, a supportive husband. He had a kind of courage that I haven't encountered much in this world, and more courage than I've ever had myself." Her voice wavered slightly, and she caught my eye. "He would be proud of his kids today, and grateful to everyone for coming."

My whole body shook. Emilie, leaning down, laid her head on top of mine. Johnny brought an arm around both of us. We lingered for a long time in this three-way embrace, watching the coffin be lowered into the ground. Mom thanked everyone in attendance personally, her discomfort at being in Watankee forgotten, or at least, momentarily stowed away.

I couldn't help wondering: If whatever had happened

to Stacy Lemke hadn't happened, where would the rest of us be? I used to have a pretty clear idea of where we would all end up, in the world according to nine-year-old me. Johnny was going to win a state title, graduate from college and come back to the farm speaking a new language of breeding and genetics. He was going to marry Stacy, of course, and produce enough strawberry-blond children to fill the upstairs bedrooms. Dad and Mom would have moved next door; on spring afternoons, they would have headed out to Fireman's Field to watch their grandchildren smash the ball off the tee. They would have lived long, happy lives. Emilie would have gone to college on a music scholarship. She might have ended up on a soundstage in Vegas, anyway, but that was only after turning down the philharmonic.

And me? Back then I'd wanted to be everything at once—a veterinarian, a detective, the celebrated reader who checked out every book in the library. I would have gone to college, too—but I would have come home on every vacation, bursting out of the car, taking the steps two at a time, not being able to wait a second longer before saying hello.

Maybe. Or maybe not. I'd lived long enough to understand that every family had its share of tragedy, large or small. No one got a free pass from heartache.

For the first time in fifteen years, I realized that I didn't give a damn what had happened to Stacy Lemke. It was sad and awful, but true; we'd let her disappearance have this strange power over our lives. What I cared about now was what I should have cared about then. My family, the five of us staying together.

A few sprinkles started then, propelling us to action. "I'd better get back to the house," Aunt Julia said. That morning, we'd helped her make up ham-and-cheese buns, a salty-sweet German potato salad and two kinds of Jell-O desserts for the funeral luncheon. She and Uncle Paul were among the first to leave, followed by handfuls of other people, in ones and twos.

"Are we ready to head back?" Mom asked, fishing the keys out of her purse. We'd come together, knowing we couldn't handle it alone. I could see how exhausted she was, how much effort it had taken to put on a brave face.

"I don't know," I said, suddenly needing more time. If I flew back to Berkeley tomorrow, there was no telling when I would be here again. But Emilie and Darby had already started walking back to Mom's car. "You know what? Go on ahead. It's not too far to walk. I'll catch up with you."

Johnny frowned, glancing at the dark clouds overhead. "It's going to start raining."

"I'll be fine. I just need to stay here for a few minutes."

"Okay, then," Mom said, giving me a squeeze on the arm.

Johnny took off his coat and draped it over my shoulders. "Don't be too long," he said.

I watched Mom and Johnny walk back to Mom's car. Darby raised her hand to wave at me, and I waved back. Johnny was right—as soon as they pulled onto the road, the sprinkles came. I slipped on his jacket, breathed in his smell.

Maybe being here, with Dad's death suddenly real, was what brought back the flood of memories. The faded wallpaper in our kitchen. The neat rows of Grandma's garden. The rungs on the ladder to the hayloft. The summer of the Hammarstrom Hitters. Racing Dad back from the barn and him letting me win. His hand on my head, tousling my always-messy hair. It was painful to remember these things. For so long when I thought about my childhood, I'd remembered it only from the moment Stacy Lemke went missing to the moment we packed Mom's Caprice Classic to the gills and headed out of town, as if nine years of life had been reduced to that short span of three months. Maybe, if I really considered it, I'd find that the next sixteen years of my life hadn't counted, either.

I knelt down, taking a handful of loose soil and sifting it through my fingers. Burying Dad here, in the small cemetery just down the road from where he'd lived his whole life, felt like a fitting final home. Dad had known this land, worked this land, loved this land. His heart attack had come midmorning, according to the coroner's report. The milk hauler had found him just after noon, only a few feet inside the barn. He'd felt for a pulse, then waited outside for the ambulance. "It must have been quick," Mom had reassured us, and we were happy to defer to her medical knowledge, happy to believe that Dad's death had been fast and unpreventable, to save us from the guilt of a father dying alone and far away.

The rain started to come down then, the scattering of sprinkles turning to determined, stinging drops.

There was a sound behind me, a quick clearing of a throat. I whirled around, placing a hand on the ground for balance. Johnny, I thought. He came back for me.

But the shadow that fell over me wasn't Johnny's, although it was familiar, in the long-ago way everything in Watankee felt familiar. Though he hadn't aged gracefully, I recognized Jerry Warczak right away. "Saw you out here by yourself," he grunted. "Figured maybe you needed a ride."

I pushed myself to a standing position. "No, that's okay. I'm planning to walk."

He stared at me. "You're so grown up."

I hitched up my pants at the knees, revealing the four-inch heels on my boots.

"You won't be able to walk in those."

"Believe me," I said. "I walk everywhere in these."

"But it's raining," he insisted. "Let me give you a ride."

I saw that he wasn't going to leave. There wasn't going to be a last minute alone with Dad. "That's fine, then." I followed behind him, my footsteps falling into the impressions left by his boots.

forty

Jerry had parked his aging pickup along a dirt road at the back of the cemetery, out of view of the main road. The outside was a mess of caked dirt, and the inside was nearly as bad. I could see that the dashboard was coated with a fine layer of dust, and in order for me to sit down, Jerry had to sweep some empty plastic soda bottles off the seat.

"Sorry about that," he said. "Not used to having a passenger." He seemed nervous, adjusting his baseball cap on top of his head, then wiping his palms on his jeans. This was how he'd always seemed to me—as if he was out of place, no matter where that place was.

"It's no problem." I reached over my shoulder for the seat belt, then had to push away some old clothes to find the holder. It occurred to me that Jerry hadn't been in the small clutch of people gathered around Dad's gravesite. "I didn't see you at the service. Weren't you there?"

He put the key into the ignition but didn't turn it. "I just couldn't… I've never been much of a religious guy. I figure the best way for me to pay my respects is when everyone else is gone, and I can drink a bottle of whiskey at his grave and think about old times."

"I can understand that," I said. Dad and Jerry had always had a special bond. What was it Dad had said once? That Jerry was like a son to him, his other son. Since we'd all left, Jerry had probably been more of a son to Dad than Johnny, more family than Emilie or me. "I'm sure he understands that, too. He appreciated all your help over the years."

"We helped each other," Jerry said, again more of a grunt of acknowledgment than actual speech. In Berkeley, people spoke quickly, glibly, ironically, and often not sincerely. Jerry would have stood out there, the way I probably stood out to him now, as good as a stranger here.

"It went both ways, I mean," Jerry continued. "He helped me out, too, a lot."

I smiled. There was a long silence before Jerry finally turned the key in his ignition and pulled forward. The jolt of the truck sent the plastic bottles scattering at my feet. The doors clicked, locking automatically.

"See," he said. "It's raining harder now."

And all of a sudden it was, as if a massive bucket in the sky had been spilled directly overhead. Jerry kept the truck in Drive, although I looked back pointedly over my shoulder, a tiny needle of uneasiness pricking inside me.

"Um, aren't we…?"

"I can turn around up here," he said, and in a minute the dirt road widened out and he maneuvered a three-point turn, bringing us back around toward the main road. I relaxed.

"Drop you off at your parents' house?"

"No, my aunt Julia's. There's going to be a little luncheon in honor of Dad. You know, you should come, too."

"That's okay." He was holding the wheel tight, I noticed, so tightly that his knuckles flamed white against his otherwise permanently suntanned skin.

"You must have known him better than just about anyone. You probably have all these stories we haven't heard," I said, realizing the truth of the statement as it came out of my mouth. If Jerry was Dad's other son, then Dad had probably been Jerry's other dad—a sort of surrogate father to him, all these years. Perversely, selfishly, I felt a twinge of jealousy, that this man who was basically a stranger had spent his lifetime close to my dad, an opportunity I'd squandered.

Jerry cleared his throat, and I understood that he was gearing up to say something important. When it came, there was a harshness in his voice that I hadn't expected. "You all just abandoned him after."

After.

I couldn't find fault with his accusation. We had abandoned Dad, even if we'd had perfectly good reasons for doing it. Johnny had left to get away from the public indictment of his guilt, and to ease the pressure on the rest of us. Mom had left because her life had become unbearable. Emilie and I—well, we were kids. I was nine years old. More to defend Mom than anything else, I said, "He could have come with us, though. The situation here—it was pretty bad back then."

"Still," he said. "To leave him alone like that."

Again, I didn't dispute this. The people of Watankee had wanted us out, and they'd succeeded in driving almost all of us away. But they had probably also needed us to stay, too, to fill the role of town villains.

Jerry was driving slowly, the rain spattering down on his windshield. He had the wipers set on an agonizingly slow speed, so that the windshield became dense with water before it was cleared. With the view out the front window obscured, it was hard to tell exactly where we were. Aunt Julia's house was less than a mile away from the cemetery—everything in Watankee was only about a mile or so away from everything else—but the trip was starting to feel too long.

Again, he cleared his throat, and I had a feeling that he was going to say something significant, although I couldn't imagine what it would be. Another accusation, a denunciation of my childhood behavior? Without warning, I felt terribly tired, the stress of the past few days catching up with me. "Jerry," I said quickly, trying to cut him off. "I understand that it must seem like—"

He persisted, as if I hadn't spoken. "Your brother wasn't guilty, you know."

I glanced at him sharply. A thought was beginning to form at the back of my mind, where I'd buried my memories of that long-ago time. I couldn't exactly put a name to it, but I was suddenly aware that I was traveling with a man who was essentially a stranger, and no one else on earth knew where I was.

He rapped again on the steering wheel, impatient. "Not that it matters anymore, what with your dad dead."

My mind seemed to be moving too slowly to catch up with his logic. What did Dad's death have to do with anything? "I'm sorry, but I don't understand," I sputtered. "Are you saying that my dad was somehow… involved?"

He turned to me. Strange, how I'd never really seemed to see him before. He was just Jerry Warczak, the guy who lived just down the road. *That poor Warczak boy,* losing one parent and then another. Now, I saw that beneath his baseball cap, his dark eyebrows had grown nearly closed. It was the sort of thing a woman would notice right off the bat, but a man might not. Had there ever been a girlfriend, a woman in Jerry's life besides his mother? I didn't think so. His cheeks were raw from shaving, with a little knot of dried blood above his lip. There were some scraggly dark hairs on his chin, as if he was trying to grow a goatee that just hadn't filled in yet. As if he was somehow still a boy, not yet a man.

"How could you say that?" Again his voice was harsh, accusatory.

"I didn't say it. I was only asking what you meant." I tried to keep an edge out of my voice, the shrill tone that tended to creep in when I was on the defensive.

"I would never say anything against your dad," he insisted, not seeming to understand my point. His eyes were dark and unreadable, and I felt something rising in me.

"That's good," I squeaked, peering out the window. *Just let me off here,* I thought. *I'll walk the rest of the way.* What would he do if I just opened the door and tumbled out, taking my chances? I felt for the seat belt clasp with my left hand.

"We're not there yet," he barked.

I closed my eyes, reaching deep within me for some words to pray. *No, God, no.* I knew now that it had been Jerry's truck that had stopped at the side of the road, Jerry's familiar face that had greeted Stacy.

"You never even realized it, did you?"

"Stop! Just stop here!" I felt sick, the bowl of oatmeal from that morning sitting heavily in my stomach. I had realized nothing. I had been a stupid girl, self-absorbed, more worried about what others believed than what I believed myself. For all these years, we had let Jerry Warczak get away with it, so absorbed in our own misery that we were blind to what was right in front of us.

He braked suddenly, and I braced myself with both palms against the dash.

"My family is waiting for me," I said, trying to cover the fear in my voice. "They'll be looking."

He said nothing, but the truck slowed further, pulling onto the side of the road. I peered out the passenger-side window, saw that we were balancing on the edge of the ditch. I would have to step out into the soft dirt in my four-inch heels, the incline leading down into stagnant water. I would roll down the hillside if I had to. I challenged the seat belt with both hands now, determined to get free.

"That one's tricky," he said, leaning over me.

"No!" I recoiled, my head angling away toward the door. I could feel his breath against my neck and smell it, too—stale, coffee-tinged. I saw in a flash that Stacy had done this, too, had fumbled with the seat belt and the door lock, had found it impossible to break free in time.

His hand tunneled into the seat by my left hip for an unbearable moment, and then the belt clicked and sprang free.

Not taking my eyes off him, I felt along the door for the lock release and gave it a sharp upward tug.

Instantly, his hand was on top of mine, forcing the

lock down. "I don't have to let you go," he said, his face too close to mine.

"But you're going to," I said, my body frozen into place. "For my dad."

He shifted back into his seat, and I unlocked the door again. *Be cool,* I thought. *Just get out of the car, run away.*

I had one foot out on the slippery shoulder of the road when he reached over, grabbing my arm at the wrist. *Please, God,* I prayed. The rain pounded against my back, soaked into my hair.

"All I ever wanted was what you had, Kirsten," he said, his eyes holding mine.

It was too open-ended, like filling in the blank for a vague question on a test. But he seemed to expect a response, and as if I'd been preparing for it, I knew what to say. "A family," I choked. "You just wanted a family."

He released my wrist, and I stumbled backward, grabbing on to the open door for balance. He hit the gas, and the truck lurched away from me. I fell to my knees, somehow managing to keep myself from completely falling. The spray of mud from his tires hit me as he gunned the engine and zoomed away. In a few moments, he was lost to the rain, and I was on my feet, running.

forty-one

Johnny met me at the door, took in my dripping, wild-eyed appearance, and placed a hand on each shoulder to steady me. "What happened?"

"We have to call the police. We have to get them down there right now, we have to— He almost— I don't know, but he could have—" I knew I was babbling, but couldn't stop myself. I closed my eyes against the memory of Jerry Warczak leaning over me, his breath on my cheek.

Johnny gave my shoulders a little shake. "What are you talking about?" Behind him, I could hear muffled voices, the clatter of plates being stacked. Aunt Julia called, "Johnny, who's out there? Why don't you let them in already?"

I took a deep breath, tried to steady myself. I couldn't be wrong; I couldn't say this now and later admit to a mistake. I closed my eyes and felt it again—Jerry's hand on my wrist, the clammy sweatiness of his skin on mine. *All I ever wanted was what you had.* My voice seemed to come from somewhere outside my body. It sounded different to me, maybe because I felt, for the first time in my life, the full importance of what I was saying. "Johnny—it was him. It was Jerry. He killed Stacy, I know it."

Johnny stepped back as if I'd slapped him. His eyes were wide. "Jerry? No. No, it couldn't be."

"Johnny, I'm telling you. There's something wrong. I know it, Johnny. I just know it."

He swore. There was a moment's hesitation while he looked at me, taking everything in—the rainwater dripping down my face, the mud spattered across his jacket, the dirt caking my boots. His eyes settled on mine, and I could see him considering. There was the man he had known his whole life—a neighbor, only a few years older than Johnny himself. And then there was me. Only since returning to Watankee had I realized what a stupid, dramatic little girl I had been, all those years ago. But I wasn't that anymore.

"Johnny," I pleaded, and he nodded twice—tentatively at first, as if he were getting used to the idea, and then decidedly. He would believe me, because he had to.

In a single move, Johnny sidestepped me, breaking into a run across Aunt Julia's driveway. His left hand fished in his pocket for the keys.

I was right behind him, throwing open the passenger door to his truck as he was starting the engine. "You're not going by yourself! You're not going without me!"

"This isn't about you, Kirsten," he hissed through gritted teeth. "This is my business to deal with."

I clambered onto the passenger seat. Steadying myself with one hand on the dash, I yanked the door shut behind me. "I'm not getting out!"

He swore again. A few sedans had parked behind Johnny's truck, blocking the exit. He considered for a second, then turned the wheel hard and gunned the truck into Reverse, his wheels sliding on a stretch of soggy lawn. I lost my balance and fell back against the door.

"Johnny!" I screeched.

"If you're not getting out, you'd better hold on," he growled. He spun onto the road, leaving deep tire grooves across the lawn.

Johnny shifted into Drive, and I righted myself in my seat, gripping the door handle. Suddenly, someone appeared before us in the road—a dripping figure, arms waving. Johnny swore again, pounding on the steering wheel in frustration. I couldn't help it: I screamed, as if I was a kid watching a movie that would give me nightmares.

But it was only Emilie, rain flattening her spiky hair. She had smears of black, blue and silver around her eyes like a Mardi Gras mask.

Emilie yanked open the passenger door. "Aren't you forgetting something?" she demanded. "Me, for instance?"

"Both of you, out!" Johnny ordered.

"Forget it!"

It was the only time I can ever remember saying something in unison with Emilie.

She slammed the door behind her and folded her arms across her chest. "You going to tell me what's going on?"

I blurted, "We're going to Jerry Warczak's. He killed Stacy." The more I let the idea exist in my mind and the more I said it out loud, the more I knew for certain it was true. Jerry Warczak, not Johnny Hammarstrom, had taken Stacy that night.

"What? Did you hit your head or something?"

"He picked me up at the cemetery. He was acting… strange." I shivered, suddenly overwhelmed by the cold, the rush of memories, the knowledge that I was setting something into motion that had long been buried, and life was about to change, again.

"Did he hurt you? Did something happen?"

I shook my head. He hadn't hurt me, but I had known the possibility was there. What if he hadn't stopped at Aunt Julia's, but kept going? Would I have dared to throw open the passenger door and tumble onto the road? Was that what Stacy had wondered, too, in her last living moments?

"Hang on," Johnny ordered and floored it, his truck fishtailing for a wild moment before straightening out. Jerry's house was only down the road, past the empty horse pastures, the barren stalks of corn, past our house, vacant now, too. The ride seemed endless, though, like running in a dream. Each second stretched long, bloated with importance. My mind was spinning, as if I was replaying a movie on an old reel-to-reel. Stacy had been walking home, her pretty boots drenched, the collar of her coat turned up to protect her face. Jerry had been driving by—coincidentally or not. He'd pulled over, offered a ride.

"You're sure about this, Kirsten?" Emilie demanded. "You'd better be sure, because Superman here—"

I nodded furiously, my words tumbling out. "Don't you remember? He was always there. He was there when you wrestled in the living room, Johnny. He was there that night, in our kitchen."

"Half of Watankee was in our kitchen that night," Emilie pointed out. "I mean, it would be nice to know for sure before Johnny here does something stupid and—"

I couldn't get the words out fast enough. "It was him! He reached over, he grabbed my wrist. He said we hadn't treated Dad right. He said he knew you were innocent, Johnny. He said he'd only wanted what we had."

"It makes sense," Johnny said, his face like stone.

Emilie swiveled in her seat to look at him. "It does? Why, because he lives alone? Because he's kind of creepy? I know a lot of men who fit that description."

I said shakily, "I thought he wasn't going to let me out of his truck."

Emilie looked hard at me and swallowed. "Okay. Let's say you're right. Are we thinking he's going to welcome us into his house and serve us a cup of tea? I mean, it's one thing to play girl detective, but it's another thing to barge into a man's house—"

Our house slid by in a blur on the left, and in the surreal way everything looked right then, I could have sworn it was moving and we were standing still. I glanced at Johnny. His jaw was set, his eyes full of an icy determination I hadn't seen in ages but still recognized. This was the Johnny who had taken down his opponents on the mats, who had strategized and planned and looked for an opening.

This was his opening.

I put a hand on Johnny's shoulder. "She's right. We can't just show up there. We could call the police—" But I trailed off here, because this brought back another memory: Johnny ducking his head to enter the back of a patrol car. Never charged, but always the only suspect.

Johnny said, "I told him. He's the only one who knew."

"Told him what?" I asked, gaping.

Then I spotted the mailbox tilting to one side, as if it had been bumped once and never righted: *J. Warczak.* How many years, I wondered, my thoughts running unrestrained, had Jerry lived here alone? How many years had passed since that night, how many months and weeks and days and seconds had he lived with his guilt?

Johnny didn't bother to ease down Jerry's driveway but took it full force, spraying a mixture of mud and gravel everywhere, taking the turn at the end recklessly, tossing me onto Emilie's lap. I'd seen Jerry's property from the road only yesterday, on my early morning jog. From that vantage point, it had looked slightly run-down—lacking, I remembered thinking, a woman's touch. Behind the house, though, his property was a hoarder's dream—jumbled piles of rusted truck parts and the skeletal remains of farm implements, with weeds growing tall between them. A chicken strutted by, its head bobbing nervously.

"Whoa," Emilie muttered, taking it in.

Jerry's truck was already there, and I half expected to find him waiting on the porch, but there was no sign of him outside the house. He'd only had a small head start, so I knew he couldn't be far.

"Johnny—" I tried again.

"And all that time he never said anything. I figured he was just being decent, not repeating everything I'd said. . . ." The look on his face was equal parts wonder and horror.

"Johnny? What did you tell him?"

Johnny opened the driver's door and stepped out into the rain.

"Now, this is incredibly stupid," Emilie huffed, as if her good sense was offended by our folly.

But Johnny wasn't in a hurry anymore. He stood there for a long moment, staring at Jerry's house, letting water drip into his eyes without blinking it away. "I told him," he said simply. "I told him Stacy was pregnant."

"Shit," Emilie whispered.

When he took a step, I reached for him, catching only a handful of fabric.

He jerked away. "I'm doing this, Kirsten."

I stepped out of the car, screaming after him as he charged across the weed-choked lawn. "What are you going to do? Johnny, you can't just go in there!"

"Johnny, get back here!" Emilie pulled her cell phone from the pocket of her skintight black jeans. "I'm calling for help."

Johnny was heading up the porch steps. Some were rotted, I noticed, the boards buckled and splintered. He hesitated for a half second over the broken screen door, as if he were deciding whether to knock.

"Oh, God…oh, God," I said over and over, not being able to form any more words. I saw Johnny turn the knob of Jerry Warczak's back door. It was open, and in a second Johnny was inside, closing the door behind him.

"We've got to stop him," I cried, seizing Emilie's arm.

She shook me off. She was waving her cell phone over her head, trying to catch a signal. "All that time, that dirty son of a bitch," she muttered.

I put my head in my hands, trying to still my thoughts. Was this where it had happened, where he had brought her? Was her body here? Not a body, I realized—not anymore. After all this time, there would only be remains, bones and fragments, the sort of thing you saw in television crime labs, pieced together by white-coated professionals. And then I gulped an uneven breath. What if she had been here all along, prisoner in this dilapidated hellhole? I turned to Emilie. "What if—"

We both heard it at the same time, the sound reverberating through the house, blasting through the roar of the rain that was now seeping into everything.

A shot.

One single shot.

forty-two

When Stacy Lemke went missing in 1995, the local papers had covered the case ad nauseam. The *Watankee Weekly,* which never had any news to report besides the weather, had kept Stacy's name alive for months—and we had thought *that* was bad. I remember the white news station vans parked across Rural Route 4, keeping their distance under Grandpa's watchful eye. At the time, the presence of a few op-ed pieces and the occasional updates on our local affiliate stations had made us feel hemmed in, prisoners on our scant 160 acres.

This time around, dozens of reporters and white utility vans descended on Watankee. They camped outside the rows of yellow police tape at Jerry Warczak's house; they followed his walk from the jail to the courthouse in Manitowoc, greedy for the footage that would explain it all. They hounded the Lemkes, too. I had my first glimpse of them in sixteen years on the evening news, the night after Johnny was shot. They must have been in their late fifties by now, but they looked much older, in ways I couldn't fully explain. Maybe it was the harsh glare of the studio lights, revealing faces that gleamed faintly orange with makeup. Maybe it was the circles under their eyes, dark as storm clouds. Maybe it was the shock of believing one thing for sixteen years and then overnight having to believe something else entirely.

And, of course, the reporters couldn't get enough of Johnny. Back then, he'd been the suspect. Now he was a victim—and a hero.

Johnny didn't want to tell the story, but it leaked anyway, the way news does in a small town.

When Johnny pushed open Jerry Warczak's front door, Jerry had been sitting in a recliner, his rifle ready on his shoulder.

"You killed her," Johnny had said, and in confirmation of this fact, Jerry had fired.

The bullet had only grazed Johnny's arm before he'd tackled Jerry, bringing him down in what I liked to imagine was the most spectacular pin of his life. Once Jerry had lost control of the gun, Johnny had simply held him in a full nelson—a decidedly illegal move, if this were high school wrestling—until the police had arrived. When Emilie and I'd pressed him later, Johnny admitted to a particularly tight hold, which had explained the screams we'd heard following the gunshot.

Jerry Warczak—it was repeated with relish—had screamed like a girl.

If it was difficult to go from chief suspect to town hero, Johnny made the transition gracefully. Everywhere he went, people said that they had always known he was innocent, that it was such a shame what had happened back then. The women patted his shoulder, the men offered him a hand to shake. If it were me, I might have been too bitter to accept these assertions, but Johnny just wasn't that kind of guy. When you got right down to it, Johnny was a better person than I could ever have imagined. He thanked everyone for their kind words, insisted rather modestly that he was no kind of hero.

In Texas, Johnny told me once, he had just been some guy who lived alone in a dinky apartment, sold farm equipment, spent long days on the roads and slept several nights a week in motels. No one he encountered knew anything about Johnny Hammarstrom, and he'd liked it that way, without his past waiting around every corner. He'd dated from time to time—not seriously, friend of a friend sort of thing, he said—and held his breath, waiting for some enterprising person to connect the dots.

In March 2012, Johnny took the stand as the star witness in the case against Jerry Warczak. By this time he'd packed up his life in Texas and moved to Watankee permanently. With Dad gone and Jerry in jail, someone needed to run the farm.

In a way, the trial was like an extended family reunion. Mom, using her accrued vacation time, stayed with Aunt Julia and Uncle Paul. Emilie and Darby came up from Vegas; I took a semester's leave of absence from my doctoral program after assurance from my advisor that a spot would be waiting for me. Each day we filed into the courtroom and took our places on one of the wooden benches, a few rows behind the Lemkes. We were a curious group: Aunt Julia, oxygen hissing into the plastic tube at her nose; Mom, wearing one of several expensive suits purchased especially for the occasion; Emilie, with her blue-black hair and off-the-shoulder throwback-to-the-eighties tops; Darby, her body swimming in an oversize concert T-shirt and the tightest jeans I'd ever seen; and me in a Cal sweatshirt, hunched over a notepad where I scribbled furiously. Suddenly it was important for me to write everything down, to own every detail.

Collectively, we focused our attention on Jerry Warczak. He had been denied bail from the beginning; by the time trial started, he was a heavier, shaggier, paler version of the man who had come up behind me at the cemetery. If it were possible for glares to bore holes through someone, Jerry Warzcak would have looked like a piece of Swiss cheese by the end of the trial.

Some of the details about that night I'd forgotten, but they came back in a sudden rush during Johnny's testimony. We heard again about his date with Stacy—a matinee in Sheboygan, hamburgers at The Humble Bee. The Green Machine hitting a patch of ice and fishtailing, landing in a ditch. And finally, Stacy pulling the hood of her coat over her head and walking away into a swirl of snow. Johnny told all of this calmly; I was reminded of the seventeen-year-old boy he had been that night, sitting at the kitchen table with the detective, pounding his fist against the wood. He'd wanted to go out there. He'd wanted to do something, before it was too late.

The defense attorney posed the question to Johnny: "But you had reason, didn't you, to kill Stacy Lemke?"

"No, of course not."

Shuffling through a stack of papers at his table, the defense attorney questioned Johnny about a conversation he'd had with "the defendant" on the afternoon of Wednesday, March 1, 1995. This clicked with me instantly; it was the day after I'd seen Johnny and Stacy arguing on the side of the road, the day after she'd pushed him and he'd fallen backward, catching himself on the bumper of his truck.

"Do you remember telling the defendant that Stacy Lemke, your girlfriend, was pregnant?"

Johnny wetted his lips. His gaze traveled apologetically around the courtroom, taking in the Lemkes, our row of Hammarstroms, and settling on Jerry Warzcak. His expression didn't change, but suddenly the vein in his forehead seemed more prominent, as if thumping with purpose. "Yes," he said.

"Some people would call this a motive," the defense attorney said mildly, turning away.

"It was a motive for me to love her even more," Johnny countered.

The worst part of the trial was the testimony of the county's forensics experts. These were the details we sometimes wanted to discuss but never could, because to say these things made them real.

Stacy's remains had been found in a fifty-five-gallon drum in Jerry Warczak's cellar, next to a water heater and towering stack of industrial-sized canned foods. If he'd ever needed to hole up, Jerry was prepared. Compared to the rest of his house, where the carpet was worn through and the linoleum was warped and spiderwebs hung from the corners, the basement was clean and well-tended. Jerry had pointed out the barrel for the detectives himself, as if he were proud of it.

After all those years, much of the evidence had decomposed, or simply dissolved. After an examination of the skeletal remains, the cause of death was ruled unknown, possibly strangulation. Stacy was identified through dental and medical records, including an X-ray of a broken arm from when she was twelve.

The last bit of the coroner's testimony, seemingly thrown in as an afterthought, was that there was only one type of DNA present in the remains. Stacy Lemke, he clarified for a puzzled courtroom, had not been pregnant.

When he heard this news, Johnny closed his eyes, his chin sinking to his chest. Had Stacy really believed she was pregnant? Had she just wanted to hold on to Johnny for a little longer, for as long as she could? I remembered the way she had been that afternoon in his bedroom, so unwilling to let go. The pregnancy might have been a trick or a trap, but I couldn't bring myself to judge her; she'd been only sixteen years old then, trying to figure out the rest of her life. Everything about her was frozen at that delicate age, no longer a child but barely a woman.

For me, it was enough—and it was nowhere near enough—that Jerry was found guilty.

We talked about closure, and putting the past behind us, and moving on. I'd heard these sentiments on television talk shows, before the cameras turned to the victims, who looked shell-shocked and blank. They hadn't figured out how to put the past behind them. They didn't know how to move on, or what they were supposed to do to move toward.

For a long time we were the same way. We tiptoed around the subject. We hesitated to say Stacy's name or make any reference to Jerry. We talked about safe things: the weather, the crops. We held our breath, waiting for the right moment to exhale.

epilogue

Dad had told me once, a million years ago, that everything worth knowing could be learned on a farm. He had valued the land above all else—the hard work it demanded, the simple routines and quiet satisfactions. It had been his father's land, and his grandfather's before that, and so on, back to the Homestead Act that had divided much of the Midwest into neat, square grids.

And so he had left it to Johnny.

He'd made the arrangements years before, mailing Johnny the paperwork in a thick legal envelope. Johnny had signed everything and mailed it back—not that he understood any of it at the time, he said. He'd been in his early twenties then, picking up odd jobs here and there, trying to keep his head down and stay out of trouble. All those years in between, when Johnny had moved from Illinois to Ohio to Tennessee to Texas, the farm had actually been in his name, with Dad listed as the official renter. Now the land was Johnny's free and clear, with none of the inheritance taxes that had crippled Jerry Warczak so long ago. His first act as a landowner was to draw up plans for expansion. The dairy would always be there, but Johnny knew the future lay in genetics and breeding. "This is what I dreamed of, all those nights when I was on the road," he told me once.

"You dreamed of inseminating cows?" I asked.

He smacked me, but lightly, playfully. "Coming home," he clarified.

I grinned at him. "The prodigal son makes good." And one by one, the rest of us began to come home, too.

Emilie took a few more gigs in Vegas before she and Darby packed up their tiny apartment and moved back to Watankee, permanently. Surprisingly, Emilie had "a little money saved up"—enough to begin some renovations on Grandpa and Grandma's old house. She'd been dabbling here and there in photography, and a new generation of teenagers used our farm as a backdrop for their senior pictures. Darby enrolled at Lincoln High School; I experienced a particularly hard jolt of déjà vu the first time I saw her in a gray Ships sweatshirt.

Mom was next, taking a head nurse position at the E.R. in Milwaukee. She wasn't ready to call Watankee home again but liked being able to drive up on a long weekend to help with a remodeling project or watch one of Darby's volleyball games. She even got over her phobia of shopping in the grocery store. To see her walk through the Piggly Wiggly now, you would think she owned the place, and it was everyone else who didn't belong.

I returned to Berkeley to finish my studies in cultural geography, finally understanding what it meant to have a sense of place. Every chance I could, I caught a flight back. Sometimes I stayed in Aunt Julia's guest room or on Emilie's sleeper sofa, but every now and then, I stayed in Johnny's house, curled up in my old childhood bed under the eaves. I could never do this without crying, but they weren't always tears of sadness. Sometimes I cried simply with relief for things being right with the world.

Being back home, it turned out, wasn't a distraction at all. I toted my laptop most mornings to the Watankee Public Library and found myself suddenly zipping along on my dissertation. Somehow, the words came more easily here.

From time to time, I thought about visiting Jerry Warczak in prison. He was at the Columbia Correctional Institution in Portage, which had famously housed Jeffrey Dahmer before him. I imagined sitting behind a Plexiglas barrier, lifting the receiver and demanding an explanation. I pictured him on the other side in his orange jumpsuit, just one of a thousand other men in an orange jumpsuit. I rehearsed the string of invectives I would let loose on him, knowing that nothing I said would matter, and nothing he said would change anything. Jerry Warczak had killed Stacy Lemke, and my family had suffered for it. In the end, I never made the trip. Jerry Warczak had stolen my childhood, but I wasn't going to let him have anything else.

The summer after Jerry was convicted, the Lemkes held a memorial service for Stacy at the Watankee Memorial Cemetery. Thousands of people attended, some from as far away as Minnesota and Iowa. Her gravestone read simply, *Stacy Lynne Lemke, 1978-1995. Never forgotten.*

Bill and Sharon Lemke were there, of course, and Joanie and Heather, too. We'd only nodded to each other politely during the trial, giving each other space, but we stood together at her gravesite and ate together afterward at a small luncheon at the Lemkes' house. Bill Lemke didn't exactly apologize to Johnny, but he offered to help him out, should Johnny ever need anything. Johnny accepted graciously, but I knew he would never take him up on that offer.

Heather and I talked for a while on the Lemkes' front porch, while Joanie's redheaded kids chased each other in circles on the lawn. Neither of us mentioned the tetherball match; it was ancient history now. We shared the basic details of our lives: my dissertation, her plans to work for a district attorney's office after law school. I thought this was a perfect fit—if she took no prisoners on the playground, she would be fierce as a pit bull in criminal court.

"You'll stay in California when you finish?" she asked, catching me off guard.

"Well, actually—" I hadn't admitted this to anyone else, and hardly even to myself. "I've applied for a few teaching positions in Wisconsin. There's an opening at Marquette, and another one in Madison."

"Good," she said, touching me on the arm. "It'll be good for you to be home."

When I returned to California a week later, the homesickness was especially strong. Darby would be starting her senior year soon, and Mom was going to help Johnny rip out the upstairs bathroom, which needed a complete overhaul. We talked every few days, but sometimes that wasn't enough for me.

Once, late at night, I logged on to Google Earth and visited Watankee through my laptop. I approached first from far away, following the ridges and crevices of the Rockies, whizzing past the flat expanse of prairie, lingering over the neat sections of green-and-brown farmland bisected by gray lines of highway, dawdling over the forests that appeared suddenly, like green heads of broccoli.

I zoomed in on the businesses on Main Street, the striped awnings and flat silver parking lots. I followed the country roads, dotted here and there with pickup trucks and the metallic blurs of oil tankers.

There was a curious absence of human life, as if the farmers in their work boots had been lifted from the fields, the women and children sucked from kitchens and backyards.

Something inside me tightened when I approached 2242 Rural Route 4. My heart ached for the old truck still rusting away behind the barn and the white homes set close together on the lush, green lawn. It didn't take much to fill the land with people I knew—Johnny and his dog, heading out to the barn; Darby with a backpack slung over one shoulder, waiting for the bus. I could even make one of those blurs into Stacy Lemke, still a sixteen-year-old girl, her red hair trailing over her shoulder, her smile wide and welcoming.

When I zoomed back out, following the neat grids of farmland and pavement, I could almost hear the mosquitoes buzzing in the stagnant water of ditches, the cows flicking flies off their hides. I licked an imaginary finger and held it to the wind, feeling the storm roll in. Then I put an imaginary ear to the ground, listening for the roots of the corn to spread downward, deep down, beyond the face of the earth.

* * * * *

Acknowledgments

If it wasn't for the inspiration, gentle support and outright arm-twisting of others, this book would never have been written. I would be sorely remiss if I didn't thank the following people: Paul and Karen Treick, who let me read long past my bedtime; Beth Boon, Sara Viss and Debbie Miller—sisters, friends and readers with impeccable taste; Ruth Batts, in the running for the world's sweetest grandmother and a faithful reader, too; librarians everywhere, but particularly in Henry County, Ohio, and Stanislaus County, California; my Treick and Rodewald relatives near or from Newton, Wisconsin, who possess only the best and none of the worst qualities of the characters in Watankee; Carol Slager, Dr. Mike Vanden Bosch and Dr. James Schaap, who inspired me at just the right time and in just the right ways; The English Ladies: Cameron Burton, Alisha Wilks, Jenna Valponi, Amie Carter, Michelle Charpentier and the inestimable Mary Swier; Aaron Hamburger, Elizabeth Searle, Boman Desai and my fellow Stonecoast slaves to the written word; Ted Deppe, for saying, "I think there's something there…why don't you keep writing?"; Suzanne Strempek Shea (the best cheerleader any writer could ask for); Beth Slattery and Paige Levin—for gewürztraminer-fueled Yahtzee sessions and talking me more than once off a hypothetical ledge; Robb Vanderstoel, who read early drafts; Rex Cline, who steered me in the right direction; my DeBoard and Davenport in-laws, but especially John DeBoard; Alanna

Ramirez (who deserves a million thanks and has good karma coming in spades); agent extraordinaire Melissa Flashman at Trident Media Group; my wise and überpatient editor Erika Imranyi and all the folks at Mira Books, including Michelle Venditti; my creative writing classes at Ripon High School; teaching colleagues who must have resisted the urge to roll their eyes every time I talked about writing; baristas at The Queen Bean and Starbucks; the friends who faithfully "like" my book updates; the three people who read my blog; and finally—Will DeBoard: husband, best friend, first reader of everything, extrovert to my introvert, grounded to my flighty, and fearless navigator of everywhere we've ever been. Thanks doesn't begin to cover it.

Questions for Discussion

1. At the beginning of the novel, Kirsten's father tells her that everything you needed to know...you could learn on a farm. In what ways does this statement prove true—both in the book and in real life?

2. Explaining death to his daughter, Kirsten's father says, "It's just how things go. It's the way things are." Is this appropriate wisdom to share with a nine-year-old girl? Why does this advice make sense for Kirsten? Kirsten references "the life cycle" throughout the novel. What does she mean by this?

3. How does Kirsten's age affect how you read/understand the book? How is it an advantage to the storytelling? In what ways is it a disadvantage?

4. Consider Johnny and Stacy's relationship from their first meeting on the softball diamond to their last, ill-fated night together. What attracted them to each other? Is Johnny's mother right when she says their relationship is too obsessive, or is this just a normal teenage relationship? How would you react if your child was in a similar kind of relationship?

5. The people of Watankee react to Stacy's disappearance by convicting the Hammarstrom family in different ways. Is it surprising that few people come to Johnny's defense? How do you think the small-town culture contributes to people's responses?

6. Family loyalty is a strong theme in the book. Is Kirsten wrong for feeling conflicted over whether her brother is guilty or innocent? If your child or sibling was accused of committing a violent crime, how do you think you would handle it?

7. After the Memorial Day incident, the Hammarstrom family begins to drift apart and eventually disperses to different parts of the country. Only John stays behind on the farm. Do you feel the dissolution of the family could have been prevented? Why do you suppose they fled, and do you feel it was the right thing to do? What, if anything, would you have done differently?

8. At the end of the novel Kirsten puts "an imaginary ear to the ground, listening for the roots of the corn to spread downward," referring to something her grandfather used to do. What is this a metaphor for?

A Conversation with the Author

What was your inspiration for *The Mourning Hours*? Are the characters or events in any way based on real life?

Most of the characters in the story are completely fictional, although Kirsten and Emilie are composites of my three sisters, my niece Kera and me. A significant portion of my life was spent in the Midwest, wearing snow boots and those swishy snow pants. My parents had these horrible cautionary tales of people getting lost in snowstorms, when it wasn't possible to see the way from the house to the barn, and that fear stayed with me through the years.

The novel is told from the perspective of Johnny's younger sister Kirsten. Of all the characters in the novel, why did you choose Kirsten as your window into the story?

The story actually began as a three-page vignette of a young girl watching her brother's wrestling match, and it grew from there. I was intrigued by Kirsten's voice—as a child, she brings an innocence and naïveté to the story, but she also has a way of seeing and knowing things that the adults around her don't. I suppose I've always been intrigued by stories where the principal players aren't the ones in charge of the story, like *The Great Gatsby*.

Watankee is a fictional town, but is it inspired by a real place? Why did you decide to set the story in a small Midwestern farm town? How do you feel the setting enhances the story?

Watankee was inspired by a small town in eastern Wisconsin, where one member of my family or another has owned land since the 1800s. The layout of the Hammarstrom farm is similar to the Treick farm—when Kirsten and her father race from the barn to the house, my childhood self is running right along with them. There's a natural beauty to a farm setting, but it's somewhat isolated, too. Watankee itself could be any small town in America—welcoming and loyal, but judgmental, too.

***The Mourning Hours* is the story of a family forced to confront the possibility that one of their own has committed a heinous crime. Each of the characters reacts differently to Stacy's disappearance and Johnny's alleged guilt. What do you hope readers will take from this aspect of the story?**

I see the Hammarstroms as a typical family that suddenly finds itself in a horrific situation. It's the sort of thing that could happen to anyone—to you or me, too. We might think we'll always support the people we love, but doubt can be a powerful force. Ultimately, this family spends many lost years apart before coming to the truth.

What was your greatest challenge in writing *The Mourning Hours*? Your biggest surprise?

At the beginning, I just let myself write and write and write, to see where the story would take me. That's undoubtedly the fun part of writing—to create something entirely new that didn't exist an hour ago. The unpleasant part is losing all those little gems that have to be sacrificed for the good of the whole—the writer Suzanne Strempek Shea refers to this as "killing your darlings." I was surprised at how the story transported me back to my own life—to the misfit young girl I was and to the obsessed teenager wrestling with first love. At times, the writing felt very emotional and cathartic.

Can you describe your writing process? Do you outline first or dive right in? Do you write consecutively or jump around? Do you have a routine? A lucky charm?

When I'm at home, it's far too easy to be distracted by piles of laundry and stacks of dishes and pets who demand attention, so I mostly write in local coffeehouses, where I can be distracted by strangers who have no claim on my life. I both credit and blame caffeine for many of my writing decisions. Each day, I have a basic idea of what needs to happen next, and I go from there. If I have an outline at all, it's very roughly sketched, and designed only to take me through the next chapter or two. There's a great E. L. Doctorow quote that I believe, too: "Writing is like driving at night in the fog. You can see only as far as your headlights, but you can make the whole trip that way."

How did you know you wanted to be a writer? How old were you, and what was your very first piece of writing?

I think I always knew I was meant to be a writer. I love to observe things; I was the somewhat weird kid watching life from the sidelines. I was (and still am) an obsessive reader, and in one way or another I've always kept a journal. I wrote my first novel when I was nine years old in a seventy-page spiral notebook. Somehow that was very easy—probably because I had a practical goal. When I ran out of pages in the notebook, that was the end of the story.

Turn the page for a sneak peek at
Paula Treick DeBoard's
THE DROWNING GIRLS.
Available now from MIRA Books.

JUNE 19, 2015
5:40 P.M.

LIZ

Someone was screaming.

For a moment, with the ceiling fan whirring quietly over my head, I allowed myself to believe it was a benign sound—the kids next door on their play structure, maybe, sliding and swinging and climbing, their voices carrying on a breeze.

I propped myself up on my elbows, blinking myself awake. How long had I been sleeping? Twenty minutes, an hour? The tank top I was wearing was streaked with dust and damp with sweat. Dizzy, I focused on my bare feet, where chipped red polish dotted my toes. On the dresser was a nearly empty bottle of Riesling, a slick ring of condensation bubbling on the wood.

I reached a hand onto Phil's side of the bed, groping and coming up empty. Of course. Phil was gone, and he'd taken everything with him—armfuls of shirts and pants, suit coats and blazers, slippery mounds of ties and belts, even the dry cleaning in its plastic sheeting. Shoes, too: wing tips, loafers, sneakers, the pair of black Converse I'd never once seen him wear. He'd taken the neatly folded stacks of T-shirts and boxers, the lumps of paired socks, the heavy woolen sweater that smelled like a Greek fishing village—or at least, how I'd imagined a Greek fishing village would smell, briny and deep down damp.

After he left, I'd searched the floor for a button, a collar stay, a lonely sock, as if I could keep that one discarded thing as evidence of our life together. For a long time, I'd wanted to go back, to pin our relationship to a wall and study it, like a specimen, from every angle. I wanted to be able to say: *Here*. This is where it all went wrong. This was the point at which the inevitable was not yet evitable.

But that was a long time ago. Months now.

I shook my head, chasing away the thoughts, and heard the screams again, over a relentless pounding of bass. Was the television on downstairs? That was the simple explanation, and for a moment, I allowed myself to be reassured by the thought of actors following a script, raising their voices on cue.

And then I remembered: the girls.

The pool.

The screams were coming from outside, distorted by the triple-paned windows, as if they were being filtered through a kaleidoscope, splitting and fracturing.

I swung my legs over the side of the bed and moved toward the door. My head pounded, an angry thing.

Danielle.

My baby.

No—not a baby. Fifteen and so angry we'd barely exchanged more than a sentence in a month.

I stumbled on the stairs, catching myself with a hand on the rail. *Steady*, *Liz*. I had to navigate around the stacks of boxes in the foyer marked *Towels* and *Office* and, helpfully, *Stuff*.

Closer now, the screams became words, and the words became language, mixed with the thumping of the stereo, the music that had been playing all afternoon.

Help!

Mom!

Ohmygodno!

I yanked open the sliding door, catching my foot on the frame in my hurry. A bright bloom of pain flowered in my vision. After the interior darkness, the outside was a trick of sunlight, bright against the water, a shimmering, endless blue. I squinted into the glare, trying to understand what I was seeing.

It looked at first like a game of tug-of-war, a three-headed, six-armed monster writhing in the water.

But of course, it wasn't a game.

It was another inevitable, a thing that had been coming and coming, a thing I'd let come. There were three girls in the water and one of them was limp, her head flopped forward, blond hair plastered over her face.

Still the shouts came, an unrelenting swirl of voices. In that half second while my mind puzzled, before my body could snap into action, I realized that the loudest voice, the one that couldn't stop screaming, belonged to me.